HOUSE OF CRIMSON ROSES

CHAD LESTER

Hardcover ISBN 979-8-9896121-5-4
Paperback ISBN 979-8-9896121-4-7
Ebook ISBN 979-8-9896121-3-0
Library of Congress Control Number: 2024910606

Fiction / Family Saga.
Fiction / Historical / Civil War Era.
Fiction / War & Military.

Published 2025

For my family.

JOHN BROWN

I

Harpers Ferry, Virginia 1859

It was night. Coyotes yipped and howled as the smell of burnt coal filled the stale air. Chimney smoke spiraled obliquely toward the quiet heavens, its sooty tendrils clouding the blood moon high above. Beyond a wash of black mist they spied only a single sentinel guarding the federal armory, the biggest in the South. Inside were some twenty thousand rifles. It was an ample enough supply of weapons to arm the slaves, John's army of the righteous. God had sent him to vanquish the slavers, the fleshmongers, the man stealers. The sinners. A bullet to the head was the only language they understood, and John wouldnt hesitate to communicate in their lingua franca.

His motley crew of raiders, three of John's own sons among them, pushed away dark branches as they made their way through the wooded labyrinth. Upon passing through lingering briers and bracken at the forest's edge, they came upon the winding blackwater of the Potomac. Beyond the weather-beaten planks of a railway bridge stood the armory at Harpers Ferry, a small town nestled between the river and the wood. John closed his eyes and took a deep breath. The air tasted of sulfur. After a pause, he gave the order. His sons climbed over the wall and leveled their firearms. The startled sentinel surrendered and the armory was theirs. It all seemed too easy, but no matter John was sure the slaves would hear of the victory and an army of God would rise up in glorious insurrection.

John pointed his rifle at the tied-up sentinel.

—I want to free all the negroes in this state. I have possession now of the United States Armory, and if the citizens interfere with me, I must burn the town and have blood.

II

Upon lightfall, when the yawning workers of the armory arrived, the raiders took them hostage. The commotion caused the residents of the town to shuffle outside in vague curiosity. It wasnt long before they elucidated the matter at hand and surrounded the armory bearing makeshift agrarian weapons. John fired a warning shot in the air. A lantern shattered against the ground. Dogs barked and the townspeople fled. John's army of the righteous had only grown to about fifty souls, mostly negroes liberated from the surrounding area. Many of them appeared to be trying to make heads or tails of what exactly was happening. Without sufficient time to train them how to use firearms, his men handed them pikes. His men began to bicker amongst themselves. At noon there was the sound of hundreds of bootsteps around them. The Virginia militia surrounded the armory and loaded their muskets. Escape wasnt an option, so John led forty of his hostages to the nearby, more defensible, fire engine house. They ran for it. A roll of smoke filled the air as the militia's rifles rattled and hot lead hissed past John's head. The back of a raider's head exploded into red mist after a ball collided with his skull—Newby was his name.

The hours ticked by and he knew they were running low on water. John stroked his long white beard with his sinewy forearm. He was strong as an ox thanks to decades plowing through the hard earth of his farm, in good shape for a man of nearly sixty. Some of his men had compared him to Moses. He secretly liked the comparison but tried not to like it too much, for pride was a sin.

Under the flag of truce, John offered to trade hostages in exchange for passage across the railway bridge. His offer was met with gunfire and the flag fell to the ashen earth. His son Watson crawled back to the fire engine house, leaving a steaming trail of blood behind him. When he made it there, he tried to plug the hole in his torso with his finger. It was no use, for the dark red blood still gushed forth. The sight was too much for raider Leeman, who made a run for it. Leeman got all the way to the riverbank. There the Virginia militia surrounded him and John averted his eyes. A shot rang out followed by a splash.

Leeman's death didnt dissuade two more of his men from fleeing their dire situation. More shots, followed by two more splashes. John's men fired upon the surrounding militia and put a bullet into the mayor. Sporadic gunfire continued into midday until John's son Oliver collapsed on the floor and gazed at his ruined, bullet-ridden torso with disbelief.

The air grew colder as the pallid sun receded behind the blackened trees. For a while it was quiet. Then the silence of night was interrupted by the cadence of trained killers marching in unison. John checked his pocket watch. It was eleven o'clock. Such an organized cadence wasnt the drunken Virginia militia, now taking turns using the decomposing bodies of his fallen raiders for bayonet practice. The Marines had arrived. Oliver's moans reverberated against the redbrick walls of the firehouse. Each cry of agony sent a shudder up his men's spines. Hour after hour he moaned and begged to be put out of his misery. At first John had tried to encourage his son, but each wail seemed to demoralize his remaining men just a little more.

III

By the time the white sun had finished climbing the autumn tree line, his boy's pulse was no longer there. John let go of his wrist and cast his eyes downward. He brushed his son's lids shut. Watson lay next to Oliver, the wound in his torso still gushing, holding a pistol to his head to end his suffering. John stayed Watson's hand.

About a hundred Marines in crisp blue uniforms stood in formation outside the fire engine house. There was a rapping against the door. A sharply dressed Marine officer under the command of Colonel Robert E. Lee demanded surrender. John refused. Moments later came a sharp blow. And another, and the wood door began to rive and splinter. With each thrust it broke apart a little more. John shot the first Marine to set foot inside. The man's brains sprayed against the redbrick walls of the engine house. More Marines filed inside and bayoneted John's men. They stabbed with wild abandon and proceeded to slaughter with machine-like efficiency. Soon the cold floor of the fire engine house was steaming with the sticky communal blood of the raiders.

John fought with everything he had until the room went dark.

IV

The federal courts declined to intervene, and the state of Virginia found John guilty. His sentence, death by hanging. John learned that Watson had died the day after he was captured. The sentence stung a little less when he learned that his son Owen had managed to escape. John offered his body as a living sacrifice to make his prophecy come true. In this way he thought himself blessed. He had sent a letter to his wife asking her to stay home in North Elba. Mary didnt listen. John had maintained his composure in battle. He had maintained composure when his sons were killed. Through the interrogations and the trial, he had maintained. He even remained calm as Mary visited his cell and tearfully held his callused hands. She struggled to speak as she broke in and out of fits of sobs and they talked about their hopes for their living children. Then their time was up. His wife tearfully crossed the threshold of his cell and exited his life.

Then hot tears worked their way down the hard lines of his weathered face.

The air was cold. The hemp rope around his neck was rough and scratchy. The gray overcast sky disappeared as a hood was slid over his head. He found it hard to breathe. John had imagined this day so many times it felt as if he were living a memory. Only it wasnt a memory, for the present was finally upon him. Rain pattered upon his tired shoulders and the wind howled through the twisted leafless branches of the dead trees around him. An old lever creaked. The trapdoor fell from under his feet and John was weightless as he fell toward Mother Earth. Back to whence he came. His memories gave way to the present occurrence. It felt as if he had been falling for an eternity when he opened his eyes. He expected to see the inside of the hood. Instead he saw the sun rising over the cedar shake roof of his cabin until its golden rays faded into a perfect and indescribable light.

The thick blond rope snapped tight.

Chapter 1

EMMA

1860, Delaware

Windswept wildflowers blew in the rolling pastures dotted with chestnut horses, their easy ruminative chewing matching the pace of life in that tranquil slice of northern country. Emma studied her reflection in the limpid water of the horse trough. She turned her head as an aristocrat carrying a panther-headed cane sauntered inside the stables. He was a middle-aged man with a cropped salt-and-pepper beard, steel blue eyes, and a fine white suit—not a speck of work on it. The man patted the muscled flanks of Dakota, a prize-winning, smoky black thoroughbred.

She brushed a mare named Cheyenne while the man talked with Master Anderson. Cheyenne was a spirited horse and Emma was the only person who could manage her. Her entire life consisted of church and horses, and that black racehorse was one of her few friends in the world. Little brought Emma more pleasure than watching the funny faces Dakota made with his lips as he reached for apples and carrots and other treats she fed him.

—Fine horse, fine horse. Sure he's not for sale? asked the man in white.

—Dakota? The fastest horse this side of the Mississippi, sorry, but I cant possibly part with him Mr. Beaumont, said Master Anderson.

—I'll triple my price.

Master Anderson's big round stomach jiggled with laughter.

—Miles, I respect your determination, but I just cant. No matter the price. I'll sell you Cheyenne. She's a bit wild, but she's pregnant with Dakota's first foal. She'll produce a fine racehorse, I guarantee it.

—I'll take her, but I do need an experienced caretaker for my stables. Do you happen to have someone? What about her?

The man pointed at Emma. Her stomach tightened. Her first thoughts were of her father and the little cabin they all had lived in for as long as she could remember.

—How much?

—Well you see, I cant part with dear Emma either. She's an exceptional groom, the best in the county, probably the state. She is a master of her craft, and I would have a tough time replacing her indeed. Besides, she's only fit for taking care of horses and the stables. She's not suitable for the fields, you know.

—Of course. Of course. Like I said, I need a skilled groom. I, too, care very deeply for my slaves. I wouldnt dare put a groom out in the fields, especially one as fair as your dear Emma. Given her exceptional skill and reputation, how about twenty-five hundred?

—Twenty-five hundred? That's generous. Very generous indeed, but I dont think I can spare Emma. She's very dear to our family.

—My need for a skilled groom is quite dire. How about you name your price.

—Well, in that case.

Emma ran to her father at the other end of the stable. He was heaving fresh straw. When she approached, he placed his pitchfork in the straw and she wrapped her arms around him. Upon hearing the news, her father began breathing heavily. His hands trembled. He told her that it was clearly a misunderstanding on her part and that he'd sort it out.

Master Anderson waved as Miles Beaumont's carriage clattered and trundled against the furrowed dirt road lined with meandering white rail fencing. Emma and her father approached him.

—Master, my daughter has this notion that you're going to sell her.

—Unfortunately, Jeremiah, I'm afraid that is the case.

Emma's father's facade cracked and his lip began to quiver. His sweaty hands fiddled with the brim of his straw hat as he held it against his chest.

—You sold us together. Right, Master Anderson?

The man scratched the back of his neck.

—Jeremiah, you're the stablemaster. I need you here with me. Dakota needs you too.

—Aint we been good to you?

Master Anderson laid his chubby hand on her father's shoulder.

—The best, Jeremiah. Emma is almost a woman now, and it's time for her to part ways. You still have some years left. Maybe you can have another child with someone. Maybe I can get you a new wife since Sarah passed on.

Emma fell to her knees and seized Master Anderson's leg. She pleaded with him to allow her to stay with her father. He pulled his foot free from her grasp and stormed off.

The dying sun set over her cedar shake cabin next to the stables. Emma had only taken two bites of her bread and found herself full. A watery brown stew of boiled offal spilled over the edges of her cracked wooden bowl as her father poured it. She took one sip and pushed the bowl away.

Emma left the old crate that was their dinner table and spent the next few hours in the outhouse dry-heaving. She stumbled back inside the cabin and collapsed onto her straw-filled mattress. Emma had met other slaves at the market. A few were covered with little more than rags that revealed hideous scars scrawled all over their backs. At the time it was the most horrendous thing she'd ever seen. Now she would gladly accept rags and beatings if it meant she could stay with her father. He was the only person in the world she had. Emma's eyes grew heavy and she drifted off into a death-like sleep.

Someone shook her shoulder. Emma pulled away. Again the shaking until her eyes grudgingly opened. The dull flickering light of a tallow candle illuminated her father's face, shining with sweat. He had a knapsack slung over his shoulder and turned and held his finger over his mouth.

—Keep quiet. Let's go.

Emma crept from her bed and slipped on her worn leather boots. Her father cracked the door to their cabin and peered out. He took Emma's hand and they slowly made their way toward the dark wooded grove just beyond the pasture. Her father held his finger up to his mouth again and they walked as quietly as they could past the kennels. A lone dog began to bay and the others joined the chorus. The kennel door creaked open and a hound's long head emerged. Usually the kennel gates were locked. Another head emerged, and another. Emma and her father backed away slowly as the dogs loped toward them.

—This way.

They ran inside the stables, the hounds not far behind, and hid behind a stack of straw. A lone pitchfork stuck out of it. Emma heard the dogs snuffing at the straw-covered ground. About to cry out, she covered her mouth with both her hands. Straw crunched on the other side of the pile. Emma pressed her back against the timeworn wood of the barn. Her father dug through his knapsack. As the hounds rounded the pile, baring their teeth, her father pulled out a small burlap bag of entrails and tossed it toward the dogs. They stopped and sniffed the bag. One of the hounds took the bag in its jaws. Another ran up and attempted to steal the scraps and a fight ensued over the smelly morsels.

They got up and ran toward the open end of the stable. As they were about to cross the threshold, they saw two silhouettes in the blackness. The hounds ran past them, baying and howling, as they ran out into the pasture after the dog with the bag of giblets. One of the two figures called out to them.

—Somebody there?

Her father looked to the tree line and then looked to the stable. He took Emma's hand and they ran back into the stable and ducked behind the straw pile once more. She peered over the edge of the pile. A dim bobbing lanternlight appeared at the far end of the stable. Her father squeezed her hand.

The light was nearly on top of them as they huddled together behind the straw pile. Dim yellow lanternlight reflected and refracted off a pudgy round face. A lurking shadow emerged from the howling dark. It was Abel, the son-in-law. Master Anderson had his chubby fingers wedged inside the lever action of a rifle. He cast his eyes downward and shook his head.

—It disappoints me that you would try to pull a stunt like this, Jeremiah. I give you a cabin, I feed you, and this is how you repay my kindness?

Her father slowly rose to his feet.

—Sir, I aint got no choice.

—Choice? You have no business making choices.

—Please, sir, let Emma stay with us. I'll do anything.

—Abel, discipline Jeremiah and see to it he stays tied up for the night, so he can think about how much pain he's brought me. Tie up Emma until Mr. Beaumont picks her up in the mornin.

Abel grabbed her father's wrist. He jerked back his hand. With one hard swing, her father's fist connected with Abel's temple. He stiffened and collapsed to the straw-covered floor. Master Anderson leveled his rifle. Emma grabbed the barrel. A shot went off and a thin ray of moonlight shone through the ceiling. Master Anderson backhanded her. She landed hard upon the ground.

Her father pulled the pitchfork free from the nearby straw pile. Before he could take aim again, Master Anderson's baggy eyes widened. Her father had thrust the pitchfork into his belly. He tried to speak, but when he opened his mouth blood oozed down the folds of his jowls, trickled down his neck, and pooled in a sticky straw-laden muddle. Master Anderson collapsed.

Jeremiah removed it and fountains of thick greasy blood geysered forth from the punctures. He walked toward the fallen son-in-law and raised the pitchfork above unconscious Abel's neck. He held it there. His hands trembled. Her father took a deep breath, and his shoulders relaxed. Then he tossed the pitchfork aside.

They ran through the sedge and wildflower-swathed pastures and climbed over the white rail fence and out into the quiet woodland. Dark, tangled branches blotted out the moonlit sky. The air was still. Emma could only hear their footsteps atop the dried leaves. Then they crossed a creek. The cold water worked its way into her shoes, numbing her toes.

She was out of breath by the time they found a curious edifice in the middle of the woodland. A tiny cabin. Half the roof had caved in and all the windows were shattered. Once the abode of an elderly slave sent to live out his days in that forgotten wilderness.

The structure buckled as her father heaved the rickety door open. After they got inside, he removed a tallow candle from his pocket and lit it. The dull flames revealed some rusted pots and pans and the remains of a cot, its fabric long since disintegrated. Bleached bones lay scattered throughout the cabin. They pulled the door shut as morning light worked its way up the ragged tree line. The sun had begun to rise. Better to move at night and rest during the day, her father told her. He said they were going to go farther north, to the Free States.

—How do we know we've reached em? she asked.

—There are some stone markers that look like gravestones along the border.

They laid out some blankets on the floor. Emma took off her shoes and poured out the water. She wrapped herself up tight in the worn patched blanket and closed her eyes.

The sharp afternoon sun shone on her face through a spot where the roof used to be. The barking of hounds echoed through the woods. Her father stood.

—We have to go.

Emma put on her boots. They were still wet and cold. The barking and baying came from every direction. Her father took her hand and they ran from the shack. The thick underbrush of briars and brambles slowed their movement. At first, her legs ached. Then they began to cramp. She ran as hard as she could.

—There, shouted a voice.

The barking of the hounds grew louder, closer. Her father led the way. As he pushed through a thick tangle of branches, he stopped and turned.

—If anything happens, keep runnin.

Jeremiah had explained that the Pennsylvania border was just a few hours' walk away. Once they crossed it, they were free. Emma struggled to catch her breath. The trees around her were spinning. Her legs wobbled as her surroundings faded in and out. Her father placed his hands on her shoulders and shook her.

—Promise. Promise me you'll get to the Free States.

—I promise.

They made their way through the thick forest as fast as they could. Her father ran ahead and stopped in an ankle-deep creek. The hope was to lose their scent by wading upward through the creek. Once again, Emma felt the water flow between her toes. The icy water stung at first, followed by numbness.

They paused to catch their breath. A hound emerged from the dark tangle of branches around them. The dog clamped its jaws around Jeremiah's leg. Another hound appeared and latched onto his wrist. Four more materialized. Two went after Emma's father and the other two after her.

He was pulled down into the creek. Emma picked up a large branch and swung it hard into one of the dog's muzzles. It ran off whimpering, but the other dog took the branch in its jaws and shook. She kicked the beast in the head until it let go. Then she swung the branch downward upon its skull. It ran with its tail between its legs. As she ran toward her father, yelling and wielding the stick at the dogs, four men with guns pushed through the thicket and into the clearing. One of them had a bloodied face with bandages Abel. Her father looked to her.

—Run. Run.

Her father's cries gave way to gurgled groans. The crystal-clear creek became pale red. Abel watched for a few moments before directing his gaze toward Emma.

—Bring her to me, he said.

She crawled over thorn bushes and raced through the thick tangle. The preoccupied dogs didnt give chase, but the men did. The underbrush closed in around her. Branches cracked behind her. Emma gained ground. She ran past the last of the trees and found herself standing in a wide-open prairie. Something stuck out above the nearby hill. Emma climbed. Soon she could see it: a stone border marker like the one her father had described. This had to be it. She commanded her legs to run faster, but they refused as she stumbled toward the border as fast as she could.

The border appeared so close, yet with every step she took it seemed as if she gained no ground. She collapsed, her legs exhausted. She lay there for a few moments, then pushed herself up with all the strength she had left. The border stone grew larger in her sight. She paused. The clatter of hoof clops behind her became louder.

—There she is.

The four horses were right behind her, galloping at full speed. She crossed the border right as Abel rode up on horseback beside her. The next thing she saw was the butt of his gun. Emma faded in and out of consciousness as they carried her back across. Voices surrounded her.

—Are we gonna kill her?

—Cant. Mr. Beaumont already paid for her.

Blackness.

Water churned from a spinning red paddle beyond the wavy teal glass of her small window. The yellow straw she sat upon vibrated from the side paddle steamer's coal-fueled engines, humming through the worn floorboards. The blades of the paddles made a thrashing sound as they pounded against the cobalt waves. Emma sat in a cramped compartment with a few familiar thoroughbred horses. She thought about smashing the window and hurling herself into the dark waters below. She wrestled with the idea until the steamer docked in Savannah Harbor.

The dock bustled with activity as all manner of goods were moved to and from the ships in the harbor. Emma was manhandled into a waiting wagon and put in the back with an assortment of other purchased supplies.

She wished it was a covered wagon. The harsh sun beat against her face as it bumped along Savannah's cobblestone streets and made its way outside of the city. Emma found herself on a furrowed road of red clay. Her hands and feet were bound. The air was hot and humid. Moss hung from the ancient oaks, and cicadas whirred. She was in a place much different. An hour or so after leaving the city, the wagon jerked to stop.

—Sweet Georgia, here we are, said the driver.

A man led Cheyenne, the pregnant mare, to the man in the white suit whom Master Anderson had called Miles. Miles tried to pat the horse's muzzle, but Cheyenne reared up on her hind legs.

—Spirited horse. So sorry to hear about Mr. Anderson. He was a good man.

—Sad indeed.

—Do I need to worry about this one?

—She wont be a problem.

Master Beaumont gestured toward a collection of cabins. The man hoisted Emma over his shoulder and dropped her at the front door of one of the cabins and cut her free. Before her was a cruel circus of the damned. A hunched-over creature, presumably a man, with bulging yellowed eyes and a crabwise gait grinned at her. Then he gave a shrill laugh and licked his cracked lips. A gaunt woman regarded her for a moment with her vacant gaze and then continued weaving a basket with her knotted hands. A few muscled toughs leered at her through dark eyes. The rest of the men and women wore rags while the feral children ran about wearing nothing. Her new master stepped forward. Emma pulled her knees to her chest.

—Here at Beaumont Hall, any woman who produces seven living children gets Saturdays all to herself.

Miles patted her head and walked off. Emma sobbed as quietly as she could. Cheyenne kicked and pulled as she was led away to a stable. Emma had never thought her dress was that nice, but compared to everyone else on the plantation, she might as well have been dressed as the plantation mistress. Two smirking young men, one of them the creature, watched her with predatory eyes. The large muscled one blew her a kiss and the other one grinned wide. She considered that it would have been better to die and be in heaven with her father. Instead, she had been sent to hell and the monsters were all around her.

An apparition-like woman in red watched her every move from the window of the palatial gray stone mansion. Another young man, slightly older than Emma, sat next to the well that stood between the mansion and the collection cabins. He was of mixed blood and had peculiar features. The coin hadnt flipped in his favor. If he wasnt in rags, she might have assumed he was a farmhand. Emma figured his mother must have been a slave, and by law that made him a slave. She shuddered when she saw his startling pale blue irises ringed with black. She had never seen anything like it nor thought it possible. Unlike all the others, he ate alone, seemingly rejected from the pack. Those haunting wraith-like eyes locked onto hers, watching her. Young Emma pulled her knees up to her chest as he walked over. She tried to hide her face behind them, unsure of his ghoulish intentions. His hand held out a cup full of water.

—Please drink.

She wanted the water, but her arm wouldnt move. It was a trick. As soon as she reached out to take the water, he would clench his hand around her arm and drag her away to his wretched haven. The young man placed the cup of water at her feet. He stepped back a bit to give her some space. Emma snatched the water and greedily slurped it down. The liquid poured from the edges of her mouth. *Who, or what, was he?*

As if she'd spoken the question aloud, he returned and held out his hand.

—My name is Isaiah.

Emma placed her trembling hand in his.

Chapter 2

ISAIAH

1860, Georgia

Miles' mansion stood at the end of a long red dirt road lined with two rows of moss-laden oaks. The gray stones of the mansion rose high above the nearby swamp. The manor was surrounded by large doric columns which formed a covered porch and second-floor balcony around the entire home. The back of the estate had a central fountain enveloped with manicured gardens flush with crimson roses. In the front, wildflowers and camellias grew in the undulating and rolling rail fenced pasture where thoroughbreds roamed. Through the wavy glass panes of the mansion stood the plantation mistress wearing a dress, also crimson, against her milky-white skin and raven-black hair. Her eyes were always upon him, though any time he made eye contact, she'd fade away back into the dark interior of that old stone edifice.

It was another day in the glary heat of the unforgiving sun for Isaiah. The other overseers were poking fun at Jed again. He was a tall man, gaunt and lanky, with dark eyes, beady and glasslike set in a writhen stubble-laden face. He lived solitary on the plantation in a shake cabin, oblong and slanted, that reeked something fierce when its flimsy plank door was open to the hot Georgia breeze. He had no wife nor kids and wore a tattered straw hat and ragged clothes, patched and repatched. The overseers had a long pheasant feather and took turns tickling Jed behind the ear. He turned and cursed.

—I'll kick the ass of whoever's doin that.

The men hid the feather behind his back and chuckled. Jed turned and then they did it again.

—It aint us, simple Jed. The overseers burst out into laughter. Jed seized the feather and began shouting expletives while the men rolled over laughing. Then he stormed off.

Meanwhile, young Lea gritted her teeth as she clutched her sweat-soaked back. Isaiah sliced a tobacco plant free with his sickle and watched as the petite woman wiped her forehead with the end of her ragged yellow skirt. Her swollen ankles wobbled every time she bent over to cut a tobacco plant and put it in her basket. It was clear that it was twice as difficult for her to stand back up with the weight of her unborn child pulled toward the red earth of the field. Isaiah took several tobacco plants from his basket and put them in hers, topping her basket off.

Jed strutted toward them, barefoot, cradling his rifle. His glass-like eyes followed Lea's every movement. When he reached them, he took the tobacco leaves out of her basket and tossed them onto the ground.

—You need to do yer own work. Now get yer back down and harvest.

—I cant. The baby.

—I said a-keep workin, damnit.

Jed struck her with a thick birch switch, again and again, until she resumed picking.

James, a giant of a man, stood nearby. His back was a web of thick, overlapping scars that wrapped around the sides of his massive torso and up his neck before terminating at his hazed-over left eye.

—It's my fault, Mr. Jed. Beat me instead, he said.

—Not again. I'm tired of whippin yer ass. You got so many scars on yer damn hide I reckon you cant feel it anyhow.

—Yessir, I can feel it, and Lord knows I deserve it. She dont, Mr. Jed.

—You say that every time. Shut yer mouth and harvest.

James had weathered some fifty-five seasons. At seventeen, Isaiah could hardly imagine the years. James treated him as if he was family and was the only person in the world he trusted entire. He despised the masters and he despised the slaves, and his singular desire was to spill a great deal of blood.

His mother was a slave. Her father was a white man. Isaiah used to pray to be anything other than what he was. Now he no longer prayed, he used his fists. Anyone who told him he had no right to be this or that, he popped in the mouth, for violence was a universal language. He didnt always win the fights he started, but it worked, and the issue had subsided in recent years.

Isaiah eyeballed Jed's Colt six-shot revolving carbine, a gift from his boss. Jed had leaned it against a tree. Isaiah went over a chain of events in his mind. He could take the gun and kill Jed. That was easy enough. The problem was the other overseers. There were about ten of them. How many could he kill? Five more before reloading if his aim was true.

He had been savoring the moment for years. He had finally grown strong enough to fight back. Isaiah knew he would die, but at least he'd finally be free. He imagined so many times bleeding out, his light fading while welcoming the cold embrace of the reaper. Today would be the day. Then his mind's eye flashed with an image of the new girl, shy and delicate. He tried to forget her. He had to stay on the path of bloodlust and retribution. He wanted to forget, but the way she had looked up at him, alone and afraid. He ran his weathered palm over his face and shook his head.

If he chose to act, he wondered if James would help. The giant man could kill three or four overseers with ease, but James hated violence, even though he had probably taken more beatings than anyone, almost always for others. Isaiah thought him peculiar. If Isaiah did attack Jed alone, he wouldnt get far. The other overseers would hear the commotion and come running and Isaiah would be taken out by a hail of hot lead before he could do much.

What would be the payoff of his martyrdom? Miles would still be alive, and he deserved to die above all others. If he was going to kill anyone, he ought to kill Miles first, not last. Then slaughter the entire household and the overseers, of course. Lastly, the other slaves he didnt like and anyone who tried to stop him. Though what if James tried to stop him? He almost certainly would. Would Isaiah shoot him? He reckoned he wouldnt. So what was the point of daydreaming about his bloodbath? Hell, who was he kidding, he needed to stay for old James. Isaiah was the only thing the man had.

Lea stumbled to a nearby tobacco plant. Jed struck her a few more times. She raised her sickle and continued to harvest. The dull clang of bronze emanated throughout the red fields as the plantation bells rang. The sun fell behind the trees of the mist-laden swampland beyond and the day's work was done.

He had never seen her in such terrible shape. James lifted her off her feet and carried her to her living quarters. He placed Lea on the floor inside her cabin. She writhed and groaned as she clutched her stomach and cried out. Lea's mother dipped a mottled rag in gray water and patted her head with it.

Isaiah retired to his cabin.

At daybreak, the bells chimed across Beaumont Plantation. Lea's mother, sobbing and wailing, pleaded for Isaiah and James to come into Lea's cabin at once. The girl lay there, her cadaverous eyes staring blankly into the eyes of her nameless unmoving infant, clutched to her breast.

Isaiah found himself digging that red earth with James. As they heaved the heavy clay, he caught a flash of red fabric. The mistress stood on the mansion balcony, gazing upon them. Jed sauntered forward.

—Leave her and get yer asses in the field. Dig them graves on yer own time.

The rest of the field slaves trudged into the red mire of the fields. Isaiah and James ignored Jed's commands and kept digging. The other overseers moseyed on over. One of them elbowed Jed.

—Look'ee here, they just ignorin you, simple Jed. I reckon we ought to give one of them the whip and put you out in that there field.

The overseers laughed.

—Shut yer damn stupid faces, yelled Jed.

More laughter, louder now.

—Is one of em doin unchristian things to ya at night in that there reekin cabin of yours? Is that why it stinks?

The overseers reeled over in a hyena-like cacophony as Jed cursed and spit and flailed his lanky arms about with violent invective. James turned to Isaiah.

—Go on. I'll take care of it, said James.

Even though Isaiah was a man now, James saw fit to protect him as if he were still a boy. He protested, but the old man was having none of it.

—Go, he said. Isaiah climbed out of the grave. Jed took a weak swing with his switch at Isaiah as he slowly walked oblong to the field. Jed then stepped to the rim of the grave and pointed his switch.

—I said get in the field, said Jed.

James kept digging. Jed stood there, mouth agape, as his hand-rolled cigarette dangled from his lower lip.

—Boy, did you hear me?

James nodded politely and then heaved another pile of dirt to the side.

—Oh, yer gonna get it now.

A hand fell on Jed's shoulder. It was Miles, dressed in his usual fine white suit. The master watched James with curiosity rather than anger.

—Let em finish, said Miles.

—But, sir, he defied my command.

Miles took a deep puff of his cigar.

—James is respected by the others. He keeps the peace. Keeps em in line. He's the most valuable man I've got. He can do the work of ten men. Aint that right, James?

—Yessir.

Miles blew a puff of smoke in Jed's face.

—You mishandled my property again, Jed. That young negress was easily worth fifteen hundred. Do you have fifteen hundred, Jed? Are you even worth fifteen hundred?

—I'm sorry, sir.

—Why'd you have her in the fields when she was so late in her pregnancy?

—Well shoot, I didnt know there was different times I should and shouldnt put her in the fields. I just reckoned her hands still worked so she ought to work.

—Well, now you know. You see, Jed, we could have had her sit down, do some bottling in the distillery or tidy up the house or any number of things appropriate for a woman in her condition, but you chose to beat her in the hundred-degree heat and now I've lost two pairs of hands.

—I'm sorry, sir, I am. I just reckoned we cant have them disobeyin us. Specially James. They was gettin all riled up when he ignored me. Defiant looks in their eyes. Surely that's cause for the lash, aint it?

Miles flicked the cigar away and gazed at its dying embers for a few moments before stomping it into the earth with his polished black boot.

—I suppose so, but let him finish the grave and bury her. Of course, I'll be docking your pay for the expense. Do be more careful next time.

—Yessir. Sorry, sir.

Miles pointed at Jed with his panther-headed cane and prodded him with it a few times. He enunciated every word in his sentence as if to make sure the overseer would understand:

—And, Jed, I expect him to be fit enough to work the next day. Mess up again and I'll have *you* flogged.

—Dont you worry, Mr. Beaumont. I wont mess up again. I'm good for my word. I aint been flogged since my navy days. Dont want that again, no, sir.

When the fieldwork was done for the day, James didnt hesitate to head over to the whipping post, where Jed was waiting. James was stripped and tied up with thin rope he could have easily broken free from. Jed leaned in close.

—Gonna beg for mercy? No, not you. I spect you like being whipped.

He gave a wide grin, revealing the few blackened teeth he had left, and his glass-like eyes lit up. He cracked his whip against James' rugged back. After the first lash struck, Isaiah's old friend stood there like a stone pillar. James didnt make a sound nor flinch as the sharp leather flayed finger-thick gashes into his flesh. Specks of flesh filled the air and blood poured down his back and pooled and steamed around his feet.

Jed stopped. He clutched his shoulder and struggled to catch his breath as he walked away. The dark skin on James' back was peeled open to reveal the pulsating pink flesh underneath. James didnt grimace when Isaiah poured saltwater over his wounds, a painful necessity lest infection set in.

Isaiah figured he could kill Jed tonight as he slept in his cabin. He could even do it slowly. Then he could go inside the mansion and kill Miles the same way, maybe a few others if he was lucky. Or he figured he could try to escape. He could escape with James.

But what about the girl?

Chapter 3

ELMIRA

1860, Georgia

Elmira wore her usual crimson dress. The neck was cut wide so that the dress hung slightly over her shoulders. It exposed just enough of her décolleté to show off her favorite black pearl necklace doubled up around her neck. She had just finished hanging her watercolor painting of a rose upon the oiled millwork of her dining room wall when Miles walked in.

—Do you like it? she asked.

—What is it?

—A rose, of course.

—Perhaps you can hang it in your private chambers instead.

Elmira took a seat at the long mahogany table and tried to read the newspaper under the sparkling iridescence of a crystal chandelier. Then she sighed and laid the paper down. Her husband leaned his panther-headed cane against the wall and sat beside her upon a matching mahogany chair.

—We must not let Noah join the army, said Elmira.

—Nonsense. He's about to graduate at the top of his class, at West Point no less. You ought to be proud of our boy.

—Our only boy.

—Yes. Only. And whose fault is that?

Elmira gritted her teeth. He knew damn well whose fault it was. Miles had caught a disease several years back and his manhood had been reduced to a doughy, uncooked banquette ever since. She dared not to think of how he contracted it. The last time they'd had this argument, Miles refused to speak to her for a month. Elmira changed the subject.

—The North's been in an uproar after they hung that troubled abolitionist, said Elmira.

—A fanatic and a terrorist.

—They're calling him a freedom fighter.

—He's a maniac. They had every right to hang him. If others dont like slavery, then dont buy slaves. Simple. But dont force it on the rest of us. Maybe they ought to lecture the Africans to stop enslaving and selling their own people by the millions instead.

—I believe their argument is that it's against God. I know the last pope opposed the practice.

—I know the arguments and I dont give a damn about the papists. I'm telling you, if these creatures arent given a firm hand they'll rise up. Then they'll spare the white man no quarter. Why would they?

—Only God knows. You're right, of course, so we must remain strong, which is why the wealth and industry of the North is not something someone in your position ought to take lightly.

—You spent far too much time in Philadelphia. We have weapons and cannons.

—That we purchase from the North.

Miles had always given Elmira a hard time for studying in Philadelphia at Madame Grelaud's Seminary as a girl. To him, she could never be a true Southerner, though she very much considered herself one. She'd fallen in love with the lush scenery, the gentle winters, and the lovely Spanish moss that dangled from the trees. There was a special rhythm and soul to Dixieland. The South was glorious, and because it was glorious she did not wish to see its sacred landscape and its noble people torn asunder by war. In her visits up north, she had grasped how woefully behind Southern industry had fallen. Miles slammed his cup against the table.

—Enough, woman. Politics is not your concern. Noah shall join the army and bring honor to this family and you shall accept it.

It was an argument Elmira had lost long ago. She had pleaded with her son not to go to the military academy, but her boy, young and full of patriotism, went with his father's advice instead. Miles' fury dissipated nearly as quickly as it had come and he lowered his voice.

—Right now, we need to focus on my reelection campaign.

He wasnt doing well in his race for congress, which was a mere week away. Word had it that it was almost a shoo-in that his challenger, Ambrose de Bellomonte, would win. Ambrose had made a name for himself during the Mexican War and rose to become a prominent, and now retired, general. The de Bellomonte family and the Beaumont family had vied for power and influence for generations. Now Ambrose had his sights on Miles' house seat. Ambrose's father had been a governor, but that was not enough. Elmira thought her husband's chances slim, nevertheless, she was the bedrock that the Beaumont family was built upon, and she vowed to support him with her heart and her actions, though for now, she only had comforting words.

—I'm quite certain your victory is all but assured, she said.

Her husband was a difficult man, but she loved him. She still remembered the way her heart fluttered when her father introduced her to her betrothed. She'd expected he would marry her off to some old high-society toad and was surprised by the handsome young man he presented to her. Miles often refused to budge on things, even when it was sensible to do so, but she considered herself a dutiful wife and mother and would suffer what she must for the sake of her small family. God had given her only one son and the Lord knew she'd do anything to protect him.

Elmira put down her newspaper and rubbed her ink-stained fingers together. It reminded her of her father's hands, stained from the long hours he'd put in at his print shop, setting type. She admired her father, a hardworking man raised in a one-room cabin who built a sprawling newspaper empire from scratch.

—You ought to manage the press better, she added.

—I cant outspend Ambrose. Even your own bloody father takes the man's advertisement money.

—If you cant outspend him, then you need to say something to get attention. To motivate people. Father always liked to print contentious articles. He sold more papers that way.

—Like what?

—Well, what is it that people dont like about Mr. de Bellomonte?

—Ambrose is soft. He wants to work with the Northerners. If you ask me, we ought to cut them loose, but he's afraid of them. Afraid he'll lose his plantation. You know what we ought to do? The South ought to strike first. Yes. Strike hard and fast before they even know it's coming. One Southerner is worth five Northerners in battle.

—Darling, our only son is going to be serving in the army.

—And he'll serve with valor. The North would never stand a chance, it would be a rout.

Elmira wished she hadnt said anything. She had already sacrificed her religion for Miles, and now he wanted her to sacrifice her only son to the army while he did all he could to goad the good public into war. She didnt know much about war, but she didnt think wanton jingoism was enough to win one. What she did know is that her dear Miles had no substance, only sinful pride, and she feared it would be the death of all of them. Miles grabbed his cane and stood up with his chest puffed out.

—Tonight, I have one last rally in Chippewa Square. I'm not going to hold anything back this time.

By midmorning the following day, Elmira and Miles found themselves on a train steaming north toward West Point. A stack of newspapers was piled on Elmira's lap, her husband's name on the front page of each. The rally had gone better than she'd expected. Ambrose de Bellomonte's latest had been described by the press as flustered and defensive, as he flipflopped between a hard line against the North and cooperation. Elmira figured that since they were heading to New York anyway, instead of telling her husband of the North's industry, she could show him.

—Darling, perhaps we could see a bit of New York City while we're passing through? she asked.

—The windows on our train car are enough. I have no need nor desire to step foot in that filthy crime-ridden stain upon our map.

She had been to the city the year before and had been impressed with its phenomenal growth. Fresh batches of European talent poured forth from ships by the thousands, the sky was filled with the spiraling smoke of industry, and new buildings were going up around the clock. While the old South was in her heart, her mind told her that it would take more than Southern courage to win against such industrial might, filthy and crime-ridden or otherwise.

—Perhaps you could convince some of their industry to move to Georgia. It might be wise for the South to improve such things before taking such a hard line on matters.

—We have no need of their industry.

—Aside from DC, you havent been to the Northern cities in twenty years. Remarkable things have happened in that time. Their industry, their commercial operations have grown incredibly. You mustnt be so rash, Miles. At least have a quick look around. It wont take long.

—I dont feel like it. I feel like sleeping.

Miles closed his eyes and placed a newspaper over his face.

A drizzle fell as their carriage pulled in front of the solemn granite campus of West Point. A grand, Norman-style cathedral towered above the morning mist. Miles took Elmira's arm as they walked along a winding path to the parade grounds. The bleachers there were packed full of people holding black umbrellas. The ceremony had already started.

When the cadet band finished, a formation of young men in gray uniforms marched to the center of the grounds. The only sound was the rhythm of shiny black boots against the pavement. Despite the academy's best attempts at complete uniformity, Elmira could still make out her son's boyish face amid the formation. His uniform was nicely pressed, and his boots polished to a mirror's shine. The realization that Noah had become a man hit her hard. She had given her baby boy to the army to be trained to kill other baby boys.

There he stood, tall and erect. Elmira tried to hold back, but her emotions got the best of her. She held out longer than her husband, as Miles had started sobbing as soon as Noah crossed the threshold of the parade grounds.

Chapter 4

NOAH

1860, Georgia

Noah rode upon a black horse. He had been pinned a brevet second lieutenant and was on leave before his first deployment. He couldnt wait to leave the plantation and was excited to go battle against the Indians. Stories of war had enthralled him since he was a boy, and he longed to battle, to kill, to bring glory to his family. His father had agreed and made every resource available to him to pursue his aims.

Beside him rode his father, Miles, on a white horse. Several hounds followed along, their noses low to the ground. The rolling pastures filled with thoroughbreds and livestock. They rode along the perimeter of their twelve thousand acres and watched as the machinery of the plantation went to work. A stream turned a water wheel, which ground corn into meal. The old whiskey still gave off a fermented perfume of corn mash and rye. Everything worked like clockwork.

They stopped their horses upon a ridge overlooking the surrounding swampland. His father owned all of it, but the only use it served was as a source of alligator leather.

—This will all be yours one day, said Miles.

—Pa, I pray that day never comes.

His father leaned over from his horse and patted Noah's shoulder. Such affection was rare. It had been a hardscrabble battle throughout Noah's life to earn such gifts. At school, at sport, at West Point, he'd fought to be the best and usually he was. Typically, his efforts had only earned him his father's criticism at best, or indifference at worst. It made him fight that much harder. Every smile, every pat—every *Good job, son*—was like a glass of iced tea on a scalding Georgia day. His father awkwardly removed his hand and returned his gaze to the swampland.

—So, have you considered taking Abigale Lee's hand?

—Ma wants me to meet some other woman first.

—There you go a-talkin to your mother again. Her and her Northern boarding school clique.

—I dont see no harm in meetin her.

—That's just what your mother wants. To have some Yankee woman get her claws around you. Son, trust me when I say that you want a woman who's beautiful, dumb, compliant, and most importantly, Southern.

—But Ma is neither dumb nor compliant.

—Tis the consequences of an arranged marriage. Be thankful I've given you a choice. But I expect that you'll make a wise choice. Such is your responsibility to the Beaumont name.

His pa always liked to remind him of the importance of the family name, which dated back to Norman times. They were of Norman heritage, who in turn were supposedly descended from the Romans. Their ancestors had conquered Britain, and now they had sailed to the New World and conquered it from the war-like, pagan savages. Their bloodline kept the family legacy immortal. Beaumont Hall was their villa, their castle, and their mark on the New World. Above the entryway of their home stood their family crest, in the center of which was a bloodred crimson rose. He replied to his father's commands the only way he knew how.

—Yessir.

Father and son turned away from the swamp on the edge of the plantation and rode inward toward a stretch of wide-open pasture. The blue sky turned black and for a moment all sunlight was blotted out by the massive conflagration above. The air around them echoed with the flapping of passenger pigeons' wings. They aimed their shotguns skyward. Two blasts rung out. Black specks fell to earth and thudded against the ground. The horses and livestock scattered while the hounds bounded forward toward the fallen birds. They fired into the black mass again, and again, and again.

—Pa, I think we got enough birds.

—Nonsense. We'll shoot till we run out of ammunition.

Noah gazed at the mass as it inched across the horizon.

—There's got to be millions, billions of them.

—All the more reason we oughta keep shootin.

And so they did.

The day was dying by the time they returned to the plantation buildings. Noah counted twelve burlap sacks full of passenger pigeons. The servants would sort the choicest birds for the family and give the remainder to the overseers and the slaves.

Noah walked past the well and toward the slave shacks with two burlap bags full of pigeons in each hand. He wandered over toward Isaiah's cabin. The young man was sitting by the communal fire, shirtless. His back was covered in fresh flog marks. Noah dropped the bags of pigeons at Isaiah's feet and ordered him to distribute them evenly among the group.

—What happened? he asked.

—Back-talked simple Jed.

—Why would you do such a fool thing?

—Why wouldnt I?

Noah huffed. Isaiah merely looked at him, stone-faced. Those pale blue eyes were an embarrassment. Those blue eyes staring from the tan flesh of that quadroon body, like a ghost haunting Beaumont Hall.

—If you'd stopped acting up, Pa wouldnt have kicked you out of the house.

—I was gonna get kicked out either way. And as for Jed, I've met smarter potatoes.

—Shut up with that. They catch you talking like that you'll get flogged again.

—I get flogged either way.

Noah studied Isaiah's face, an abomination if there ever was one. Why should he even bother? Isaiah had once lived in Beaumont Hall, in a room next to his own. Still, he was to lower his eyes when in the presence of his betters.

—You oughta be more careful.

Isaiah gave a weak laugh and pointed to the mansion.

—It's all a roll of the dice, ya know. I could be in there with fine clothes and you out here in rags.

By all rights, Noah should have punished Isaiah for such flippant remarks. His pa certainly would have. He held back and thought himself weak for it.

—And in such a case you'd behave no differently. Especially you. You've got a taste for blood. I know it and you know it. In that vein, I must admit we are similar. Though I spect you'd be far more ruthless than Ol' Jed. Jed acts the way a dumb animal does, but you, I could see you being a ruthlessly efficient killer. Remember our old lessons together, about Thucydides?

—I remember.

—Then you know the strong do what they will, and the weak suffer what they must.

His ma had made Isaiah his childhood companion. Noah figured she'd wanted someone for him to play with since she and his pa couldnt produce any more children. Noah got along well with Isaiah for the first twelve years. They did everything together. They played with toys, played in the swamp, and out in the pastures. When they became teenagers, the fighting began, as it often did with boys. Ma broke the fights up. Pa encouraged them. Eventually Ma started insisting on granting Isaiah an allowance and finding him a suitable woman for courtship.

His pa wasnt pleased, for people would talk, and the talk would take a toll on the family name. There was an argument and another and another. Isaiah caught on and began to ask too many questions about his status. At first, Miles had brushed the questions aside.

Perhaps if Ma had left good enough alone, Isaiah might still be living in Beaumont Hall. Though being strong willed as she was, the arguments increased until his pa put his foot down and cast Isaiah out into the fields. He figured it was more out of spite to her than anything Isaiah did. At the time, Noah had cried and sobbed and protested Isaiah's exile. He'd been corrected by the snap of the birch. Indeed, he needed correcting quite a few times before he accepted the truth.

As for Isaiah, he was corrected by those who had once called him master. The first day he was sent out, he was stripped naked and beaten by the field slaves. The beatings continued for months on end. Eventually Isaiah grew strong and began winning.

Noah turned and walked past the central well and around toward the back of the house. He came up to the whipping post and he found James tied to it again. His father stood next to Jed as they debated what punishment to mete out. Noah lowered his head and tried to enter Beaumont Hall from the side before his father could notice him. It was too late. The man raised his arm and motioned for him to come over. He obeyed. Miles pointed to James.

—Noah, James here yanked Jed's whip out of his hand when he tried to discipline one of the negresses. What do you think we should do about that?

—Give em the lash, sir.

His father took the lash from Jed's hand and gave it to Noah. He had flogged people before, but never James. When Isaiah still lived in the house, they'd often visit James together and he'd tell them tall tales and always had some sort of treat to give them. Usually fresh peaches and apricots he'd pilfered from the storehouse.

Noah unfurled the whip. He squeezed the cowhide handle as tight as he could to make the tremble in his hand go away. He raised the whip over his head and cracked it against James' back. After two lashes he stopped. That displeased his father.

—Well? What are ya waiting for? Give him one more lick.

He took a deep breath and meted out the punishment. Afterward, James was cut down and returned to his cabin. James neither asked for mercy nor flinched when he was lashed. It was something everyone took notice of. Sometimes it seemed as if James were the leader of the plantation rather than Miles, for James was willing to work and suffer for his flock.

The following Sunday afternoon, Noah rode out alone to ensure the plantation was working as it should. Runaways were becoming increasingly common, and one had to be vigilant. There was another reason as well. The black horse he rode was named Bucephalus. His father had given the horse to him as a boy and now the horse had grown old and sick. This was his last ride. He had a pit dug on the outskirts of the plantation and collected river rocks for a cairn. It was out by the swampland, so he figured his pa wouldnt make much of a fuss. He planned to ride his horse out to the edge of the plantation one last time and then put it out of his misery. Then he'd walk back and get a few negroes to bury it and use the rocks to create a large cairn atop the grave. His father would have chided him for such sentimentality.

The gnats were terrible as they approached the edge of the plantation. As he reached the grave, the horse collapsed. Noah fell off to the side and Bucephalus rolled over on top of him. The entirety of its weight pressed down upon his chest. His horse lifted its head sideways from the ground and brayed and then laid it down forever. Noah tried to cry out, but he couldnt, for the air was being pressed from his chest.

Noah used all his strength in an attempt to pull himself out from under the beast. It was no use. He fell back. He was only able to inhale tiny breaths. Just enough air to keep him alive for maybe a few hours while the gnats and the flies and the creeping things sucked at his eyes.

He was watching the birds fly overhead and waiting to die when he heard a rustling behind him. A black man, woman, and child looked at him. They all carried pouches and it was clear that they were runaways. Noah held out his hand and tried to speak but was unable. They looked at him for several moments as if trying to figure out what to do. They whispered among themselves and then disappeared into the woods.

So this is how it ends. This is God's plan for me.

His vision was getting blurry. The light was fading. He blinked and made out a dark figure standing over him. Noah saw one eye white and glazed over and the other a deep brown. It was James. Noah had put out a prayer that someone might save him. Now he knew he was as good as dead.

—Just do it. Just kill me, he mouthed breathlessly.

James squatted down. Noah felt his chest fill with air. He began breathing and coughing, coughing and breathing. His eyes widened in disbelief as the old man heaved up the dead horse. Noah quickly crawled out from under it. James then dropped the horse with a thud.

Noah climbed to his feet. He felt along his belt for his revolver but it was gone. He looked up and saw it in James' hand. The giant was holding it by the barrel.

James handed him back his revolver. If he'd been in the old man's position, he would have simply shot him and run off. The man before him was either an idiot or a saint. He dusted himself off and awkwardly tried to stand proud and erect. They walked quietly back toward the center of the plantation where the main house and slave cabins were. After walking for several minutes, Noah spoke.

—Why did you help me?

—Couldnt just leave ya there.

—But I flogged you just yesterday.

—I forgive you.

His neck and face grew hot with blood. He stomped out in front of James and blocked his path. Then he unholstered his revolver and held it down at his side.

—Who the hell are you to forgive me?

—Creature of God. Like you.

—You aint nothing like me.

James appeared neither angry nor afraid. That somehow made Noah angrier. He had struggled to push the childish relationship he'd had with the monster out of his mind. James looked at him with his good eye.

—You're different than your pa.

—You know nothin of my pa.

—Known him longer than you and I know you didnt whip Isaiah when you had every excuse to. Ya know, you and him look an awful lot alike.

The remark angered him and his shaking hand pointed the pistol at James.

—You need to shut up with that.

—You asked me to look after him when he was kicked out the house. Was a kind thing you did.

Noah swallowed hard. He lowered the pistol. It took his trembling hand several attempts to get it back into his holster. He turned around and stormed off. Noah fogged out his thoughts with several glasses of brandy as he sat on the balcony and watched the sun recede behind the tree line. His father sat next to him.

—Lookin forward to heading out to the frontier? asked his pa.

—Yessir, cant wait.

Chapter 5

EMMA

1860, Georgia

Emma cried herself to sleep for the first three days, but on the fourth she found she no longer had tears to shed. She was given an old horse blanket to sleep on, which she kept in a far corner of the stable. Her new routine wasnt much different from her old one. She mostly cared for the thoroughbreds. Despite her attempts to stay out of sight, she always felt eyes upon her. The mistress of the house rarely left it, but she seemed omnipresent, always watching Emma through the wavy glass of her study with her piercing gaze.

Emma's wooden bucket was heavy enough without any water in it. When it was full, she could barely carry it. Her request for a smaller bucket was met with laughter and derision from the overseers. She counted. Twelve more trips to fill up all the horse troughs. A nearby group of girls weaved baskets. They sneered as she walked past. Unlike her, they worked in the fields and wore ragged clothes. They'd taken to calling her *the horse princess*.

As she carried the bucket from the center well to the troughs, her foot caught a rock. Water splashed down the front of her dress. The group of girls giggled as she wrung out her skirt. Emma wanted nothing more than to be invisible. If she couldnt be invisible, she hoped she could at least not draw attention to herself. But the problem with minding your own business was people always minded yours. The tallest girl put down her half-made basket and stood in Emma's path. Emma tried to walk around. Again the girl stepped in front of her. She tipped Emma's bucket and water poured over her once more. The girls chortled and squealed like brazen piglets.

She took her bucket back to the well and filled it up again. The bucket grew heavier with each trip. She could feel the strain of the tendons in her small, tired wrists. Now all the girls blocked her path. The tallest one grabbed her by the hair.

—You aint better than us.

The girl pulled back her fist. Emma's grip began to fail her as the thin rope handle cut into her palms. Then the bucket became weightless. She turned to the side to find Isaiah holding it. He grabbed the other girl's wrist with his free hand. The group of them froze, wide-eyed.

—Move, said Isaiah.

He released the girl's wrist. The tall girl and the others slowly left. Emma had heard that the strange young man had a reputation of fighting anyone, no matter how suicidal his odds might be. Women, it seemed, were no exception. Still, he didnt come across as a brute. Just unusual. He kept to himself and only talked to his mother and the giant man, James. Isaiah filled all the horse troughs to the brim. Then he reached out to pet Cheyenne.

—Careful. She's wild, said Emma.

Isaiah nodded and proceeded to pet the horse. She had never seen Cheyenne so calm around anyone. He turned to her.

—You gettin enough to eat?

—I am.

Isaiah handed Emma a peach from his pocket.

—Here.

Emma took the marbled red-and-gold fruit. She took a careful bite into the soft flesh. Its sweet juice filled her mouth. Isaiah began to walk away. Emma swallowed hard and shuffled after him and tapped his shoulder.

—I have some leftover porridge. Would you like some?

Isaiah shook his head.

—For supper? You can take it with you.

With that, he walked away.

Later that day, Emma heaved straw with a pitchfork into the horse stalls. Two young men approached. One of them was just as muscled and large as James and still growing. His name was Damian. The other was a small, sinewy, skinny creature with a misshapen underbite and red-veined yellowed eyes, bulging and bird-like. He stumbled about strangely, with double-jointed knees, and approached hunched over and slightly crabwise, always with a wide vacant grin pinned across his Godforsaken visage. That was Sid, who was known to always follow Damian around imp-like. The others warned her to stay away from them, but they had said the same thing about Isaiah.

The young men rested their elbows on the surrounding rail fence and leered at her as she heaved straw. The big one, Damian, spoke.

—Dont mind me, just enjoyin the view.

Sid gave a strange gurgled yet shrill laugh. Emma turned to the side and continued her work. Damian crawled over the rail fence and put his muscled arm over her shoulder.

—How bout you keep me warm tonight?

She slid her shoulders out from under his arm and hurried to the far end of the stables. Damian and Sid pursued her. Emma's tear-filled eyes searched for allies. Normally she feared the advances of the overseers. Now she wanted nothing more than for an overseer to come. Cornered in the stable, she picked up her pitchfork and pointed the implement at Damian.

—Touch me and I'll run you through.

Damian gave a broad smile while his imp Sid clapped and hopped about on his skinny anemic legs and discolored spittle sprayed forth from his twisted mouth as he carried on with his strange shrill laughter.

—You dont wanna spend the night?

—I'd rather sleep next to a horse.

Sid's ridiculous chortling slowed to a stop.

Damian grabbed his crotch.

—If it's horse cock you want, I've got one right here.

The pitchfork trembled in Emma's hands. She wanted to curl up and hide in a corner somewhere, anywhere. Emma prayed Damian wouldnt test her, for she wasnt sure if she could carry out her threat.

—Get. I'll tell the masters.

—Masters? Have you been round back and seen the pit?

—Full of rottin livestock and neeegroes, added Sid.

The imp clapped and chortled as Damian removed his rag of a shirt and flexed. Then Sid removed his shirt, revealing his twisted torso, sinewy and hunched, and flexed as well.

—Hot out here, said Damian.

—Yeah, it's hot, said Sid.

Disgusted but convinced the two young men werent worth impaling, Emma stormed off to the other side of the stable. They pursued. Damian approached and grabbed her arm.

—Rude to walk off like that.

His grip tightened. He squeezed so hard his thick thumb pressed against her bone.

—Stop. You're hurting me.

—Say please.

Sid's bulging eyes now glowed as his head weaved side to side with that grin, that vacant grin, painted across his face.

—Please.

He smirked and let go. Emma eyed a pile of horse manure at her feet. As Damian and Sid turned to one another and shared a laugh, she bent over and picked it up. When Damian turned back around, she slammed the patty into his face. Sid stood scared and slack-jawed as Damian wiped the warm, sticky mess out of his eye sockets.

—Oh, you gettin it now.

He and Sid closed in around her. Right then, Jed sauntered up to the stables.

—Let her work. You two apes, quit foolin round.

Damian glared at Emma and sauntered off with Sid in tow, scuttling behind him with his crabwise gait. Emma wanted to hide in the stables for the rest of the day, but she knew she couldnt.

The dull bronze chime of the evening bells rang. The cabin area around the old well was filled with life as everyone returned from their labors. Emma finished grooming the last thoroughbred for the day. What Damian and Sid had said about the pit bothered her. She tried to ignore it but found herself walking toward the location of the supposed thing. In a secluded part of the plantation, next to the edge of the swamp forest, was a great pile of red earth which rose as high as a cabin.

As Emma crept toward it, the stench of rotting flesh filled the air. She stood on the edge of a large pit full of dead livestock. There were cows and chickens and other poor creatures she could no longer recognize. Diseased animals that couldnt be eaten.

She scanned the awful pile carefully. Damian and Sid must have been teasing her. Emma let out a sigh of relief and turned away, but then she caught something out of the corner of her eye. She knew she shouldnt turn her head and look, but she couldnt help it. It was a skull. A human skull, its jaw agape, with dried flesh and tufts of black hair still clinging to it. Emma breathed hard and heavy as she backed away from the pit.

Voices. She heard two men murmuring on the other side of the dirt mound behind her. Her curiosity got the better of her. Peeking around, she saw Isaiah and James. They had sticks in their hands and were pointing to a map drawn in the soil. They were arguing over directions. Isaiah wiped the map away and traced out a new one.

—There's a safe house just up the trail from Dead Man's Creek, he said.

—How'd you hear bout that? asked James.

—I was given a pass to the downtown market a few days ago. Randall, from the Owens' plantation, told me bout it. He knows three families that have passed through.

—I suppose it's the best shot we have.

Emma struggled to hear the conversation. She peered farther over the side of the mound. James turned his head and she found herself looking directly into the monstrous man's good eye. Flies suckled on the gaping wounds of his flayed back. His torso was as muscled as an ox's and one of his arms was as thick as her waist. His body had cuts and scars that looked like spear wounds. Everything about the man told her that he must have been a killer.

—Emma, said James.

—What are you doin here? Isaiah asked, turning to see her as well.

—I came to see the pit. To see if it's real. I promise I didnt hear anything.

—That means you heard everything.

—I didnt.

By instinct, the lies flowed from her mouth. Isaiah approached and placed his hands on her arms. His callused fingers felt rough against her skin. He seemed to look right through her.

—Tell no one what you heard today. It's all our lives if you do, said Isaiah.

—I didnt hear anything.

—Promise me you wont say a word.

—I promise.

Emma peered over his shoulder at James. The monster of a man stepped forward. She wasnt sure if it was her nerves or her heartbeat, but she swore she could feel the earth tremble with his every step. Isaiah released her. James held out his massive hand, each finger as thick as two of hers.

—A pleasure, young lady. He spoke with an accent she couldnt quite place and shook her hand with surprising delicacy.

Isaiah departed. When he had gotten out of earshot, Emma turned back to James.

—He doesnt like me, does he?

—I think he likes you just fine.

—He dont act like it.

—He aint afraid of much, but he's afraid of you.

—Of me?

James plopped down upon the earth with a thud. Emma sat beside him. When Emma asked why Isaiah was so cold, James revealed that Isaiah's mother, Mary, had once been the prettiest girl on the plantation. Even prettier than the plantation mistress. Emma found it very hard to believe, looking upon the weathered and hunched-over woman now. Nobody knew for certain what, but something had happened to her. By the time Isaiah came along, her mind was broken. As for Isaiah, James was the only thing the young man had. James stood, held out his hand, and helped Emma to her feet.

—War is in the air. When the time comes, we're heading north. We'd like to bring you with us. Dont give me your answer now. Sleep on it. Cause if we get caught, well, let's just try not to think about that.

Emma retired to her stable for the night. She finished wiping herself down with a wet rag in the inner corner of the stable she called home. There wasnt much to it. Just her straw mattress and an upside down pail with a tallow candle sitting atop it. She hung her dress on a rusty nail sticking out from the wall. She missed the days when she could bathe in the cool, clear waters of the creek next to Anderson Stables. As she was about to blow out her candle, she heard the crunching of straw.

Two creeping shadows approached.

—Isaiah? James? Is that you?

Chapter 6

ISAIAH

1860, Georgia

He tossed and turned atop his itchy straw mattress. He tried to bury such transient thoughts so he forced his eyes shut, but she lingered, gliding softly and apparition-like through the anima of his being.

Isaiah sat up with his tired back soaked with a cold sudor. He stumbled outside his cabin trance-like and placed his hands on the weathered bricks of the well and gazed downward into the rippled reflection of the white moon above. As he gazed into the abyss below, he considered that Emma had come from a better place. Her clothes were nicer. Her eyes were bright, her hair was long, thick, and shiny, and she talked differently, though she tried to hide it. She told everyone within earshot that she was dumb as an ox, but he knew otherwise.

Isaiah heaved the well's bucket upward and then ladled some of the dark water into his parched mouth. Earlier that morning he had caught himself staring again. Her hair had come loose. He'd watched as wayward strands of Emma's long, curly locks kissed her neck. With her thumbs she grasped the loose, spiraled strands and pulled them back up under her headwrap. His eyes had started at her delicate wrists, moved along her shapely arms, and stopped at her chest. Emma's headwrap fell from her hand as she tried to tie back her hair. She bent over and the neck of her dress fell to the earth. He knew he shouldnt look, so he turned his head, but his eyes remained fixed. Emma stood back up and adjusted her hair. His leering gaze met with her pale brown eyes, bright and intelligent. He turned away and pretended to be busy.

Isaiah stopped his lucid dreaming. It would pass. It always passed. It needed to pass. He put the ladle back in the bucket and lowered it until he heard the echo of a deep splash. He walked back toward his cabin but paused when he heard a shuffling sound from within the stable. He continued walking, then stopped midstep. He turned and headed toward the stable. He stopped and put his hand on the nearby fence.

—Must have been the horses, he muttered to himself.

Isaiah turned to leave. Then a muffled shriek came from behind him. *None of his business.* He willed his legs to walk back toward his cabin, yet there he stood. He remembered when he'd been kicked out of the big house, stripped and beaten in front of the entire plantation. Afterward he lay there, alone and in a pool of his own blood, and James came up to him and stretched out his massive hand. In his hand, a cup of water.

James had done that despite being ordered by Miles himself not to. After Isaiah drank the water, James was directed to the whipping pole. From that day on, he was always at James' side. He didnt even know James' origins. No one did. Whoever he was and wherever he came from, those were things James kept to himself.

Isaiah only knew that James was a God-fearing man and his only friend.

Isaiah took a cautious step inside the stable. Something rustled. The yellow light of a tallow candle revealed mottled shadows wrangling against the wooden planks of the stable wall. He peered through squint eyes. The dull candlelight landed on Emma's face, contorted and nearly cowed. She was thrashing and flailing on her back. Then he made out two more figures grabbing at her, toying with her. Emma thrust her foot repeatedly against Sid's twisted chest while Damian pulled on her skirt.

The girl punched the side of his meaty head with no effect. Sid chortled, his bird-like eyes wide and crazed. She kicked wildly while Damian unbuttoned his trousers. Sid looked at Isaiah and licked his lips.

—Go find yer own bitch, said Sid.

Damian dropped his drawers to his ankles. Each of Emma's kicks and punches grew weaker than the last. His heart pounded as his clenched hands shook. Damian locked eyes with him and smiled a grim smile.

—James, James, help, he mocked.

Isaiah ran to him and thrust his foot into Damian's exposed groin. The muscled youth keeled over onto his side, grabbing his battered instrument. Sid tried to desperately hobble away but Isaiah grabbed him and popped him in the throat. As Sid collapsed, Isaiah jumped on top and pounded him.

Emma climbed to her feet and kicked Damian in his groin and ran. A moment later, Damian slowly rose and pulled up his drawers. He grabbed Isaiah's shirt and threw him off Sid with one arm. Isaiah stood and faced him.

He took a swing at the giant. It landed weakly against his muscled jaw. Damian swung and Isaiah's vision went black. His shoulder hit the ground hard. Damian's ugly mug faded in and out of focus. A powerful kick landed against his stomach and he was out of air. He rolled onto his back, wheezing and moaning. A massive foot rose above his face.

Isaiah closed his eyes.

A flurry of footsteps, followed by a loud crash. When he opened his eyes, Isaiah saw two blurry figures. He blinked hard and saw James grappling with Damian. James ended up on top and pounded Damian and pounded his muscled arms into Damian's face and torso.

When James lifted his blood-soaked fists, Sid tried to run away. James grabbed him by the neck with one hand, his waistband with the other, and threw him. He landed with a hard thud on the earthen floor. His eyes remained open and unblinking with white spittle drooling oblong from his misshapen mouth, his vacant smile still in place. James returned to Damian as he lay in the dirty blond straw, moaning and gasping. He pulled his fist back. He stopped at the sound of clapping hands.

—That's enough, James. I do enjoy a good fight, said Miles.

Jed, his bottom lip fat with snuff, stood at his master's side.

—Looks like there was quite the brawl in here, said Miles.

—They tried to rape the girl, said James.

Miles sucked on his cigar and let out a thick plume of smoke. Jed coughed.

—Of course, that type of uncivilized behavior isnt tolerated here at Beaumont Plantation. After all, this is a Christian plantation. Jed, put Damian and Sid in the stocks for three days. No food, no water. God will decide if they're to be forgiven.

Jed whistled. Four more overseers came and dragged away the limp bodies. The room began to spin and get blurry again. Isaiah saw a flash of crimson fabric and then everything went dark.

Something tickled his nose. Isaiah's eyes fluttered open. Long locks of loose hair hung over his face. Emma gently wiped the blood from his face with a damp rag. His head was in her lap. Despite the throbbing pain throughout his body, to lie in such a place made it worthwhile. A powerful pat fell upon the front of his shoulder.

—You did alright. We're gonna get out of here. All three of us, said James.

Chapter 7

ELMIRA

1860, Georgia

Elmira watched through her window as Isaiah worked the fields. His face was swollen and he clutched his side as he worked. She wondered if Miles would have come to her rescue, risking life and limb, if she'd been attacked. She pushed the uncomfortable thought aside. Damian and Sid were still in the stocks. Sid didnt look like he was going to make it. Then again, he never looked like he was going to make it since the day he was born. Though probably not this time. Miles had washed his hands of him. He wasnt much of a worker anyhow. A pair of hands fell upon her shoulders. Startled, she turned.

—Noah?

Her son stood behind her. She placed her hands on his cheeks and kissed him and then embraced him until he gently squeezed free from her grasp. Then they walked through the sumptuous passages of Beaumont Hall. Noah paused and pointed to one of Elmira's watercolor paintings.

—You're gettin better.

—Thank you. You clearly got your good taste from me.

When they got to the attached greenhouse, they sat in white wicker chairs. It was Elmira's favorite room because it was Noah's favorite room. As a child, he'd always loved to run between the ferns and little fruit trees and to sail toy ships in the fishpond.

Elmira was excited for Noah to meet Caroline. Caroline was the daughter of one of her close friends from Madame Grelaud's Seminary. Of course, Elmira saw a little bit of herself in the young woman. Caroline was educated, sharp witted, yet tactful. She was a bit homely, but she was pleasant. Elmira couldnt help but be impressed by the way she managed a household. She'd be a fine daughter-in-law to carry the torch of the Beaumont name into the next generation. She took Noah's arm and turned to him.

—Darling, you must meet Caroline. She's such a lovely girl.

—You and Pa just cant seem to wait to marry me off.

—You cant blame a lonely woman for wanting grandchildren, can you? We've got seventy-five rooms in Beaumont Hall and most of them are empty.

—I would be much obliged to give you those grandchildren. I need to wait until after my term of service though.

—Why?

—I dont need any distractions, the air smells of war.

Elmira was unsettled by such talk. Miles spoke of war as if it were glorious. Her father had served and said it was barbarous. The thought of her son on the battlefield made her stomach lurch. Elmira shifted to happier thoughts. To marriage and the laughter of grandchildren. She'd continue to press her son, for she wasnt one to give up so easy.

—Would you at least like to meet her? Courtship can take years, after all.

—Pa wants me to marry Abigale Lee Daniels.

—I'm sure he does, and I'm sure your father would marry her himself if he had the chance. A big purse, a big bosom, and a small brain. I do so hope you arent seriously considering the idea?

—She's nice, and she's pretty, real pretty.

—When she births six children and those glorious breasts of hers are slapping her knees, all you'll be left with is the wretched person left inside. Then you can ask yourself if marriage based purely on appearance was a wise idea.

Noah laughed.

—You're beautiful, and you turned out alright.

—Why, that's different. I've been blessed with both beauty and brains. I'm an extreme rarity, like a red diamond.

—I wouldnt dare disagree.

—And what does this…Abigale like to do besides walk about cross-eyed, flaunting her cleavage?

—She likes to train and ride horses.

—I've heard she likes to ride gentlemen as well. Half of Chatham County, from what I'm told.

—Mother, you're much too harsh. You're saying Pa didnt marry you because of your beauty?

—Your pa and your late grandparents were nearly bankrupt. My father wanted to expand his newspaper empire into Savannah. Though destitute, your grandfather Beaumont was a man of great influence, and he had Beaumont Plantation. I was the trade. Your father was nineteen and I was fourteen and you were born a year later.

—Then it was happily ever after?

Elmira gazed through the glass panes of the greenhouse for several moments.

—Everyone got what they needed, I suppose. As for my beauty, your pa just got lucky.

—Well then, if Abigale's got money…

—It's important that you cherish the woman you marry.

—Sure.

The hot blood of anger climbed up the back of Elmira's neck. She seized his hand and squeezed it hard.

—Dont you ever take those sacred vows only to show your wife coldness and indifference.

Elmira's knuckles turned white as she squeezed her son's arm and dug her nails into his flesh. He appeared startled.

—Promise me.

—Of course.

—Say it.

—I promise.

Elmira relaxed her grip and offered a thin smile. Noah rubbed his reddened arm and examined it to see if her nails had broken the surface.

—Good.

—Ma, you need not worry about me. I'll be fine. I promise you those grandchildren, in due time.

Naturally, Elmira ignored her son's hesitancy and had already invited Caroline to visit several days previous. The Beaumont family waited on the long porch as a black lacquered carriage trundled down the avenue of oaks and stopped before the front door. A servant walked to the carriage and opened the door, revealing a bright splash of cornflower-blue fabric.

A petite young woman with porcelain skin and brown hair tied in a simple bun emerged from the carriage. She smiled and shuffled toward them while a servant carried the luggage behind him. She turned and pawed at the suitcase handle.

—Oh, I got that, mister, thank you.

She tugged on the luggage but the servant wouldnt let go.

—I must insist, said the servant.

She nodded and stumbled forward to the base of the stairs, Noah catching her fall. Her big brown eyes widened and her small mouth parted as she caught Noah's visage. She awkwardly straightened herself and held out her lace-gloved hand and Noah took it and bowed slightly.

Later Elmira watched from a distance as her son took Caroline's arm and showed her around the plantation. They had tea together and Caroline, being from the city, was quite interested in the animals of the plantation, particularly the alligators, which she had never seen before. Noah was happy to oblige and took her to the swamp. That evening she came back filthy, her cornflower-blue dress covered in mud, but with a big bright smile. She couldnt tell precisely how well they were getting along, but things seemed to be going better than expected.

She prayed Caroline would cause Noah to reconsider his priorities.

A few days later, Elmira walked with Miles, Noah, and Caroline through Oglethorpe Square in Savannah. Elmira leaned her red silk parasol against her shoulder and Caroline carried one of cornflower blue. It was nice to see the city. Because Beaumont Plantation was next to swampland, it was nearly always wrapped in a veil of fog. In the city, the sun was out, which made for a pleasant day to walk in the square. Spanish moss hung elegantly from the oaks, making the trees appear as if they were weeping. The somber-looking branches were bejeweled by the iridescent, blue-green feathers of Carolina parakeets perched upon their branches.

Miles often said he hated the squawking of the birds. Elmira had always thought they were singing. Noah agreed. Caroline scattered some breadcrumbs and tried feeding them.

As the birds pecked at the crumbs, Noah bent over and picked something off the ground. It was two lovely feathers that changed color as they shifted in the sunlight. He gave one to Caroline and the other to her. Elmira smiled, probably too broadly, but she didnt care. She removed her hat and placed the feather in the strap, and Caroline, imitating her, did the same. It was always the little things Noah gave her that filled her heart with the most pleasure.

—So, son, is your heart with the Southern cause? asked Miles.

—Yessir, heart and soul.

—Would you fight for it?

Elmira clenched her jaw. The remark made her blood boil. If he wanted war, he ought to fight in it himself. Of course, she decided to make her remarks a little more gently.

—He doesnt need to fight because there isnt a war. We're still part of the same union, said Elmira.

—There wont be a union for long if they elect Lincoln. I'll tell you that much. This was meant to be the United States of America, not the United Provinces of America. States have rights.

Elmira took Noah's upper arm into her hand and looked up at Miles with pleading eyes.

—Why must we ruin pleasant scenery with such unpleasant talk?

—Unpleasant? The greatest thing that could happen to the South is to be free from the shackles of the North.

Miles turned to Noah.

—Would you serve under Lincoln?

—No, sir. Absolutely not.

—I tell you this, even if he were to succeed, one day they shall tear down any monument to him and work to grind his memory to dust. There will be no gratitude for him, for the masses are fickle and forgetful.

Caroline's face became painted with worry as she pulled herself closer to Noah's free arm. The lush green square seemed to turn to gray. Just when it appeared certain Elmira's day had gotten worse, her eye caught a familiar face in the park. It was none other than Ambrose de Bellomonte. She pulled on Noah's arm and tried to guide him out of the square before Ambrose could notice them, but it was too late. She found herself trapped in his stare and he made his way toward them. Ambrose removed his hat and bowed.

—Good day to you all.

The man shook Miles' hand, forced pleasantry between two gentlemen. Then Ambrose took Elmira's hand to kiss it. She tried to pull it back, but he clenched his hand tight around her wrist. Miles didnt intervene, merely rolled his eyes at the formality. After all, he had done the same to Mrs. de Bellomonte on numerous occasions.

Noah seized Ambrose's hand before his lips could make contact. Elmira watched the veins of her son's hand bulge as he squeezed. They both leaned forward, their noses almost touching.

—That gesture isnt necessary, sir, said Noah.

—I see you're not accustomed to good manners, said Ambrose.

Elmira pulled her hand free and wiped it on her dress. Noah flung Ambrose's hand away.

—My mother does not require your lips upon her flesh, sir.

—Your name is Noah, right?

—That's right.

—I'll remember that name. Noah Beaumont. I'll remember it indeed. Good day to you all.

Chapter 8

NOAH

1860, Wyoming Territory

Noah's horse looked as tired as he was. He had ridden far from the last train depot and any semblance of civilization. Initially, he'd been excited to be assigned as a cavalry officer. Now he found himself sitting atop a sweating horse. He wasnt sure if his shiny leather riding boots and tasseled Hardee hat were worth the saddle sore. As he rode, he considered that he could have married lovely Caroline and would now be enjoying her company—rather than his horse's. With tears in her eyes, she had embraced him for quite some time before she got in the carriage to return home.

Fort Laramie appeared on the horizon. He had expected a great bastion with tall walls of impenetrable masonry and cannons jutting out at every angle and a great wide moat surrounding it. Instead he found a collapsing adobe edifice surrounded by several plain wooden buildings and, to his astonishment, an even greater number of teepees. He had been assigned to the frontier fort to protect settlers and traders from the savages, yet here they were living among the army.

His horse weaved through the covered wagons, passing amid the sprawling hodgepodge of buildings that stood upon a sea of windswept plains beneath a sky thick with silver clouds. Herds of cattle grazed in the surrounding grasslands. Two small winding rivers, their waters calm, ran adjacent to the so-called fort.

His horse trotted down the road and up to a wayward cow. The beast made no attempt to move and cared little if he was an officer or not. It just stood there crapping in the middle of the road. Now it occurred to him what the lingering smell in the air was. Noah sighed.

He rode around the unmoving cow and down the long road furrowed with the hopes and dreams of poor settlers heading westward. He reached the fort, climbed off his horse, and tied it to a hitch rail. To him, the place was more of a town that happened to have soldiers in it than a military installation. It was a far cry from West Point, where military discipline pervaded every aspect of everyday life. Fort Laramie was a disorganized gaggle of activity, and it couldnt even hold everyone who arrived. Many camped outside the barracks in their wagons, while a few had set up tents interspersed with the natives. Settlers busily loaded their wagons with supplies before making their way to the Oregon Trail or to seek their fortune in California. Traders peddled their goods and haggled with the leather-clad natives.

Noah thought he was supposed to fight the savages, yet here folks were conducting business with them, even the soldiers. He didnt understand.

As he wandered the fort, a few soldiers showed him the respect he was entitled to and saluted. A few ignored him. When he approached those to admonish them, they slipped away into the crowd. Noah couldnt fathom such disregard of his station. It took several times of saying *excuse me* and gentle prods to make his way to the commander's dwelling. Just outside the building, he saw a soldier plant a kiss on the round cheek of a native woman and take her copper hand into his own.

Noah walked up to the soldier. The man promptly stood at attention and saluted.

—Welcome to Fort Laramie, sir.

Noah returned the salute and proceeded to circle the soldier. He studied the Indian woman and she looked back up at him, her face stoic and indifferent. She was short and robustly built with long straight shiny hair as dark as pitch. She wore a simple, light gray prairie dress, similar to the ones the ladies back in Georgia favored, only it was adorned with colorful native jewelry.

—What the hell do you think you're doing to that…woman? asked Noah.

—Kissing her, sir.

—Dont be an ass.

—Sir, she's my wife.

—What?

Speechless, Noah dismissed the soldier. Then he reported to his post commander, a colonel, his first commander outside of the academy. He stood at attention and saluted.

—Lieutenant Beaumont reporting as ordered, sir.

—At ease.

The colonel rambled off his expectations of Noah, strutting about like a peacock all the while. Noah could detect the sharp odor of whiskey from the colonel's mouth. After what must have been an hour, the instructions stopped.

—Well, any questions?

—Any recent attacks from the savages?

—Not since the Grattan Massacre. Been quiet ever since.

The room became silent. Noah had something on his mind he wanted to ask, but at the same time he didnt want to risk offending his new commander on day one. He simply stood there doing his best not to look nervous.

—Well, what is it?

—Sir, why are we letting the savages live here?

—Where else are they going to go? They need food and provisions like everyone else.

—But, sir, why are our men being allowed to marry them? It's an abomination, sir.

—Son, all the laws of God and man cant stop people from fornicating. I dont consider it a military matter.

—But, sir.

—Dismissed.

The days grew long. Noah found himself being forced to learn words of the native languages. Instead of gun battles with savages, he found himself acting as a sort of sheriff to resolve petty disputes, miscommunications, and arguments about trade mostly. At first, he had simply yelled louder. He gave on-the-spot English lessons, pointing to things and screaming their names. His face would grow hot and he'd wave his arms around and mess up his hair by running his hands through it out of frustration. The natives were more amused than frightened by his antics.

On a hot summer day, Noah sat on horseback between two separate herds of cattle. Or at least that was what he'd been told they were. The cows all looked to same to him. Two men were arguing over the ownership of a cow, one tall and one short. The third cattle dispute that week.

—You know damn well that's my steer.

—Bullshit, I paid good money for that animal. I have a receipt.

—Bullshit? I got your bullshit right here.

The tall man unholstered his revolver. Then the short man unholstered his. Noah put his face in his palm and sighed. He was a military officer. An instrument of war. It wasnt his place to counsel people and solve their personal problems, yet here he was doing just that. Noah had complained to the colonel about it, but the colonel had stopped him midsentence and told him that Noah's job was whatever the army said it was.

Noah dismounted his horse and stood between the two angry men and held out his arms. He motioned for them to lower their irons. Slowly they lowered and holstered them.

—No need to spill blood over a cow, said Noah.

—But it's my cow.

—No it aint.

—Which cow is it? asked Noah.

The men pointed to a cow that looked like all the other cows. Noah walked up to it. He circled the animal and looked for a brand or mark of some sort. There was none. He inspected the other cows. No brands on any member of either herd. It seemed neither of these men knew the first thing about herding cattle. They seemed to lack any semblance of common sense.

—Gentlemen, why arent your cattle branded?

Both men shrugged. Their trembling hands each held the grips of their pistols. Noah patted the flanks of the cow and circled it one more time to make sure there werent any marks he had missed. There were none. Noah unholstered his revolver. The two men's gazes shifted toward him.

He shot the cow in the head.

—Cut it in half, he said.

Noah mounted his horse and rode off.

The air grew cold and the silvery sky gave way to white. No matter how many layers he put on, it was still cold. The fire in his wood stove never went out. He mostly passed the time in a haze fueled by ale or whiskey or whatever drink the traders brought in. He prayed for war. He was trained for war and it seemed that there was none to be had. He wished the Indians would make a move and raid a wagon train or steal some cattle or something so that he could prove himself in glorious battle. Instead he was huddled in a blanket an Indian had made and watched the cows crap outside his window.

On a featureless autumn morning, he patrolled the immediate area with a few men. Then the inside of his chest quaked and rumbled with a thunderous drumbeat. The ground below him shook. A great clatter of hooves emanated from the prairie. He tilted his head to the side and tried to figure out which direction the noise was coming from.

—Sir, we need to go, said his sergeant.

Sergeant Wade Walker was a good old boy from Tennessee and Noah's only real confidant in the unit. Noah motioned for Walker to wait as he listened. It was an unfamiliar sound though it sounded similar to a herd of cattle or horses. He began to ride up toward a hill. Then he felt a hand on his shoulder. He turned and Walker regarded him with an expression, deadly and serious.

—Now, sir.

—Savages?

—Now.

They drove their horses as hard as they could back to the fort. As his unit rode up to their stables, a massive sea of brown spilled over the hillside. The rafters of every building rived and rattled. His horse was uneasy and jerked from side to side. Noah blinked hard and widened his eyes at the coming wave.

Bison poured into the plains. Thousands of them, millions. He watched, his mouth agape, as the bison continued to flood into the area around the fort. It was a clear day and he could see for miles in every direction and the massive creatures had already filled the horizon as far as the eye could see. The majesty of it all.

Walker told him that he'd once had to ride at least six days on horseback to reach the end of a bison herd like this. The bison gathered along the undulating shores of both rivers. Some of them trudged through the shallows and reached the other side and soon the beasts surrounded the water. Then they dipped their heads and began lapping at it. Noah watched as the thirsty animals drained the river dry before his very eyes.

The Indians and the settlers took potshots as the herd passed. They didnt even need to aim to hit something. A few of the mighty creatures were able to take a hit. Others fell over and were trampled by the rest of the herd. Even after one or two hundred beasts were felled, people continued to fire into the mass.

It took a week for the herd to finally pass. When the mass of animals finally fell out of view, Noah rode out onto the plains. The once tall green grass was now trimmed down to the roots. The entirety of the region was covered in manure and pulverized with cloven hoofprints and littered with hundreds of the fallen beasts. Enough of the animals had been shot to feed and clothe a small army.

Even without telegraph wires, the news spread quick. It had all happened so fast. Lincoln was elected, and South Carolina seceded. Noah knew it was only a matter of time before his home state followed suit, his father would see to that. If he stayed in the Federal Army, he would have to fight not only against the armies that the South was raising, but his own home.

Tennessee sounded like a beautiful place, the way Walker described the scarlet and yellow leaves of autumn trees clinging to the sides of slate mountains, and Noah found himself longing for a place he had never seen. When Walker suggested that they go to Tennessee together and sign up for whatever military unit they could find there, Noah agreed.

Noah stood at attention before the post commander. The colonel slouched behind his desk, unamused. The man knew why he was there and probably had already made up his mind not to grant Noah's resignation.

—Speak, said the colonel.

—I am tendering my resignation, sir.

—You're going to throw away your career, your honor, over what? A bunch of negroes?

—States' rights, sir.

—Bullshit. You're a fine officer. Resignation denied. Dismissed.

—I'm leaving, sir.

The colonel placed his revolver on top of his desk. He spun it a few times until the barrel stopped and pointed at Noah.

—Then you're a deserter. Tell me why I shouldnt shoot you right now?

—Sir, my home is in the South. What use am I to you if I love the people I'm supposed to fight against?

—Beaumont, you do know that if I meet you on the field of battle, I wont hesitate to kill you?

—I know, sir.

The colonel rocked back and forth in his chair. The creaking of the wood was the only noise in the room. He dug through his wastebasket and took out a crumpled-up piece of paper. He smoothed out the creases with his hands and studied it for several minutes. Then he dipped his pen in an inkwell and signed the paper. The colonel got up from his desk and shoved the paper into Noah's hand. Noah saluted. He returned the salute and lowered his hand and extended his palm. Noah shook it.

—All the same, Godspeed, Beaumont.

As he rode out onto the plains after, he looked at Fort Laramie one last time. It soon disappeared into the distance. Then he heard the hard wooden gallop of hooves, closing in fast. When he turned his head, he saw Walker riding up. Unlike Noah, Walker couldnt resign, so he had deserted. Noah figured they'd best get a move on before the others rode out and hung ol' Walker.

They dug in their spurs and rode yonder toward Tennessee.

Chapter 9

EMMA

1861, Georgia

Miles patted the muzzle of one of his thoroughbreds and then meandered over toward Emma. She cast her eyes downward in the hope that by not looking at him she'd somehow make herself invisible. Then he spoke to her.

—Got a husband yet?

—No, sir.

—Dont you worry. I can find ya one.

—Much obliged, sir, but no need.

—You're not getting any younger.

She felt dirty. Emma had thought about ending it all more times than she could count. She'd close her eyes every night and then be disappointed when they opened in the morning. It had been that way for a long time. For years, every night was a dreamless, deathlike sleep. Now she'd begun to have dreams again. She couldnt remember what they were when she woke up, but she knew she had them.

She knew the world wouldnt give her happiness. In fact, Emma was convinced the world wanted nothing more than to take any morsel of joy she had in her life and devour it in front of her. If she wanted any semblance of happiness, she would have to seize it. Until such a time, she was just a bright little soul clinging to an indentured corpse. Still, she held true to her dangerous and foolish dreams no matter what depravity she would be forced to succumb to.

She'd found kindness in James. Then there was Isaiah. She liked James. Then again, everyone liked James. Even the masters considered him first among the slaves despite his occasional insubordination. He was by far the best worker on the plantation and generally kept the peace. The wounds on his back never seemed to get the chance to heal completely before he was flogged for some minor offense, which almost always involved protecting someone weaker. It was strange. The masters mocked him and flogged him but at the same time, in grudging respect, they often reduced the harshness of his punishment. She couldnt wrap her mind around it. All she knew was that the world didnt deserve someone like James.

It was James who'd taken her to the local chapel. On Sundays, Master Beaumont gave out passes to attend church for any slave who had good behavior, whatever that meant. Every Sunday the congregants would get on a crowded wagon and head out toward a rickety wooden chapel out in the countryside. It wasnt far from the plantation then again, the plantation was so large that nothing was very far away from it.

At a communal fire pit, Emma snagged a sweet potato that was roasting on the hot coals with a pointed stick. After the potato cooled a bit, she held it out to Isaiah. He suggested she keep it but she insisted that he eat first. He blew on the sweet potato a few times and took a bite. It seemed to her that the swelling in his face had gone down, although he still managed to look severe and intimidating despite his battered visage. She found it hard to squeeze a single word out of him. Most of what she knew of him came from James. His ma was broken somehow and couldnt really carry on a conversation. Emma leaned to Isaiah and tried once again to coax a conversation out of him.

—Has Miles tried to marry you off yet?

—No.

—Are you, you know, plannin on it?

—No.

—Why not?

—I refuse to give him my children.

—What if you escape?

—I dont think that far ahead.

—You're just going to be alone till you kick over?

—I reckon.

He always brushed off her probing with as few words as possible. She decided to get under his skin a little in the hope it would evoke some sort of emotion at the very least.

—I caught you reading the other day. Where'd you learn to read?

—I was just lookin at the pictures.

—Pictures, huh?

—That's right.

—I didnt see no pictures in that book.

—Must have just turned the page.

Emma huffed and rose to her feet. Isaiah's eyes rolled up to her. She had unwittingly caused herself to get upset, but she no longer cared.

—Do you think I'm stupid? she asked.

Isaiah seemed tongue-tied. He started speaking and then cut himself off multiple times. He paused for several moments before letting out a sigh of frustration.

—I dont think you're stupid. I think you're clever in more ways than you could know.

The remarks cooled her temper, but she found herself unable to shake her annoyance.

—I'm goin.

—Stay, please.

She considered storming off but relented and sat down next to the fire. Emma turned the glowing coals and placed a few more sweet potatoes on top for the morning. To her surprise, Isaiah started a conversation for once.

—Did your parents get along well enough when your ma was still alive?

—The world around them wasnt happy, but they had each other.

—What do you suppose the difference is between marriage and courtship?

—Courtship is polite. Spouses fart in front of each other.

There was a crack in Isaiah's stony facade as the hard line of his mouth gave way to laughter. They laughed together for a time. It was nice. Emma hadnt laughed in so long. His usually cold eyes revealed a sparkle. There was a soul inside of him after all.

Chapter 10

ISAIAH

1861, Georgia

When the bells rang at sunset, Isaiah returned to his cabin with tired hands and a sore back. His mother didnt bother to look at him, she merely continued working on her baskets. Inside, fresh flatbread had already been prepared for him and two wooden cups of water had already been poured. Isaiah was surprised that Emma had invited herself in. She scooped stew into two wooden bowls. He didnt require kindness, nor did he want it. His desire entire was the slaughter of Miles and his retinue—or escape. Perhaps he could even have his own plantation to lord over one day.

—What are ya waiting for? Eat.

Emma spoke in a surprisingly authoritative voice for such a petite young woman. He sat down and they ate quietly together. His mother finished her stew first and went to sleep. When Isaiah finished, Emma placed some leftovers in the corner of the cabin.

—For your lunch, she said.

Emma walked to the doorway and stood there silently for several moments as if waiting for something. Isaiah scratched the back of his head. Emma finally broke the awkward silence.

—Would you like to see me tomorrow?

—I would.

—Good. We ride out to church at sunrise.

—Church?

—You dont go?

—Never.

—Well, that's where I'll be.

At sunrise, Isaiah found himself on a wagon full of parishioners. Emma sat next to him. Isaiah hated such crowded spaces, but he felt his arm press against hers in the narrow confines of the wagon and he no longer minded.

The wagon soon pulled up to a wooden chapel. It was so dilapidated it seemed faith was the only thing holding it together. James got out of the wagon first and held out his hand. Emma took it and climbed down. The congregation was run by a preacher who had somehow managed to gain his freedom. Isaiah thought the pastor was a fool to stay in the South. Prayers wouldnt keep him from being kidnapped and resold.

During the service, Isaiah stood beside Emma and James. He mumbled his butchered rendition of Amazing Grace along with the rest of the congregation. James had tears in his eyes and sang in a deep bass. Emma belted out the hymn at the top of her lungs. Her voice was the most pleasant thing he had ever heard. It seemed that only Isaiah was incapable of singing.

After the singing came the preacher's message. Isaiah felt his lids grow heavy, and the room around him went dark. He felt a sharp prod in his side. He opened his eyes and found Emma right in front of him. Her eyes bulged in anger and she prodded him again, hard. He sat up straight.

The preacher was waving his arms and shouting. Isaiah stared blankly at the wall behind him and didnt pay attention to what he was saying for the most part. However, he caught one fragment of the sermon that angered him.

—Repay no one evil for evil but give thought to do what is honorable in the sight of all.

James and Emma stood, shouting, *Amen*. Isaiah remained seated, his arms crossed.

He thought it tripe. If he had the chance, he'd slaughter every single person who had wronged him. What idiot would leave such matters of vengeance up to some invisible man in the sky? He had wanted to believe at one time. Before, when he thought the world was a beautiful place. What good had it done him? Let the simpletons have their God and let him have blood.

The preacher droned on and Isaiah gave an audible sigh. Again, he felt a sharp prod in his side. Now it was really starting to hurt. Emma glared and scowled at him for a few moments, then turned her face to the front and gave a serene and gentle smile.

After the service, she lectured him on proper decorum in the chapel and gave a long list of reasons why he should listen to her. He thought about backtalking her or walking away, but James stood behind the little woman with his massive arms crossed, nodding his head in agreement with every point she made. James interjected.

—There's a special plan for you, Isaiah. I believe that. So help me God, I'll come back from the grave if you stray from the path of grace.

They were the only two people in his life who meant anything to him, so he stood there silently and took it.

It became a routine, church every Sunday, and Emma ate with him every evening. He lost track of how long it had been since she first started coming over. Every night before she left she'd wait at the doorway silently. Patiently. Isaiah would bid her good night.

On this night he eagerly awaited a knock on his ramshackle door. He knew it would be Emma and did his best not to look anxious. Their conversations were often short and forced. She sometimes asked probing questions about his past, which Isaiah would brush aside as swiftly as he could. As they ate their meal, Emma interrupted the silence. She stood and crossed her arms.

—Who am I to you?

—A friend. A dear friend.

—Does a mere friend feed you, tend to your wounds, and look after you the way I've looked after you?

Emma cast her eyes downward and exhaled. She told him that after tonight, they could no longer be together. That it wasnt proper for her to spend every evening in a man's cabin.

—But I want to see you.

Emma's eyes watered.

—Dont you understand?

She turned and opened the door. Adjusting her head wrap, she began to walk out. Isaiah knew he was about to lose her for good if he didnt do something. While he looked up and saw only dingy gray clouds, she saw rays of light penetrating the overcast sky. He didnt understand how she could see any glimmer in the dark hell they were living, but she did.

Isaiah went to her and took her hand.

—Dont leave.

Emma pulled her hand away.

—I have a heart. Every time I walk up to your door it beats a bit faster. Every time I leave, it feels a bit colder, and you've done nothin to warm it.

Truth be told, he feared opening his own heart more than he feared the lash opening his back. Despite his best efforts, the young woman had taught him love. Part of him despised her for it, for he didnt understand the world anymore. Isaiah could not deny his affection for that young woman who had made herself the rock in his life. He took her hand again. She looked up at him with her watery brown eyes. Emma pulled her hand away once more. She faced him as if thinking of a final thing to say. He took her by the shoulders.

—It aint true that you are nothin to me. You're everything.

Emma made a half-hearted attempt to pull away. She crossed her arms, tilted her chin up high, and cast her eyes off to the side.

—I've already decided to leave.

—Stay, please.

—I'm not some temporary companion.

—Then stay with me. Until death do us part.

Emma slowly turned her head and looked at him, her face glistening with emotion. She wiped her eyes with the hem of her dress. Then she straightened her back and crossed her arms once more.

—What do you mean?

—I'm going to get us out of here. Then we can carve out a life together.

—Are you makin promises you cant keep?

—I was plannin to die. I was going to kill Miles and as many of the overseers as I could until I was killed. Then I met you.

—Talk straight. What are you tryin to say?

—Let us be married.

Emma's smile returned and her head fell against his chest. He felt her arms wrap around him and laid his head against hers.

—Then I will be your wife.

He gently pushed her shoulders back and the warmth of her soft lips melted his frozen soul. Her chest rose and fell and her heart pounded against his.

Chapter 11

ELMIRA

1861, Georgia

Elmira came down from her chambers. She stood at the foot of one of the twin winding staircases that graced the grand foyer of Beaumont Hall decorated with marble and bronze busts and stodgy paintings of long-dead members of the Beaumont bloodline. A servant arrived and handed her a cup of steaming coffee on a freshly shined silver platter.

She seated herself on a nearby couch in the foyer, then took a deep breath of freshly brewed coffee. As she sipped it, Miles paced back and forth in front of the two front doors adjacent to her.

—Darling, you've been pacing for hours.

—How can I possibly sit?

Just as Elmira was about to respond, there were three loud thunks against the doors. Miles counted to ten before opening them.

—Telegram for Mr. Miles Beaumont, said the courier.

—Yes, yes, that's me.

—Sign here.

As soon as Miles finished scrawling his signature, he tore open the envelope and unfolded the letter inside. He gazed upon it with dead colorless eyes and a bland visage. Elmira placed her coffee cup on its saucer and cocked her head.

—Well?

—Ambrose de Bellomonte, 49 percent of received votes. Miles Beaumont, 51 percent. My God, I've won.

Elmira sprang from her seat and ran forward to embrace her husband. He turned his back to her, ignoring her outstretched arms as he walked toward a bronze bust of his grandfather. The telegram fell from his hand and onto the polished marble floor. The object that had given him so much pleasure at one moment was discarded the next. He stood erect with his hands behind his back, gazing at the lifeless statue.

—The Lord has answered my prayers.

Elmira wanted to try to hug her husband again, but if Miles wouldnt even embrace her during his highest moment of elation, then he never would. He never had been much of a lover. Even before his illness, they hadnt slept together very often. It was a miracle they had a son at all.

That evening, there was another knock on the door. Elmira opened it to reveal a sturdy man with a square jaw and dark baleful eyes. They were the eyes of a general, a professional killer who wouldnt hesitate to slaughter any person he came in contact with, if so ordered. The eyes of Ambrose de Bellomonte. He removed his top hat and bowed.

—Good evening, Mrs. Beaumont. Looking beautiful as always. Ambrose tried to kiss Elmira's hand, but she pulled it away.

Miles elbowed past her and greeted his defeated competitor.

—Mr. Ambrose de Bellomonte. What a pleasant surprise.

Ambrose pulled at the individual fingers of his white glove, then stuffed the glove in his suit pocket and held out his hand. Miles extended his in return. As the two men shook, their knuckles turned white and the tendons in their wrists bulged.

—I came to wish you congratulations, said Ambrose.

Both men squeezed even tighter as they stared one another down, unblinking.

—Indeed. The people have decided, said Miles.

—You've had some good fortune, Congressman, but fortune comes and goes, now, doesnt it?

—Good fortune and a golden reputation.

—I rather think reputations are much like silver. They can be tarnished, debased even.

—I doubt that very much.

—I suppose time will tell.

—I suppose it will. Good day, Ambrose.

Their hands unlocked. Ambrose gave a curt nod, then climbed aboard his black carriage and put his top hat back upon his head.

Yet another day was fading. Blue evening twilight shone through the warped window glass of Beaumont Hall and Elmira sat in solitude in the great room of her mansion staring out that window at the creeping starless night. Miles was now away most of the time, supposedly focused on his congressional duties. Elmira tried not to think of his other interludes. She socialized as much as any high society woman, but it left a sour taste in her mouth.

Gossip didnt interest her anymore. The quest for recognition was an endless endeavor, and now she preferred the seclusion of Beaumont Hall's cold stone walls over superficial companionship.

Was the army feeding her son well? Did he have warm enough blankets? She replayed her attempt to convince Noah to attend the University of Georgia over and over again. She had gone through the trouble to try to secure him admission, but he only had dreams of military valor. How she missed him, for he was the only sunshine that graced Beaumont Hall. While Miles was cold, Noah was warm. Still, much as she'd hated it when Noah left to do his duty, endure it she must. For a woman could have no greater hardship and no greater joy than motherhood.

On a cool winter day, Elmira was passing the time as she usually did. She sat on the second-floor balcony and observed the goings-on of Beaumont Plantation. Something new had caught her interest.

She watched as Isaiah followed the new stable girl around like a puppy dog. Isaiah always gave Emma the sweetest part of his daily rations, peaches and apricots. Miles had never done such a thing to her. Every chance they got, the two would find some hidden corner to sneak off to. They'd hold hands and Emma would rest her head on his shoulder. Intrigued, Elmira spent the next several weeks watching with interest from different vantage points inside Beaumont Hall.

One evening, she watched as Isaiah took Emma's hand and pulled her behind the stable. Elmira struggled to get a good look. She pressed her face against her bedroom window and squinted. The fading sunlight reflected off the young couple's enjoined lips and the sparkle in Emma's eyes. Emma smiled. That girl never smiled. And that smile, the innocent smile of first love, caused Elmira's pulse to quicken. Why was *she* being given the gift of happiness? It enraged her. She stood in her great home surrounded by fine things that others could only dream of, yet she was alone and *that girl* was not.

At lunchtime the following day, Elmira walked off the mansion porch toward the overseer. Jed was sitting on a tree stump, slurping down some awful concoction he had mixed together in a discolored wooden bowl. Even though he sat quite some distance away, she could already smell him. She had often complained to Miles about the man's slovenly appearance and frightful hygiene, but Miles brushed her concerns aside like every other suggestion she made.

—Jed, Jed.

The overseer popped to his feet and stood as erect as his slight hunch would allow.

—At yer service, ma'am.

—Bring me Isaiah.

Jed scratched his balding head.

—Well shoot, let me think where he is. The ugly inbred one died in the stocks. The big strong one survived the stocks and is in the field. The biggest strong one is also in the field. The fancy-schmancy horse groomer is still in the stable.

Elmira sighed and rolled her eyes as Jed disappeared into the field, mumbling to himself. She fluttered her fan while she waited. The overseer at last returned with Isaiah.

—Isaiah, it's been a long time.

—What do you want with me?

—Watch yer tongue, boy.

—No need for that, Jed. Isaiah, I saw how you defended that stable girl.

Isaiah narrowed his downcast eyes. Elmira could tell he was trying to read her intentions. He probably already realized that she knew about his subsequent interludes with the girl.

—No need to worry. I am in need of a new personal servant, that's all.

—Miles wont allow it.

—Miles isnt here. And besides, he isnt upset with the matter anymore.

—I'd prefer to stay in the field.

—You're not in the business of deciding anything, dear Isaiah.

Isaiah was led by Elmira through the heavy wooden doors of Beaumont Hall and into the grand foyer. A rainbow of colored light shone through the stained-glass dome above, depicting scenes of conquest and mythological beasts. The squared foyer was held aloft by marble columns. Between the pillars were busts of Miles' heroes: kings, emperors, generals, and the like. Silk carpets with ornate flower patterns graced the smooth oak floors.

Isaiah stepped toward one wall and studied one of Elmira's watercolor paintings. The fact that someone was paying attention to her work pleased her.

—What do you think? she asked.

—It's beautiful. Magnificent, even.

—Beautiful?

—Sad, but beautiful. The artist is like the blood-red rose in this painting: beautiful, sharp to the touch, and alone.

Perhaps. It seemed she had educated him a bit too well. Shaking it from her mind, she clapped her hands. A hidden door behind another painting opened and three female servants appeared.

—See to it that he is cleaned up and made presentable.

They shuffled Isaiah into the servant passage behind the painting. Elmira wondered if it had really been so long since he was last inside. Isaiah and his mother Mary had lived inside Beaumont Hall as house slaves for more than a decade. Lessons on just about everything had continued until they were cast out into the fields.

Elmira ate alone and sipped a bottle of fine wine. Isaiah came. He wore fresh clothes. His hair had been trimmed, and he smelled of fresh citrus.

—Much better. Sit. Eat with me.

The young man wore a perplexed expression but did as ordered. She enjoyed having someone to converse with, and Isaiah was the only one she found worth talking to. Although now, things were different. He was always guarded. He no longer trusted her. Perhaps she couldnt blame him.

Months went by. On one balmy afternoon, Isaiah stood at Elmira's side, fanning her on the high balcony while she sipped her afternoon tea and read a book. He didnt look happy, and it bothered her. However, she reminded herself to snuff out such embers of compassion lest they catch fire.

Elmira jumped to her feet when she saw a carriage moving along the oak-lined road toward Beaumont Hall. She ran downstairs, into the foyer, and out the front door.

The carriage stopped in front of the mansion. Miles climbed out and stepped toward her. He said nothing, just gave her a simple nod like he had only been gone for a few hours, then walked inside the mansion. An old general with a big round belly and a walrus mustache followed. He bowed.

—General Willard, madam. Pleased to meet your acquaintance. My God, the stories of your beauty are true indeed.

—Why are you here?

—A few of the congressman have asked for my expertise on federal fortifications and other, more secretive, matters.

—If you'll excuse me, General. I havent seen my husband for a very long time.

Elmira ran up after Miles into the house and blocked his path as he tried to enter the great room. He threw his hat across the parlor.

—Lincoln. The bastards elected Lincoln. This is it, the last straw.

—Dont be so upset. They say Mr. Lincoln is quite dedicated to preserving the union. It seems likely that he'll compromise.

—I'm not interested in preserving the union. It's high time for a divorce.

Elmira followed him to his office, where he sat down in his tall leather chair. On the wall behind him was a large map of the United States. Hundreds of books lined the walls. Miles shuffled through the drawers of his mahogany desk until he found a pen.

—I'm not upset. I'm a man of action.

—What are you writing?

—My letter of resignation from Congress. We're going to send a message that the North cant push us around. We're going to secede from this rotten union, and then we're going to remove the federal government from the South forever. With cannon fire if need be. The South cant have Lincoln's troops on our doorstep.

—We're sitting on a dry tinder of war and you're trying to light the spark? Noah's still in the army. Are you mad?

—Yes, I am mad. The abolitionists think they have a right to interfere in our sovereign affairs. Ever since we hung that fanatic, they've been trying to force their views down our throats. No more.

—What about our son?

Miles didnt answer. He put his signature on a letter and placed it in an envelope, then shouted for an attendant who'd been waiting in the foyer. He handed it to the man, who briskly walked off with it.

—Excuse me, I have important business to attend to.

Miles left and the general followed him into his office. Elmira slumped onto a couch in the library. She wiped her wet cheeks with the back of her hand. Miles was in office because of her. She had goaded her father into printing articles about him. She had knocked on doors for him, handed out flyers for him, and raised money amongst high society for him. Elmira hadnt done it because Miles was the most competent. She'd done it because it was her duty to advance her family's station and because she loved him. But was the feeling mutual? Miles' cold disposition had mattered less when Noah lived in the house. Now that her boy was gone, she seemed never to escape the shadow of despair.

The morning sun crept over the fields as a chorus of cicadas whirred. Consumed by thoughts of war, Elmira had tossed and turned all night. Noah had sent a letter a while back and said he was due to arrive for leave any day now.

She heard the front doors open and then slam shut. She quickly rose from her bed and descended her grand staircase calling her son's name. Lost in her thoughts, she slipped and stumbled down the final steps. Something stopped her fall.

—Easy, Ma, said Noah as he caught her.

With tears running down her cheeks, she embraced her son.

—Thank heavens, Noah, you're home, she said while planting kisses on his cheeks. —It's so wonderful you were granted leave.

—I'm afraid I'm not on leave, Ma. I resigned from the army.

She feigned concern but was ecstatic, of course. Now Noah could return to Beaumont Hall and find a wife and the hallways would echo with the laughter of grandchildren. Then a sobering thought crept into her mind.

—But…why did you resign?

—To serve the Southern cause. Fort Sumter has surrendered and now we need to push onward to final victory.

—My God. Noah, please dont go. Stay here with me. Help run the plantation. We need you here. I need you here.

—I have to fight, Ma. Honor demands it. I'm a son of the South and I'm going to do right by my homeland.

Noah picked up the newspaper and flipped through a few pages as Elmira's eyes began to water up with despair.

—Looks like that codger Ambrose de Bellomonte has come out of retirement.

She pressed her wet cheeks against her son's chest.

—Dont go. Dont go.

Chapter 12

NOAH

1862, Tennessee

Tennessee was beautiful. It was even grander than Sergeant Walker had described it. There were great gorges and cascading rivers, but most of all he liked the way the tree-covered mountains, in their multitudes of colors, peeked above the low-lying morning mist. They stiffened his spirit even more. The South was a gorgeous place, worth defending. Still, it was a shame to cover such lovely scenery with blood.

Noah had wanted war, and he'd gotten it. He had expected the Yankees to surrender a long time ago and found it strange that they still fought against the inevitable. Or at least he thought the Yankee surrender was inventible. Fort Henry had just surrendered to the Federals, captured by a man by the name of Grant. The South was full of God-fearing people and the North simply didnt have the Almighty on their side. Noah prayed for victory every day, for he knew the loss of Fort Henry must be just a temporary setback meant to test their faith.

He had been at war almost a year now and still hadnt had the opportunity to gain his first kill. He was assigned as a staff officer and spent his time with maps and doing chores for his commanders instead of fighting. What he wanted was to spill Yankee blood and earn his honor. He was shuffled from commander to commander and moved around so often that none of them had bothered to learn his name.

One cold morning, his friend Walker poked his head in his tent and handed Noah a cup of steaming hot coffee. Something that was becoming increasingly precious.

—I convinced a wily lieutenant colonel to consider you as a staff officer, said Walker.

—How?

—Friend of a friend.

—What's this lieutenant colonel's name?

—Nathan Bedford Forrest. The fellow is a wizard in the saddle. One of the best commanders we've got. I've been assigned to his unit. Come with me.

Noah had heard of the fellow. Forrest had begun making a name for himself among the men, and the position immediately piqued Noah's interest. The Confederate States Army was in such disarray that he didnt bother to ask for permission to seek out a new command. Such efforts usually went nowhere anyway. He simply rode out to the Third Tennessee Cavalry and reported to Lieutenant Colonel Forrest in person.

Noah was immediately impressed by the man, who casually mentioned that it was *a heap of fun to kill Yankees*. Forrest was a plain-talking yet intelligent fellow who had enlisted as a private and risen to his current station. Though Forrest had no formal military education, he'd created the most feared cavalry unit in the South. The man was clouded with a mythology of heroism and bravery that had spread rapidly through the ranks. Forrest even had a rags to riches story as well. Noah had no idea how much of it all was true, but even if only half of it was, he had finally found the leader he needed.

Noah explained that he was seeking glory and wanted to spill Yankee blood. That seemed to please the Lieutenant Colonel. It turned out that staff officers under Forrest's command were expected to fight alongside him much like Alexander the Great's companion cavalry. That prospect excited Noah more than anything. Forrest agreed to take him on as an *aide de camp*. Later, Noah learned that the Federals were marching toward Fort Donelson, which sat along the Cumberland River. Forrest promised him much blood.

Noah rode at Forrest's side into the woods. The Federals were tightening their pincers around Fort Donelson, and Forrest's men were ordered to delay their advance. Noah's stomach tightened when he saw blue kepi hats amongst the trees. He looked to Forrest to see if there would be any sort of consultation or prebattle assessment. Forrest gave but one order.

—Charge.

Bugles rang out and Noah could scarcely believe what was happening was real as the trees around him zipped by in a blur. He could hear lead bullets hissing past him and the sharp crack of bark as they hit the nearby trees. Gray smoke filled the woodland and it became difficult for him to see what was happening. His body felt stiff, and warm piss ran down his leg and into his boot.

Their cavalry picked off Federals left and right. Some of the poor bastards tried to run. It was the worst thing they could have done. Forrest's cavalrymen cut them down with their sabers as they tried to outrun their horses. The smoke made his eyes tear up and he choked on it as he aimed his revolver, desperately in search of a target. There seemed to be no lines of battle, just people everywhere trying to slaughter one another. He had spent years studying blocks and arrows on old maps that illustrated the great battles of the past. It all seemed useless now, for the battle had devolved into utter chaos.

A shot tore through the air behind him. Noah wheeled his horse around and saw a Federal private before him. The Yankee private's hands trembled as he tried to ram a cartridge down the smoking barrel of his rifle. Noah aimed his revolver at the soldier. The private looked up at him with wide and frightened eyes. The boy couldnt have been older than sixteen and didnt look much different than himself.

Noah told himself to squeeze the trigger but he was frozen in the boy's gaze. His finger simply would not move. He reminded himself to breathe and then felt his own hand trembling. Noah swallowed hard. He repeated the mantra over and over again inside, to be a man and to do his duty. Still his trigger finger would not obey. For a moment it was as if the entire world had melted away and it was only him and the Federal private alone in a black void standing there, staring at one another. He heard a voice and the void disappeared and once more he was back in the chaos around him. The private dropped his rifle and slowly lifted his hands.

—Shoot him, shouted Forrest.

Another part of his mind took over. It was the part the Army had put inside him. They had conditioned him to obey. No matter what, he must obey his commanding officer. In response to the words, his finger pulled the cold steel trigger without reservation, without hesitation, without thought.

His revolver recoiled upward. The gray smoke from the barrel dissipated as he carefully guided the pistol downward to fire another shot. There was no need. The boy lay on a bed of dried leaves with a bleeding hole in his chest. The private mouthed the word *Mama* and supped several shallow breaths before he lay still, his eyes gazing upward. A pool of blood slowly expanded over the leaves around him.

Noah couldnt take his eyes off the boy until a shell exploded a few yards away and frightened his horse. It took him a few moments to regain control. He shook his head in an attempt to snap himself out of it. For a moment he felt exhilarated he had finally done it. He had finally gotten his first kill. Then the boy's face flashed in his mind's eye and the moment passed. Noah began to feel creeping dread work itself into his consciousness. He ran his palm over his face and pushed the thought down as far as it would go. There was no need to remember, he needed only to forget. Now he had truly earned his spurs as one of Forrest's Yankee killers.

The Federals fell back but Forrest ordered his men not to pursue. He said they needed to break out of the Federal forces surrounding them. Their victory was a temporary one.

Fort Donelson surrendered to the Federals. By the grace of God, Forrest's unit had been the only one to escape. Perhaps his prayers were paying off. As they rode out toward Nashville, Walker rode up beside him. They rode together side by side. Walker's face was a welcome sight. Walker had been in the army for longer, and Noah often bent his friend's ear for advice and help with military matters that were new to him. The last thing he wanted was to look like a know-nothing officer in front of his men. Walker always spoke to him in blunt terms and made no attempt to kiss his ass because of his status as an officer or as one of the wealthiest men in the South. At first, the lack of deference offended him, but eventually it grew on him. He knew Walker was a man he could trust.

—Kill anyone? asked Noah.

—I shot so much lead into their ranks that I must have killed something.

—A good day's work.

—I suppose.

—Suppose?

—I gotta wife and two boys. At this point I just hope I come back with all my arms and legs.

They had lost Fort Donelson, but they had not lost the war. Noah couldnt help but be impressed by the way Forrest directed his men in and out of the Federal lines. He did so with such speed that the Yankees were left licking their wounds before they could catch Forrest's cavalry. He truly was a wizard on the saddle and Noah couldnt help but admire the man. They ripped down telegraph wires, burned storehouses and wagon trains, tore up railroad tracks, and in general wreaked havoc upon Grant's supply lines.

They had been assaulting Federal supply lines nonstop for more than two weeks. Both he and his horse had saddle sore. His body had never been so tired in all his life, yet despite his exhaustion he found himself unable to sleep. He tried to be happy, he'd been granted his request for leave and would take it within a fortnight.

He rolled over and over in his tent and forced his eyes closed. When he did, he saw the face of the Federal soldier he had shot. He sat up in a cold sweat, his eyes open. He told himself to stop thinking, to stop remembering, but his mind didnt obey. He prayed and asked God to let him sleep, but the Lord didnt seem to hear him. Lying back down, Noah closed his eyes. As soon as he did, the young soldier's face came back into view. He sat back up and slapped himself.

—Be a man, he said.

He knew he was being ridiculous, but somehow he had managed to convince himself that the Yankees were all great burly men with fire in their eyes and blood dripping from their hands. He hadnt prepared himself that he might come across a boy who didnt even need to shave. Of course, there were lots of those boys in the Confederate army, so it shouldnt have been a surprise to him.

It hadnt felt like killing when he shot that boy, it had felt like murder. Hell, he was almost certain the boy had never been with a woman. The young Federal soldier had probably signed up like himself, itching to find glory and serve a worthy cause.

No. The young soldier needed to die.

It was him or me.

Noah shook his head in his dark tent. All men were rotten creatures anyway. Why should he feel shame? He told himself to quiet his thoughts and reminded himself that his sacred Southern cause was noble. Then he thought about the Wyoming Territory. Maybe when the war was over he'd load up a covered wagon and go there and start anew. He'd take the Beaumont bloodline to new frontiers like his fathers before him. He didnt need a grand estate, he needed quiet. He dreamed of marrying Caroline and living out his days on their ranch with their children. Maybe Walker would move out west with him. He could loan him what he needed to get started, and if he couldnt pay it back, well, Walker could count himself lucky. It would be a simple life but a good one, a peaceful one.

Noah dug through his haversack and found his flask. He opened the cap and his tent filled with the sharp odor of Tennessee whiskey. The entire contents were gone in three gulps. Then he lay back down, his eyes wide open.

Chapter 13

EMMA

1863, Georgia

Even though it wasnt far away, Emma and the others did-nt know much about Fort Pulaski. None of them had ever seen the place. They knew it stood at the mouth of the Savannah River and they knew it once was a Rebel fort. They even knew it had been surrounded by Federal ships for the longest time. Hushed voices across Beaumont Plantation spoke of its capture by the Federals. God's wrath was coming. The quick victory the Confederates had talked about hadnt materialized. Would deliverance finally come? Emma hoped for such, yet she refused to allow herself too much hope. For too much hope might lead her into an emotional gorge, and should the floodwaters of despair come rushing down, she might go under.

Emma's heart ached for Isaiah. It had been a long time since he was sent to the mansion. She rarely got to see him, so she savored small ways of making love, happy just to have their hands touch or even to see a flash of his face from a distance. Why did he have to go to Beaumont Hall? Just as her flower of happiness was about to bloom, it was cruelly snipped from its stem. But then again, what was love but beautiful misery?

Master Beaumont paced outside the stables with heavy bags under his eyes. Emma tried to stay out of sight, but Miles and Jed walked up to her.

—Why hasnt a pretty lady like you gotten pregnant yet? Aint you with Isaiah now?

—Sir, the Devil has cursed me with a rotten womb.

—That right?

Master Beaumont took hold of her arm. He pulled her close. She stood there, frozen. Emma's long curls fell to her shoulders as he removed her headwrap and dropped it on the ground. He held her locks to his nose and inhaled deeply. Her skin crawled.

—Very lovely hair. But there's no need for it, is there? You dont need to look pretty. You cant bear children? That right?

—Yes, sir. Sorry, sir.

—Jed, cut off her hair. She doesnt need it.

Emma cried out as Jed pinned her to the ground. He snipped off her graceful locks with a pair of rusty shears.

—If you want pretty hair, then make children.

Emma didnt let herself sob until after Master Beaumont and Jed left. Would Isaiah still find her attractive? That evening, she spent an hour touching up her mangled hair, cutting it so it would be even throughout.

It was a rare treat when Isaiah came to the stables. He did that night, and Emma ran into his arms. She realized she didnt have her headwrap on and she pushed him away to retrieve it. He refused to let her go. He touched her now-cropped hair.

—I heard.

Emma lost her composure. She buried her face into Isaiah's chest as his arms wrapped around her.

The months dragged on. When Emma's hair grew, she'd cut it short again lest the masters do it for her. Isaiah was away most of the time. Once in a great while, they'd sneak in a kiss or share an embrace. She hoped he wouldnt forget about her. He ate good food and wore nice clothes. There were plenty of young, beautiful girls working inside Beaumont Hall, and Isaiah was the only male working in the mansion. And who was she? A stable girl who smelled of horse. One late spring afternoon, Emma patted Cheyenne's muzzle.

—At least I still have you.

Emma coughed as a light breeze blew dust from the road in her direction. She held the back of her arm over her eyes to keep the dust out until the breeze shifted. When it did, she saw a column of soldiers in gray uniforms marching toward the plantation. Several empty wagons followed closely behind. An older soldier, with stars on his collar, dismounted from his horse and stood erect. Miles strutted out the front door of Beaumont Hall. The soldier saluted. Emma listened closely as she brushed Cheyenne.

—How much do you need? asked Miles.

—As much as you can provide, Congressman, said the soldier.

—The Northern anaconda contracts its coils. The cowards are tryin to starve us out. Why dont they fight like men?

—I agree, sir. Now, about the food?

—Dont you see all these mouths I've got to feed?

—With respect, sir, the army is hungry. We cant win the war without food.

—Go to the other farms.

—We have already emptied their granaries, sir.

—Take what you need and get back to the front lines and win this war.

The old soldier clicked his heels and about-faced. The rest of them began loading sacks of grain, baskets of potatoes, and all manner of foodstuffs into their wagons. When daylight shone on the floor of the granary, mice ran out. The soldiers stomped on them. To Emma's horror, they collected the dead rodents in a sack and tossed it in the back of a wagon with the rest of the food. They nearly cleared out all the grain. If even soldiers were driven to eat mice, what would happen to her?

One soldier tried to put a bridle on Cheyenne, but the horse turned around and kicked at him.

—Sir, what are you doing? asked Emma.

—We need horses.

—Please, sir, take one of the others. Not this one.

—Take the mare, not my racehorses, said Miles.

—Congressman, the states are in dire need of horses and everything you can spare for that matter.

—I said you can have the mare. I'll also lend the cause some of my negroes and my stores, but if you take my racehorses I'll shoot you myself.

The soldier grabbed Emma's wrist and gazed upon her hungrily.

—How about this girl, can we take her?

—No. Not her. I need her. I'll have one of my overseers assist you.

The soldier released his grip.

—Yes, Congressman.

It took a few soldiers to force Cheyenne into a bridle and drag her away. While Emma thought it silly, she couldnt stop herself from weeping.

The bells rang six times. They meant only one thing. It was one of Miles' Sunday gatherings. Everyone who lived and worked on the plantation was required to attend. They met under the shade of oak trees, whose old limbs formed a pleasing arch over the dirt road beneath. Miles stood in the center of his congregation of the wretched. Isaiah stood at Elmira's side. Emma's eyes met with his. He almost seemed like a different person in his fine black vest and shiny leather shoes. Only his eyes, those striking blue eyes, remained the same.

—Let us take a moment to pray for my son Noah who is fighting against the Yankee devils. Devils with great horns who wish to flay us all alive. They want to take all the negroes away and do horrible, ungodly things to them. They prayed.

—I have an important announcement to make. Because we are charitable people and because the war must be won, we will be donating much food and supplies to the war effort. We'll all have to tighten our belts and make do with a little less. I expect each and every one of you to be frugal with your rations.

The entire plantation began to murmur. A few hands rose. Miles pretended he didnt see them.

—Dismissed.

As the weeks went by, it didnt take long for the hunger pangs to set in. Emma felt guilty for her own discomfort when she saw James in the food line. He was hunched over and his right hand had a slight tremor. He had probably lost the equivalent of her entire body weight, yet he was still massive. James' muscle was an asset during times of plenty. Now it was a burden. He ate his stew in one gulp and proceeded to lick the tiny bowl. Emma knelt next to him and held her bowl up to his mouth. She didnt need to eat much, and she could go without food longer than James.

—Eat, said Emma.

—I cant take a lady's food away from her, said James.

She placed her hand on his cheek and gently guided it toward her bowl. Peering into his good eye, she nodded.

—Just take a little. Please.

—How can I resist that sweet face? You remind me of my daughter, said James.

—You have a daughter?

—Never mind what I said. I must be tired.

—Take another sip. Please.

—That's very kind, but I'm full.

Shouting erupted in the food line. Someone was thrown to the ground. Damian yanked a food bowl from an old man and ate it in front of him. James struggled to climb to his feet as Jed whipped indiscriminately at Damian and the others. Even though the whip fell against Damian's massive torso, he acted as if he didnt feel it. He had decided to trade pain for food.

—Wait yer turn, wait yer turn, yelled Jed.

Damian ripped another bowl of stew from someone else's hands and slurped it down before stumbling away. Usually, the overseers would exact a terrible price for such behavior, but even they were hungry and tired. He had taken a gamble and gotten away with it.

That night, Emma curled up into a ball and pulled an old horse blanket over her body. Sahara lay next to her. The foal's warmth was welcome on cold nights such as this. Emma lay her head on her straw pillow and drifted off.

—Wake up, Emma, wake up, said a voice.

Her eyes fluttered open. It was Isaiah. He dropped a burlap bag at her feet, then scurried off and came back with a shovel. Isaiah brushed the straw aside and began digging a hole. Emma opened the bag. It was full of cans of food, bread, and a few vegetables, no doubt pilfered from the mansion pantry. Isaiah tossed the bag into the hole. A large shadow stood in the doorway and blotted out the moonlight. Emma's eyes shifted toward the nearby pitchfork. The figure moved closer. James. He knelt beside the two of them.

—We're finally gettin out of here, said James.

James erupted into a coughing fit. Isaiah cast his eyes downward at the sound of his friend's illness. Emma took one of James' massive hands.

—When?

—We'll head out tomorrow night, all three of us, he said.

The next morning's dew was cold against Emma's bare feet. The weight of the two big water buckets dangling on either end of her carrying pole dug painfully into her small shoulders. Her heel slipped off a smooth wet rock, and she struggled to keep her balance. The water buckets swung in opposite directions. She had just a few more paces to go before she made it to the horse trough. When she took a step forward, her ankle rolled. She tripped and fell and she found herself covered in mud.

Isaiah was sweeping the portico. He dropped his broom and ran over. Her cheeks grew warm with embarrassment as he pulled her to her feet. They always tried to keep their love a secret, but her heart overpowered her mind and her fingers interlaced with his.

—Isaiah, hurry up, barked the mistress from the porch.

Isaiah pulled his hand free and returned to the house. Emma found herself locked in Elmira's gaze. The mistress's hands were on her hips, her mouth was sealed tight, and her eyes narrowed with disapproval. Elmira's dress fluttered as she turned around and disappeared inside the mansion.

The sun receded over the red fields. Emma peered over her shoulder before putting a handful of oats in her mouth. They were meant for Miles' horses, but food was scarce. They were dry and hard to chew, but at least they lessened the pain in her stomach. Between her and James, she knew the food she had wouldnt last long. They needed to escape tonight.

Emma hadnt had a chance to wash her mud-stained clothes. She breathed a sigh of relief as the last bell of the day rang throughout the plantation. As she made her way inside the stable, her heart stopped.

Elmira stood inside with her arms crossed. Jed was at her side, stroking his whip. In all Emma's time at Beaumont Plantation she had never once met or spoken with the house mistress. What had she done? She had followed every rule. She worked hard. Emma went out of her way to never bother anybody.

—Emma, darling, have a seat, said Elmira.

She sat wordless on a nearby bale of straw.

—I see you've got yourself a little boyfriend.

—I dont have a boyfriend.

—I know what a lovestruck girl looks like when I see one. I've been watching you two for a very long time.

—No one is in love with me.

—Well, Emma, I'm glad he's not your boyfriend, because I've sold you. But you're going to a good place, much better than here. You'll eat better, so dont you worry.

Emma's hands trembled when she registered the words. Her eyes welled up as she took quick, short breaths.

—I dont want to be sold again, she muttered.

—I know you dont, but I cant have Isaiah getting distracted from his job.

—Distracted? How?

—You're the distraction, my dear girl.

For the briefest moment she envisioned herself choking Elmira. The image passed and she came to her senses. Emma trembled as tears streamed down her cheeks. She nodded.

—That's a good girl. You leave this evening. Jed, restrain her up for the night. I dont want her emotions getting the better of her.

Elmira's hard expression gave way to a thin smile. The feathers in her hat wafted in the evening breeze as she stepped out of the stable and walked toward Beaumont Hall. Jed chained her to a large log and left.

When the day began to die, Emma found herself in the back of a wagon. Isaiah stood at Elmira's side high on the mansion balcony while the mistress fluttered a silken fan. The wagon jerked forward. She didnt cry. She simply gazed up at Isaiah and tried to sear his face into her memory. The gray stone silhouette of Beaumont Hall grew smaller as the wagon made its way along the bumpy road.

Chapter 14

ISAIAH

1863, Georgia

As the wagon that carried Emma disappeared under the avenue of oak trees, Isaiah resolved to find her. When Emma touched his hand, when he caught the sweet scent of her hair, the misery around him melted away. Isaiah wanted nothing more than her embrace, for of all the riches in the world, she was the only gem he desired.

A few days later, as Elmira took her afternoon nap, Isaiah crept into Miles' office. He used to play in there with Noah when he was a boy. His favorite hiding spot was still the space under Miles' desk. Of course, they only came inside when Miles was out on his so-called business trips. As big as it was, he never felt comfortable inside the house. The very walls seemed to be watching his every move. On rare occasions, in the dead of night, when he was all alone, he thought he even heard the walls cackle.

He shuffled through the master's desk drawers until he found a yellow slip. A bill of sale with yesterday's date. *TO EDEL DAIRY FARM. 1 STABLE GIRL. AGE 17.* At the bottom, Elmira's signature.

He gazed at the vast assortment of books in the mansion library. Thousands of books were stacked high on ornate walnut bookshelves. Today he was in need of a map. He needed to narrow down where Edel Dairy Farm was. His fingers ran past old volumes on the bookshelf and stopped at a section full of rolled-up maps. He unrolled one of the local area and ran his finger over the various locations. He soon found it, Edel Dairy Farm. The place had been there for generations.

A sharp tap came on his shoulder. He dropped the map he was holding and turned around. Elmira. She wore a hat with pheasant feathers to match her dress. A crimson ribbon kept her curled black locks in place. Elmira picked up the book Isaiah had dropped and flipped through the pages.

—A map?

—I was lookin for a map…of Athens. To study.

He felt stupid the second he said it.

—Then why are you looking at a local map? Dont be upset about the girl. There isnt much food these days. Her living conditions will be much better. I did her a favor, Isaiah. I did it for you.

He hated the words that spewed from her mouth. The only response he could think of was to give a meek nod. Elmira cupped his left cheek in one hand and kissed the right.

That night he went to his mother's cabin and told her where he was going and told her that he'd come back for her. Mary simply grunted in acknowledgment with her knotted hands resting in her lap. She didnt so much as look at him. Her gaze remained fixed and empty at the wooden cabin wall.

Isaiah met James by the stables. The man erupted into a coughing fit and nearly fell over. When he recovered, he tied up their food stores in a cloth for the journey ahead. His old friend had always seemed strong, invincible even. Now James appeared gray and withered from the disease that had overtaken the plantation. Isaiah knelt down next to his old friend and pleaded with him to come. James shook his head.

—I'll just slow you down.

—Put your arm around my neck. I'll help carry you.

—Go get the girl. When I feel better, I'll be right behind you.

That night, the rain spat and pattered against the old wood of the kennels. The hounds regarded him with bleeding eyes and curious noses. Isaiah unlatched all the cages and the dogs darted off into the pasture led by their noses to smells exciting and new.

Then Isaiah ran into the pasture toward the surrounding swamp, toward Emma. A few of the horses got startled and darted off. The rainfall intensified and thunder clapped and the pasture quickly became mired with the muck of pockmarked hoofprints. Progress was slow as the cattails and barreled knees of bald cypress came into view. Soon he would disappear into the dark waters and make his way into the deep swamp and, eventually, Emma.

As he reached the edge of the pasture, he heard the sucking sound of hooves cupping against mud behind him. He looked behind him but couldnt see anything in the moonless dark. The cover of the swampland wasnt far. He ran. Then a large silhouette, darker than the night around it, came up from behind him. He heard the all-too-familiar click of a hammer being thumbed back.

—Halt, said a familiar voice.

Isaiah lifted his hands slowly as he heard the snorting of a horse.

—Let me go.

—I cant do that.

—You know what they'll do to me if you take me back.

—I know Pa would kill you if you were caught by anyone else, and you would be caught. The Home Guard is all over the place, and let me tell you, they love catchin runaways and deserters.

He felt his tired hands being bound with rope to be replevied to a fate unknown. A lantern flickered to life, revealing Noah in a dirty gray Confederate uniform. His bloodshot eyes had heavy bags beneath them. He was no longer clean-shaven and had grown a scraggly brown beard. Isaiah noticed that Noah's eyes no longer gleamed of lurid lapis. They had glazed over into an almost gray color. It looked as if he had aged ten years in the short time he was gone. He led Isaiah back to the heart of the plantation and tied him to a whipping post.

Now he found himself surrounded by the entirety of the Beaumont clan. Miles stumbled forward. Isaiah realized that in his rush to find Emma, he had been careless. He should have waited.

Elmira walked up to him.

—After all I've done for you, she said.

—Noah. Get a board and a sledgehammer, said Miles.

Noah raised an eyebrow and tilted his head, acting as if he didnt hear his father's commands clearly. Isaiah knew what they intended. Hobbling. The practice involved putting a thick board between the ankles. Then a sledgehammer would be swung against the offender's foot, snapping the ankle. When the foot finally healed, it would be permanently contorted. He would be forced to use a walking stick for the remainder of his life. Isaiah had only seen Miles implement the punishment once before the runaway hadnt survived.

—Pa, are you sure about that?

—Boy, I said get the board and the hammer.

Noah didnt move. Miles shot a glare at Jed. The overseer left and quickly returned from the tool shed with the implements of punishment. Elmira stood in her husband's path.

—I shall not have him mutilated, said Elmira.

Jed put the hammer and board on the ground next to Isaiah's feet. Miles pushed Elmira to the side. He gestured for Noah to tie Isaiah's ankles to the board. Noah's continued refusal to move made Miles furious.

—Get on with it.

—Pa, he wasnt running off. He was just looking for the stable girl and got lost. That's all.

Miles muttered something under his breath and then yelled at Jed. The lanky head overseer ran over and fastened the board to Isaiah's ankles. The thin rope was so tight it cut into the flesh. The pain didnt last long as his feet quickly grew numb. Miles pointed toward Elmira.

—Jed, take the missus indoors.

Jed took Elmira's arm. Noah stepped forward to intercede but his mother yanked her arm free. She stood erect and her eyes burned white hot. The petite woman arched her back and turned toward Jed as her bloodred dress fluttered in the breeze. She looked more imposing than all of them combined. She spoke through clenched teeth.

—So help me God, Jed, if you ever touch me with those rat claws again I will gouge out those dumb eyes of yours with my bare hands.

Jed's eyes bulged as he took in shallow breaths. He held up the palms of his hands and shook his head at Miles.

—Boss, I dont wanna get involved.

Elmira hiked up her dress and walked up to her husband. Her eyes locked on his. Miles raised his hand above his head, ready to strike. Elmira stepped closer still. Miles lifted his hand higher. Now she stood chest to chest with her husband, her gaze unflinching. Miles scowled and swung at Elmira's face. Before he could make contact, Noah's hand seized his arm. Miles pulled, but his son clenched even tighter.

—Pa, get some rest. I'll handle it.

Miles' face burned red. He tried to pull his arm free but Noah would not let go. He pulled again, not strong enough to free himself from his son's grasp. Miles shook with unexpressed rage and glared into his son's eyes.

—You've had a long day, Pa. Get some rest.

Miles gave a curt nod. Noah released his grip. The master rubbed his red wrist with his other hand and glared at Elmira as he walked into the mansion. Elmira and Noah shared a word out of Isaiah's earshot. She put her hand on his cheek. Then Noah cut Isaiah loose and kicked aside the hobbling implements. Elmira stepped toward him.

—You've been spared the worst of it, she said.

With that, Elmira turned and left.

—He aint happy, Isaiah. If I do nothin, he might be fixin to kill you tomorrow when he sobers up. So, you got a choice.

Noah gave Isaiah two choices of punishments to choose from. Humiliation in the kennel or six lights raps with a birch. Isaiah chose humiliation. Noah gave an incredulous look.

—What? It's six raps, not even hard ones. You'll be back in your warm quarters tonight.

—No.

—Just take the birch.

—No.

—Well, you're being stupid. I'm orderin you to take the birch.

—No, you said I had a choice. I want you to sleep in your warm bed, right next to my old room with all our old toys in it, while I sit and shiver in this here filth all night.

—You think I dont know what it's like to shiver in filth?

—You know what, I want two nights. You pride yourself on bein a man of honor, so honor my choice.

—Fine.

The previous night's thunderstorm and the hooves of the plantation's beasts had turned the grounds into a thick sludge of mud and horse manure. Isaiah was already covered in it from head to toe. He had no way to shield his body from the cold rain in the confines of the wrought-iron dog kennel Noah locked him in. He was forced into a permanent stoop, as his head hit against the top of the cage if he tried to sit upright. He clutched his arms and shivered.

In the blackest hours of the night, James appeared outside his kennel. The man's condition had taken a turn for the worse. James forced an old horse blanket through the bars of the kennel.

—Take this.

Isaiah wrapped himself in the blanket.

The following morning, the overseers dragged Isaiah out of the kennel in front of the others as a warning. At Jed's encouragement, a few of the field slaves threw apple cores and peach pits at him while others covered their mouths and turned away. After Jed was content that Isaiah had endured enough ridicule, he put Isaiah back in the kennel. Once Jed left, James spoke.

—This could happen to any of you.

Some of them, those who had thrown things earlier, cast their eyes downward. Several nodded. A few gave dismissive waves and stormed off in spite.

Another night passed. Elmira knelt down outside his cage. She held a steaming mug of tea through the bars and lifted it to his mouth. He wanted to spit it in her face, but he was so cold and so thirsty he couldnt bring himself to do it. He pulled away as the woman tried to wipe the muck from his face.

—Dont hate me, Isaiah. You know I was against this. You hurt me when you ran off like that. I know you liked the pretty stable girl, but she's in better hands now. Miles would have forced her to bear children. Now she milks cows for a living with other women. And as for you, you'll be back inside the house in no time.

—I'd rather die here.

—Stop being stubborn. You're going to need to be less willful. Now please understand that you're very dear to me, Isaiah, I need you. As I said, I'll give you clean clothes and fresh food once you're free from this awful cage.

She wiped clean a spot on his forehead and then she kissed it and left. Noah had stood beside her the whole time and said nothing. Before he followed, he tossed Isaiah a small flask.

The dreary gray sky faded to black. James again appeared outside his kennel. He opened the door. He placed some fresh clothes and a satchel full of provisions at Isaiah's feet. James coughed into his hand. When he finished, his hand was covered in bloody phlegm.

—Run, he said.

—Come with me.

—Get on outta here.

Isaiah put the clothes on. James told him the path to Edel Farm was clear. There were only a handful of overseers now, many having been drafted. As for Noah, it seemed the only thing he did on his leave was sleep. Isaiah was hugging his old friend when Jed appeared.

—Get back in yer cage. Who said you could let'em go?

Jed wasted no time exacting punishment. He whipped wildly at James and Isaiah. James walked toward him. The overseer struck him again and again with his lash, but James continued, one step at a time. The lash tore into his face, it opened up his chest, it flayed his bulging arms, but still he moved ever closer to the overseer. Jed stumbled back as he closed in, continuing to swing the lash with wild abandon.

—Get back. Get back.

James was almost within arm's reach now. The overseer's face grew distraught. James wrapped his massive hand around Jed's throat. His yellowed eyes bulged as he dangled helplessly, his flailing feeble lank arms unable to hurt the giant before him. A pool of urine formed in Jed's trousers and began dripping down his pant leg and onto the mire below. Jed gurgled as his dry tobacco-stained tongue writhed about from his purpled writhen face. Then his vacant glass eyes rolled up into his deep-set sockets. James clenched his jaw and let out a sigh. Then he tossed the scrawny overseer like a ragdoll. Jed hit the ground a great distance away and lay there, filth covered, in a grotesque pile as he moaned and supped for breath.

James dropped to his knees. Through his labored and heavy breathing, he muttered—Lord, forgive me my trespasses as I forgive those who trespass against me. He clutched his side and spit up blood. As Isaiah held his hand, he locked his good eye onto Isaiah. The light was fading.

—Promise me you'll be a good man, Isaiah.

—I promise.

A gentle smile worked its way up the corners of James' mouth. James released the grip and his hand fell to his side. Isaiah noticed it was covered with blood. He looked at James' hands and saw both palms were bleeding from circular wounds.

Isaiah's eyes welled up. He shook his old friend several times, but old James did not respond. He wanted to cry out, he wanted to sob, but then he heard one of the overseers calling for Jed. He gazed upon his friend one final time.

—Goodbye, James.

He went to the stables and helped himself to the fastest of Miles' prized thoroughbreds and rode off.

Chapter 15

ELMIRA

1863, Georgia

A week after Isaiah fled. If Isaiah returned, her husband would hang him for taking one of his prize horses, though he seemed distracted by other matters as of late. Elmira sobbed alone in her chambers. She hadnt even bothered to get dressed. Noah's leave had expired and he set off on his horse to rejoin his unit the day previous. She regained her composure and dragged herself out of bed to get Jed to run some errands for her.

She walked about the plantation, calling for Jed. He could not be found. She asked the other overseers if they had seen him, but they had not.

—Well, I'm paying him and I expect him to work. Find him, she demanded.

An hour later, two of the overseers returned with grim expressions. They directed her to a tree not far from the main road of the plantation. The stink of rot filled the air. At the trunk of a fruitless fig tree sat a man in a ragged straw hat with his head slumped over. She slowly walked toward him.

When she reached the man, she gasped and turned her face. It was too late. The image of maggots pouring out of Jed's contorted mouth was already seared into her mind and now it was shifting the contents of her stomach. That and the strange, discolored boils mottled all over his skin. She pressed her hand against her lips. It was no use, she retched. After she had finished, she wiped her mouth and turned to one of the men who'd led her there.

—My Lord, how long has he been out here? asked Elmira.

—Bout a week, we spect, said the overseer.

—How did nobody notice him when he's been lying dead right next to the main road for a week?

—Well, he aint got no family. No friends. Hell, he aint even got a dog.

—What happened to him?

—Looks like some sort of disease. I tell you what, I've seen a lot of diseases, but nothin like that.

—Well, bury him...or something.

—Ma'am, it might be best if we say a few words and take him to the burn pit. Dont want...whatever that is spreading. Probably ought to burn his cabin too.

—Fine, just handle it.

Elmira stepped inside the Episcopalian church she had married into for solace but it just didnt feel right, it never had. Her family were English Catholics, recusants. After her ancestors' estate was seized, they'd lived quietly until their descendants had a chance to settle in Maryland. Of course, they did so in order to keep their faith, yet here she was living as an Episcopalian. Those were the things she'd had to do in order to marry into the Beaumont family. It was her duty to support her father, and she'd done just that. She gave a silent prayer in the empty church and left.

Miles was always in Richmond, and now her dear Noah and even Isaiah had left her. As for Isaiah, she found him somehow alluring. Perhaps it was because everything he said seemed genuine. Perhaps it was because Noah and Isaiah had grown up together. By all rights, she should have hated him for what he was. Still, his mind was sharp and he was eager to learn from her even more so than her own son. Now even he wanted nothing to do with her.

Over the following weeks, she ate very little and rarely got dressed. She preferred to stay in her chambers alone and look out the window. Sarah knocked. Elmira didnt bother to answer, for she knew her servant would barge in anyway, as was her routine.

—Mrs. Elmira, you really ought to get out of this house.

Sarah had prodded her for the last few weeks to get up and leave her chambers. Elmira played the game and went along with Sarah's conversation.

—And go where?

—I hear Judge Foster is throwing a ball.

Elmira perked up. A ball? Every day over the last week, Sarah had come up with new ideas that Elmira dismissed. Maybe it was time for her to get some fresh air.

—Get me my dress.

Her carriage jerked to a stop. Elmira looked at the palatial stone mansion outside her carriage window. It was built in the style of a Tudor-era English country manor. Two fountains sprayed water on either side of the pebble road leading to the entrance.

An officer, his gray uniform bejeweled with gold buttons, took her hand with his white glove and she climbed down from her white carriage. It was pulled by four white draft horses with ostrich-feathered headdresses.

Inside, the lively music of the band was drowned out by the chatter of high society. Streamers and flags, stars and bars, hung from the ceiling beside glittering crystal chandeliers. Officers on leave and ladies in brightly colored gowns danced upon the polished floors of the mansion's ballroom.

Within minutes, her head was swimming. Only then did she register that she had already downed three glasses of champagne. Judge Foster was a stern-looking man with wild gray sideburns, but he was a gentle soul. Once he caught sight of her, he weaved through the crowd and made his way toward her.

—Mrs. Beaumont. It is a surprise and a pleasure.

—Congratulations on your re-election.

—Thanks to the support of fine people like the Beaumont family.

Judge Foster was the archetype of a high-society man. Once one has all the money one could want, one desires power, and once one has power, one desires to keep it. When a man is already rich, favors and reputation become more valuable than currency. Elmira was very good at securing and bestowing favors and always keeping her word on behalf of the Beaumont family. While the Beaumonts weren't as financially wealthy as the de Bellomontes, they were far richer in terms of favors banked.

—It's our pleasure.

—A dance?

It had been so long. Once the band started anew, Elmira recognized the song and knew what dance was called for. She wasnt sure if she'd remember the steps to the Gothic Dance, she hadnt done that particular one for years, but once her feet began moving, the steps came naturally. With the dance finished, the judge bowed and went on to meet with other guests. Out to collect and give favors.

She felt a tapping upon her shoulder. Elmira turned and came face-to-face with a Confederate officer. It was clear that he was younger than she, but by how much she did not know. He was tall, with fair brown hair and a closely trimmed beard.

—The Elmira Beaumont. I had imagined you as someone much older and frumpier. But you are stunning. Truly stunning.

—Please dont forget the Missus, Mister?

—Colonel Pierce Westbrook, ma'am.

—And you're on leave?

—No. I'm an engineer in charge of building fortifications around our fair city.

—Defensive fortifications? Should I be worried, Colonel?

—Please, call me Pierce. No need to worry. General Lee has whipped the Yankees at Chancellorsville. I'm told it was a great rout.

Elmira nodded. She did not smile nor show any hint of satisfaction with Pierce's remarks about the recent Confederate victory. Her only care was that Noah would return home unscathed.

—A pleasure, Pierce. Now, if you'll excuse a frumpy woman.

He blocked her path and bowed slightly.

—I beg your pardon. You're not frumpy at all.

—And you're not a glorified construction laborer in a pretty uniform. Good day.

—Your reputation precedes you. Indeed, you are a dragon woman, who blows fire in my face without cause.

—The burns will be an improvement, I think.

—Perhaps, but it is better to be a monster on the outside than on the inside.

—Are you suggesting I'm a cruel and hard person?

—It wasnt a suggestion.

—I suppose it's better to be seen as hard, rather than impotent.

—You are an unparalleled woman, Mrs. Beaumont. Dance with me.

—How can you dance with that sword dangling about? Do you battle with it or are you trying to compensate for something?

—Neither. Decoration, I assure you. But it is long, isnt it?

A chuckle slipped from Elmira's mouth, though she quickly quashed it. Pierce looked at her with a cocky assuredness that was both repulsive and alluring. The center of the ballroom began to clear. The band turned the pages of their sheet music.

—There are several other ladies to choose from. Good day, Pierce.

—But none of them are Mrs. Beaumont.

Elmira felt a smile crawl up her cheek. She hadnt smiled in a long time. She forced it away and tilted her chin up. Pierce handed his sword to a comrade.

—Of course they arent.

Pierce took her hand. She was offended by his forwardness. After all, she was a Confederate congressman's wife. But she did not pull away.

—They're playing music for the Redowa. Perhaps you arent familiar with the dance, Mrs. Beaumont? Is it too spicy for you?

Elmira seized Pierce's free hand.

—Try to keep up, Mr. Westbrook.

The band played. The fast-paced dance required not only intricate footwork but stamina as well. As the music went on, it became a sort of battle between her and Pierce. They each tried to outdo the other in terms of grace and elegance. To Elmira's surprise, the man kept up. When the music stopped, her heart was pounding. She fluttered her silken fan over her reddened chest. He seemed amused.

—What are you smiling about? asked Elmira.

—You are a fierce one, Mrs. Beaumont.

Pierce took her hand once more. He kissed it. Perhaps he kissed it for far longer than she should have allowed, but her hand did not move.

—You may call me Elmira.

Chapter 16

NOAH

1864, Tennessee and Georgia

Dried autumn leaves crackled under the hooves of Forrest and Noah's horses. The beasts' eyes burned like hot coals as their nostrils steamed with cool morning vapor. Black, leafless branches around them zipped by in a blur. Word had it that General Sherman was massing troops around Chattanooga. At Fort Pillow, Forrest had found a Yankee seed that had to be eradicated before it could take root. The apocalypse was coming for the Yankee devils. The fort was surrounded, it would be either surrender or death.

Noah's horse struggled to keep up with Forrest's horse. Earlier, the now-general had ordered a detachment of his men to attend to Fort Pillow while he managed the mopping up of renegade Tennesseans, homemade Yankees, that plagued the countryside. Now they were trying to make it to the besieged fort as quickly as possible.

Noah, a major by this point and Forrest's chief of staff, rode alongside the general and Walker. His friend didnt look well. Walker's face was ashen, and his hair appeared brittle. Men fell ill all the time, he must have caught something. Dysentery was going around. Noah had just had a bout of the flux and was glad it was over. Walker looked gaunt with heavy bags under his eyes. He had trouble keeping up. Noah asked Walker if he was alright, and his friend told him it was nothing to worry about.

Hot lead hissed by Noah's ear and it startled his horse. He patted its mane to calm it and then removed his flask and shook it. His whiskey was getting low and that gave him great anxiety, more so than the Yankee sharpshooters in the trees. They were hiding in the woods surrounding Fort Pillow, and despite their best efforts to root them out, Noah's unit had already lost several horses on the way to the battleground.

They rode up a hill and the fort came into view.

Fort Pillow was a modest mound of earth arranged in a half-moon shape facing outward from the Mississippi River with just a few cannons jutting from its sandbag-laden mud walls. The front end of the fort was surrounded by a second ring of earthen works and manmade ravines while the rear part, the open end of the fort, led to a vine-strewn bluff that descended sharply down toward the river below. Some six hundred Federal soldiers were crammed together within.

The battle had already commenced, and the outer ring of the fort had already been taken by Forrest's men. Tree trunks cracked and clods of earth kicked up into the air as the Federal gunboat floating on the river beside the fort fired shells toward their positions. Trees were by and large the only casualties for the Confederates were well hidden under the cover of the woods.

With the surrounding woodland secure, Forrest had his troops unleash hellfire of their own. First, they fired upon the gunboat. It eventually moved away from the shore to escape the relentless barrage. Now Forrest's sharpshooters' full attention was directed at picking off the officers within the huddled mass of Yankees. Their low earthen walls left them little protection from the Confederates' higher vantage points. Chaos consumed the inside of the fort.

Forrest ordered his men to cease fire. A temporary truce was called, and he handed Noah his terms to give to the trapped Federals inside. He rode out to the fort waving a flag of truce. Noah dismounted his horse and handed the reigns to Walker. His boots sank ankle-deep into the mud as he walked toward the fort alone.

He passed by the contorted bodies of dead young men lying in the muck and soon reached the innermost walls. There he handed the document to a waiting Federal solider. The contents of the ultimatum were as follows:

> *Major Booth,*
>
> *The conduct of the officers and men garrisoning Fort Pillow has been such as to entitle them to being treated as prisoners of war. I demand the unconditional surrender of the entire garrison, promising that you shall be treated as prisoners of war. My men have just received a fresh supply of ammunition, and from their present position can easily assault and capture the fort. Should my demand be refused, I cannot be responsible for the fate of your command.*
>
> *Respectfully,*
> *N.B. Forrest*

Noah could see the barrels of the Confederate sharpshooters poking out from the trees around him. Hot, wavy air rose from above the barrels of cannons inside the fort. The chaos waned as the Yankee commander inside wrote his response. Upon receiving it, Noah trudged back toward his horse and rode out for the hill overlooking the fort that Forrest was waiting upon. General Forrest read the letter aloud to his staff officers.

> *General Forrest,*
> *I respectfully ask for one hour consultation with my officers and officers of the gunboat. In the meantime no preparation to be made on either side.*
> *Very respectfully,*
> *L.F. Booth*

As Forrest mused over the letter, a scout reported that two Federal steamers loaded with guns and infantry were steaming down the river. He calmly folded it and put it in his pocket.

—He's tryin to buy time. They've got twenty minutes to surrender or there will be no quarter. I'm not bluffing. I'll slaughter them to the man if I must.

Noah returned to the fort once and handed a new letter with the general's deadline. A soldier soon handed him a simple response:

I will not surrender.

After Noah gave the message to Forrest, the general was elated rather than dismayed. In the years he had known him, he had found Forrest to be a peculiar man. He was one of those rare people who seemed immune to the fatigues of combat and the mental trials of having to deal with death and suffering on a regular basis. Rather than attempting to escape such horrors, Forrest relished them. Not only that, he seemed to attract other such peculiar men to serve under his command.

The silence of the truce was broken by the call of the Confederate bugle. Forrest's horse reared up on its hind legs and he waved his hat high above his head. The order to take the fort had come.

—No quarter, boys. No quarter.

The woods echoed with the unmistakable shrill of the Rebel war cry and filled with rolls of gray smoke as lead balls cut through the air and into the bodies of the penned-in Yankees. Tree limbs cracked as cannonballs from the fort tore into the surrounding woodland.

The sharpshooters picked off the Federal officers first and moved down the chain of command. The Federal gunboat sat idle in the river, its gun ports still sealed shut from the unrelenting rain of sniper fire. Emotions grew hot when word spread that half of the Yankee soldiers were runaways and the other half Confederate turncoats and draft dodgers.

The Confederates climbed up over the half-moon berm walls of the fort, with some of the men standing on others' shoulders to get inside. As the Confederates seized the perimeter of the fort and descended into the interior, the trapped Yankees fled to the open end of the fort. Some tried to fight back while others tumbled down the steep bluffs to escape. Several of them waded out into the Mississippi in a futile attempt to reach the ships anchored in the distance. Those who didnt try to escape fought valiantly until they were cut down by the attacking Confederates. As a whole, the outnumbered Federals were incapable of resistance. Noah was elated.

Hundreds of corpses littered the ground. Those who were still alive tried to surrender and a few fell to their knees and pled for mercy. They were ordered to stand and then bayonetted. Others cried out to God, but God did not answer. Noah saw Walker waving his arms, trying to get the men to cease the unnecessary carnage.

—They're surrenderin. They're surrenderin, damnit.

It was no use. Bloodlust and rage had taken over. Despite the burden, Noah was in favor of taking prisoners, for if men knew they were going to live and be treated well then they would surrender more easily in future battles. After all, the Federals were doing just that to great effect.

—Sir, they're surrendering, he said to the general.

—Good. Now shoot them like dogs, hollered Forrest.

—Sir, we've already won.

—Are you getting soft on me, Beaumont? Are you gonna feed all those hungry mouths with that West Point education of yours?

—Sir, it's against God.

—We're Yankee killers. That's what we do, kill Yankees. That's our purpose from God.

Forrest had proven that he wasnt one to make idle threats. Noah's elation gave way to horror. He didnt think the carnage could get any worse, until it did. Ammunition ran low, so the Confederate soldiers held their rifles by their barrels and swung them like clubs. They mashed the heads of the Yankee soldiers until their eyes fell out and their skulls cracked open. And they continued mashing their heads until the contents spilled out onto the ground. A few pulled out Bowie knives and gutted surrendering soldiers. One Yankee collapsed while trying to hold his entrails inside only to have his throat slit moments later. All the while, the Rebel soldiers yipped and bellowed atop the sticky, blood-sodden earth.

—No quarter. No quarter, the men yelled.

The military objective had already been achieved. What Noah saw now was nothing more than a sinful orgy of bloodlust. Had they no honor? No shame? No God? Noah's stomach lurched as he saw a Rebel slice the flesh of a dead soldier's forehead and peel the scalp off. He held the scalp over his head and bellowed. The men around him cheered. Then he slid it on a bloody hook with the other man-pelts dangling from his belt.

Noah had served under Forrest for years. He knew the man. The actions didnt surprise him, but he had reached his limit. Deep down, he knew the offer of allowing the Yankees to become prisoners of war amounted to little more than Punic faith. He'd wanted to believe in his general. Never before had the men devolved into such godless barbarity at such a scale, and he had already seen much horror.

Noah vomited.

The Mississippi turned red. Then, with nothing left to kill, the carnage stopped. The men had had their fill of blood. Noah's hands trembled as he gazed at the noseless faces and red skulls glistening in the dying sun. The entirety of the riverbank was awash in blood, entrails, and brains. Bodies floated down the Mississippi, never to have graves. Noah rubbed his eyes in the hopes that it was a figment of his imagination or his exhaustion. When he pulled them away and blinked, the river was still red. Where was God? Where was God?

That night, he trembled in his tent, his eyes wide open. He was out of whiskey and couldnt sleep. The fog from the booze had disappeared for the first time in months. The smell of blood filled his nostrils. The only thing in his mind's eye was the act he had just taken part in.

About a week later, Noah no longer shaved and no longer cared if his uniform was in order or not. He knew he had to get out from

General Forrest's command. Sure, Forrest was a brilliant tactician, but he was the most amoral officer Noah had ever met. For years he had tried to push such thoughts away and made excuses for why the man behaved the way he did. Now he could no longer deny the truth.

Noah went to go find Walker. He wanted to tell his friend that he was leaving. He had thought about leaving some time ago, when he began to question some of Forrest's methods, but had stayed on mostly because of Walker's presence.

Even after looking all over the camp, he could not find Walker. Then Noah walked past some horses and noticed that Walker's saddlebags and things were sitting atop a tree stump. Noah checked every tent once more and couldnt find his friend. He eyed an outhouse and knocked on the door.

No one answered.

Noah opened the door of the outhouse and found him. His friend sat there slumped over to the side, the flux had taken him. He cried out and pulled up Walker's pants. Then he heaved his body out of the outhouse. He sat there with his friend's head in his lap and broke down.

A few days after Walker's death, he had given General Forrest a number of excuses as to why he needed to transfer to a different unit. Now, he stood before Forrest inside the general's command tent. It turned out that Forrest finally had an answer to his request.

—I found a commander who needs a staff officer, said Forrest.

—Who, sir?

—Major General Ambrose de Bellomonte.

Forrest crossed his arms and smirked. The general's eyes challenged him to submit, to be a good lap dog and come crawling back to his master with his tail between his legs. Noah wasnt sure if honor existed anymore. Maybe it was an artifact from the age of chivalry. Maybe it never existed. It was no matter, he needed to leave.

—Sir, anyone but him.

—Take it or leave it, Beaumont.

It was clear that he was being forced to stay. Of all the generals in the CSA, Forrest had reached out to the one man he knew Noah loathed more than any other. Still, he'd rather serve under his family's enemy than fight alongside the devil. And so he agreed.

—Are you sure? Forrest asked.

—Yes, sir.

—So be it.

Noah became an *aide de camp* under Major General Ambrose de Bellomonte. They were in the Confederate Army of Tennessee, led by General Johnston. Inside de Bellomonte's tent, a lieutenant polished an extra pair of the major general's boots. Ambrose insisted that only an officer was able enough to polish his boots.

Ambrose's beard was in the fashion of Napoleon III and his uniform was by far the gaudiest of all the officers'. Massive gold epaulettes graced each of his shoulders to match the gold-plated buttons shimmering off his chest for all to see. He had a saber, also gilded in gold and silver and slung around his waist. Despite his haughty flamboyance, Ambrose had a reputation as a competent commander who was cool under pressure. He was neither too aggressive nor too passive in battle. His men didnt feel like he was throwing away their lives needlessly. Despite their family history, Noah had to admit that Ambrose had strokes of strategic genius from time to time.

Noah marched south from Chattanooga with the battered army. His canteen was empty. The youngest soldier in his new unit handed Noah his own. He took a sip of the fetid water and thanked the boy. The Federal Army had taken Chattanooga, the Gateway to the South. Now the Yankee hordes were slaughtering their way after them into Georgia, their vicious eyes set on Atlanta.

Noah's men were short on everything. Their uniforms, if they had them at all, were in tatters. Food was scarce. They had to pillage the farms of the people they were supposed to protect. Every other day at roll call, someone came up missing. It usually meant one of two things: they had either deserted or they were lying dead in a pool of their own filth, the glory of war. His men often prayed to let the Lord take them in battle before the dysentery did. Noah no longer prayed. He had a permanent ringing in his ears and his hands trembled if he didnt get any whiskey.

They came upon steep cliffs that rose over a valley known as Buzzard's Roost. There was a tiny town nearby called Dalton. The men set up camp. Noah walked to the command tent. He stood at attention and saluted. Major General Ambrose de Bellomonte returned his salute.

—At ease.

—General Johnston ordered us to dig in. We are to make this place a Yankee graveyard.

—Yes, sir.

Noah about-faced and began to leave.

—Halt. Who said you could go?

Noah turned around. Ambrose strutted up to him and leaned forward until they were nose to nose.

—The latrines are overflowing. It's unsanitary. Dig new ones.

—I'll assign someone at once, sir.

—No. You do it.

—Sir, I'm supposed to be your staff officer.

—Your job is whatever I say it is. Now go.

—Yes, sir.

Noah about-faced once more and began to leave.

—Halt. You have not been dismissed. You'll leave when I tell you to leave.

—Yes, sir.

Noah turned and stood at attention. Without a word, Ambrose left to use the latrine and didnt return until twenty minutes later. Noah remained at attention the whole time. Ambrose then went about his business barking commands and studying maps. He poured some brandy for his sycophantic staff officers and lit up a cigar. Noah could feel his swollen ankles rub against the inside of his hard leather boots. He was exhausted from the march, or retreat, to use the honest word, from Chattanooga. His knees wobbled.

—Beaumont.

—Yes, sir.

—Dig those latrines.

It was midnight by the time Noah finished digging the new pits. He collapsed into his tent, asleep before he even hit the ground. Though he was technically an officer, he might as well have been a private.

Noah was assigned to take a dead captain's place for the time being. He knew it was an excuse for Ambrose to put him on the front line. He didnt care.

A string of gray Confederate pearls dotted the top of Rocky Face Ridge. Their firearms were trained on the valley below. They were dug in along the leading edge of the ridge, and Noah sat in a trench full of muddy water with his men. He could feel it seep into his boots. Most of the men around him were beat down and ragged. Others were sick, and a few were covered in boils, still they were ordered to hold the line.

The first thing he heard was the drumbeats in the distance. Then the artillery.

Dirt and shards of bark exploded around him. He dove down. His knees and elbows and face became wet with the muddy water. The Confederate artillery returned fire. The smoke made the trench suffocating. He peered over the trench. His eyes widened. Flags emerged from the woodland. Massive columns of blue marched toward his position. Cannonballs plowed into the Federal formations. Many of the men below were torn in half, some were decapitated, and others exploded. The smoke cleared. The star-spangled banner appeared once more, flapping in the air, and the Federal ranks reformed and continued their march forward unabated.

The rain sizzled as it steamed off the barrel of his rifle. Noah looked to the men to his left and noticed that the soldiers beside him were aiming above the heads of the Federals. Others weren't shooting at all. Instead, they were helping with loading and other menial tasks. It was something he had observed before but thought nothing of it.

Now it seemed they were missing on purpose. Weak stomachs.

He choked as an earthen berm exploded beside him. One of his men was knocked off his feet and began rolling down the steep hillside toward the oncoming Union troops. The teenage soldier tried to hide behind a tree stump as the Federals took potshots at him. He tried to climb back up to the remnants of the protective earthworks, but the ground was too steep.

Noah shoved his rifle into the hands of a nearby soldier.

—Hold this.

—Sir, I know what you're thinking. Dont. You cant help him.

—Dont you tell me what I cant do.

His men tied a rope around his waist and held the other end. Noah got on his hands and began crawling through the muddy hillside toward the kid solider as lead balls whistled over his head and clods of dirt kicked up around him. The men cheered when he reached the soldier. Noah wrapped his arms and legs around the man.

—Pull, you bastards, pull, he shouted.

The men pulled as the Yankees continued taking shots.

Then there was cheering, louder than before. He wasnt sure why until he realized they were both over the berm, behind the earthworks. His men were patting him on the back and shaking his hand.

Noah wasnt sure how much time had passed when the gunfire stopped. He leaned against the trench, soaking wet, his elbows in the dirt propping up his rifle. He gazed at the fallen trees, the mangled earth, and the war dead around him. The field before him was a godless expanse filled with hundreds of corpses of men in the prime of their youth.

He knew men on both sides were praying. Noah considered it useless. Were their prayers answered when their brains were blown out, when their bodies were torn apart by cannon fire, when they died in the latrines? His government had mandated him to murder in the hope it would solve their political problems. Yet no one in Richmond was out in the mud getting their hands dirty with death. At least Brutus had the integrity to use the dagger and dip his hands in Caesar's blood. He couldnt imagine a modern politician doing the same. He thought that they ought to go back to Roman rules: senators leading the battles from the front.

He wasnt the only one that took notice. Every day at rollcall they had fewer men. Most of which had deserted in the night. If they were caught, they'd hang, but most were never seen again. He took a breath and reminded himself why he was there. He counted himself as a sinner for the Southern cause and hoped the cause was noble enough to risk damnation for. He wouldnt desert, despite the horror around him devouring his soul. Besides, even if God was up there, he didnt care.

The Federal troops fell back, leaving behind the countless guttural moans. Some were Federals, others Confederate. He couldnt tell anymore, for the entrails of brothers, sons, and fathers were spread out together in a great canvas of death. His men who lived cheered. Noah stayed silent.

Chapter 17

EMMA

1864, Georgia

The cows werent cooperating. Emma veered to the side as a massive hoof kicked backward. She tried to milk the cow, but it wasnt in the mood. The war had taken its toll on Edel Farm, now even the cows rebelled. She had only managed to fill the bottom quarter of the bucket. As she pleaded with the cow to help her out, a large shadow appeared over her. It was Nora, the head house slave.

—You better fill that bucket.

Before Emma could respond, Nora whacked her across the back of the neck with a switch. Numbness was followed by searing pain. The pain was worse when the thin wooden rod struck again, this time at the edge of her ear. She instinctively shuddered every time Nora's large shadow approached.

—You hear me?

—Yes, Nora.

—That's *yes, ma'am* to you.

Emma felt the sharp pain of the switch again.

—Yes, ma'am.

—Dont know why they decided to keep your scrawny ass.

—I wouldnt be so scrawny if you'd stop eating my food and everybody else's.

Whack.

—You sayin I'm fat?

Emma bit her tongue and kept her eyes toward the ground. She wanted nothing more than to rip the stick from Nora's hand and give her a taste of her own medicine. Yet she kept her composure. Edel Farm wasnt a pleasant place, but she could imagine far worse places she could be sold off to. Everyone knew Lincoln's army was coming. They just did not know when. Until then, Emma hunkered down inside herself and continued to feed the fire of her soul. She wouldnt let Nora or anyone else quench it.

Nora put her hands on her hips.

—I aint fat. I'm curvaceous. I'm gorgeous. And you better believe I'm fabulous.

Whack.

—Dont you ever talk back again.

Whack.

The Edels only kept female slaves. They were allowed to sleep inside the farmhouse in a large room with a wood-burning stove and a row of bunks. Real beds. Not a filthy rag stuffed with straw like she'd had at Beaumont Plantation. Mrs. Edel expected everything to be kept clean and orderly and, unlike Elmira, she wasnt a woman who was afraid to get her own hands dirty. As for Mr. Edel, he was a quiet distant man. He had a bit of a complexion that caused whispers throughout the farm.

While food was still scarce, Emma ate far better on the Edel Dairy Farm. Mr. Edel and Mrs. Edel showed no affection for their slaves, but at least they didnt possess a sadistic need to punish, they left that to Nora. Nora gave the cow a whack for good measure and then wagged her finger at Emma.

—I'll be watchin you, she said.

The beastly woman walked off to bother someone else, and Emma exhaled. Nora required all the other girls to give her a portion of their rations, and with the war and the blockade, there wasnt much to go around. If they didnt, she'd deliver a sharp crack of a switch against the offender's neck. The woman always carried it around and snapped it against things to frighten the others and remind them of her power over them.

As Emma was eating her lunch that day, Nora took an orange from one girl's plate, a peach from another, and sipped a little milk from a third, and then she reached over to take Emma's cornbread. Before she got her hand on it, Emma shoved the entire thing into her mouth.

Nora's eyes widened with a combination of incredulity and rage. Nora grabbed the back of Emma's neck and slammed her face down onto the table.

—Spit it out.

Emma chewed as fast as she could. Nora wasnt able to get much leverage in their awkward position, and the blows of her switch didnt sting. Then Nora tried to squeeze the morsel out of Emma's rounded cheeks to no avail. All the while, Emma chewed defiantly.

After she swallowed the last of her cornbread, Nora screamed. The other girls covered their mouths and laughed. Nora tore open the back of Emma's dress and set to relentlessly beating her bare back with the switch until a voice echoed throughout the room.

—Enough of that, Nora. I need you in the kitchen, said Mrs. Edel.

—Yes, Mrs. Edel, I'll be right there.

Emma turned and faced Nora. Part of her unbuttoned dress hung over her bare shoulder. Nora crossed her arms and gave her a cold stare. Emma straightened her back and tilted her chin upward. She would rather get beaten than go hungry. Emma could still taste the cornbread, it was good. Nora offered a litany of curses and stormed off.

The girls were all in their bunks and they knew that Lincoln was freeing slaves. Most agreed to drag their feet and work as slowly as possible, no matter how many times Nora whacked them. The war was on everybody's lips. That night, like every night, the girls whispered in hushed tones in their bunks after the candles went out. They called the stream of war updates they received the *grapevine telegraph*.

—The Federals defeated the rebels in Chattanooga, whispered one of the girls.

—Where's that? asked Emma.

—Just across the border from Georgia, in Tennessee.

—Are they coming here?

—I met a girl in the market who says General Sherman is marching toward Atlanta. Some say he's coming for Savannah.

—Who's General Sherman?

—A Federal general. They say he's one mean son of a bitch.

—Or an angel of judgment.

—The masters say he's the devil incarnate.

—If he is, then he's our devil.

The following day, a small group of Confederate troops had set up camp in the pasture at Edel Farm. Emma figured it had something to do with the defense of nearby Savannah. A few of the men wore makeshift uniforms and several of the soldiers lacked shoes, and when the breeze shifted she could smell the stink of their unwashed bodies. Every day they collected a supply of milk and flour and other goods and loaded them onto a wagon. A day or two later, the wagon would return and the process would repeat itself.

One morning while the soldiers were collecting food from the Edels, she noticed a rather different soldier. If he could be called a soldier. He was a boy, perhaps nine years old, with moppy brown hair. He had the neatest uniform out of all of them and carried a drum.

The boy caught her staring and approached. Emma cast her eyes downward and resumed feeding the chickens. The last thing she wanted was to get the attention of the Rebel army. She heard that some slaves were seized by the army to dig trenches and build fortifications.

—Hello.

The boy's greeting froze her. She wasnt sure what to do and wished he had never seen her. She simply returned his greeting, gave a polite nod, and resumed her work. The boy followed her as she conducted her chores. She wanted to tell him to go away. However, the day was dull and her curiosity got the better of her.

—Where are you from? she asked.

—A house high in the mountains.

Emma gave a forced smile and tried to busy herself with other chores at the far end of the farm. Still, the boy followed her. Then the boy dug into his pocket. When he removed it, his hand was full of several candies in bright-colored wrappers. He unwrapped one and tossed it in his mouth. He stared at her with blinking, curious eyes for several moments. After looking side to side and over his shoulder, he held out his hand.

—You can have one.

She wasnt sure if she should take the gift or not. Emma cautiously took one of the candies and thanked the boy, who then wandered off and explored the farm.

Chapter 18

ISAIAH

1864, Georgia

The stench of cow manure filled the air. He rode atop a hill overlooking a pasture with hundreds of head of cattle. He dismounted his horse and climbed over a wooden fence. There was no one outside, so he sat and waited.

Nearly an hour had passed with only cows in sight. He got up and began to mount his horse when he caught something. He held up his hand over his brow to visor his eyes against the midday sun. He saw a figure through squint eyes. A woman, her dress fluttering in the warm breeze. It was a girl walking toward a milking barn. He squinted.

It was Emma.

He let go of the reins of his horse and walked toward her. She held her hand over her eyes and gazed in his direction. His moment of elation was interrupted by someone calling out.

—Who goes there? the voice demanded.

He stopped. He made out several dirty white tents on another hill nearby. Four Confederate soldiers, rifles slung over their shoulders, began to climb up the hill he was on. He clenched his teeth and looked to his horse. Then he turned and looked toward Emma. He struggled to gauge the distance, but he knew it was too far. Isaiah mounted his horse.

—Did you hear me? demanded one of the Rebel soldiers.

The soldiers grew closer. The last time he'd acted rashly out of passion, he'd nearly gotten himself hobbled. He took a breath and one last long look at Emma and galloped off. To where, he didnt know.

Isaiah slept in the swampland next to his horse and awoke to a stomach churning with hunger. He ate berries, and grass, and whatever he could find in the swamp. It was not enough. How could he free Emma if he couldnt even feed himself? Even if he had a rifle, he couldnt free her alone. He squeezed the bridge of his nose as he thought through his options, none of which was good. He only knew that he needed a gun in his hand and an army behind him.

Isaiah mounted his horse and rode toward Atlanta, toward the Federal army. He rode into the nearest tree cover he could find. Instead of dry woodland were still black waters and submerged bald cypress trunks. He tried to lead his horse into the chest-deep water. A peculiar log drifted by. Upon the log he spied a slit pupil against an iris the color of the swamp itself. His horse was having none of it. It tried to pull and jerk itself free from his grasp. He covered the horse's eyes with his shirt and calmed it. Then they entered the dark water.

For two days he traversed the swamp, his horse in tow. On the third, he hit dry land. When he did, he lay down just inside the tree line and slept until evening. Once awake, he rode as fast as he could through the open fields and pastures, only stopping to sustain himself on crops and the occasional chicken seized from its coop. When dawn arrived, he fled back into the cover of wilderness with pilfered roughage for his horse.

He did that for several days, until he came across a wide river. He was about to get on the road and pass over the bridge when he noticed that it was guarded by troops. The current of the river was too fast for him and his horse to ford or swim, but he knew attempting to cross the bridge was a death sentence. He didnt know how long the river was. How many miles could he ride until he found a spot narrow enough to pass? Even if he was willing to ride along the river for several days, he didnt have the time. He was growing hungrier with each passing hour. The ribs on his horse were beginning to protrude, along with his own. He always let the horse out to pasture under nightfall, but the hard ride was taking a toll on the both of them.

Isaiah watched the soldiers on the bridge from a distance. He counted nineteen of them, and of those nineteen, half looked as if they could barely stand, and the other half looked ill. As the day began to fade away, they created a campfire and most of them gathered around it. Only two guards remained at their posts on the end of the narrow bridge. They appeared to be playing poker.

That night, Isaiah watched as two fresh guards were posted at the ends of the bridge. The rest were asleep in little makeshift cabins cobbled together from nearby trees. The two fresh guards looked just as tired as the ones they'd relieved. Isaiah mounted his horse.

He rode back down the road some distance and then wheeled the horse back around. It began to trot forward. He couldnt see the trees beside him much less the bridge in front of him. The horse began to pick up speed. It was too dark and Isaiah still couldnt see the bridge, but he knew it must be close. He dug his heels into the flanks of the horse and it began to gallop.

He saw the whites of the first guard's eyes as he rode by at full speed. The second guard heaved his rifle to his shoulder as Isaiah passed. Both yelled at him to stop. The sky briefly lit up with the flash of muzzle fire before giving way to darkness once more. He dug his heels in harder and the horse continued down the road.

After some time, Isaiah stopped in the middle of the road. He tilted his head and listened for hoof clops or footsteps or any indication that he was being pursued. There was only silence. Still, he didnt want to take his chances by being out in the open, so he dismounted his horse and again entered the deep wood. He couldnt see, and he didnt dare try to light the tallow candle he had brought with him. He just kept moving northward, as silently as he could.

Atlanta was now behind him and Sherman's army was somewhere in front of him. He passed through a clearing next to the calm waters of the Etowah River. It was graced with grand pyramidal mounds of earth, an ancient city. The dwellings and edifices were long gone and all that remained was an echo of ages past. Only ghosts dwelled there now. Like the thousands of people of the dead city in which he now stood, he knew his flesh was only for the moment and was fated to be ash for the rest of eternity.

His horse was gasping for breath. His legs could feel the rattling of the horse's lungs as they made their way along a road that cut through the surrounding woodland. He decided to climb off and give the animal some rest, but before he could the horse fell over dead beneath him. He spilled off onto the road and pulled his leg out from under the horse. He patted the muzzle of the poor animal that had done everything he had asked of it. Campfires dotted the horizon. Their number was beyond counting. As the sun rose, he made out blue uniforms and knew he stood before a Federal camp. It had to be Sherman's army.

Isaiah cleaned his clothes in a nearby river to make himself as presentable as possible. He wasnt sure what would happen once he walked up to the Federal camp. Would they detain him? Would they shoot him? He figured it didnt matter. He was half-starved and had already traveled this far. Besides, he needed a gun in hand and an army behind him to free Emma. If he couldnt get that, he had nothing. His only real option was to push his shoulders back and walk up to one of the sentinels guarding the camp.

—Halt. Who goes there? The sentinel glared at him with tired gray eyes. Isaiah noticed the glint of the morning light crawled along the blood groove of the soldier's bayonet pointed at his neck. He held his trembling hands up.

—I'm here to enlist, said Isaiah.

The man narrowed his eyes and studied Isaiah for several moments. Then the man slowly lowered his rifle. Isaiah was ushered through a maze of tents and directed to stand in a line that must have been hundreds of men, many of them runaways. He was finally close enough to hear the voice of the grizzled man sitting behind a desk under the shade of a maple tree.

—Pioneer. Next. Pioneer. Next. No. Sorry, coloreds can only be pioneers, not infantry soldiers. Why? General Sherman's orders. Take it or leave it. Alright, welcome aboard. Sign here. Next.

Isaiah had read about pioneers. Their work consisted of building fortifications, creating pontoon bridges, and assisting the engineers. Isaiah didnt want to be a pioneer. He wanted to spill blood.

It was midevening by the time he made it to the desk. The sergeant briefly looked up from his papers and narrowed his eyes.

—What are you?

—Sir?

—You got something in you. Injun? Mexican? Negro?

—Why?

—Field Order No. 16. I cant take colored folks into the army. Other armies under other generals maybe, but not this one.

Speechless, Isaiah cast his eyes to the ground. He wrung his hands together as his mind searched for a good answer. The grizzled sergeant looked both ways and leaned forward.

—If you're half-Injun, I can take you. You're half-Injun, right?

The sergeant leaned forward even closer. His eyes bulged and his head nodded in affirmation ever so slightly.

—Yes, sir. Half-Injun. Absolutely.

—I knew it. We need as many warm bodies as we can get.

The sergeant went inside a large tent and came out with a little wooden table. He unfurled a document and scribbled away.

—Name?

—Isaiah Beaumont.

The sergeant laughed.

—Beaumont? As in *the* Beaumonts?

—No, sir.

—Of course not.

Isaiah took the paper handed to him by the sergeant. He began to read it, and the sergeant became annoyed.

—Just sign the damn thing.

Isaiah complied. Even if there was something in the writing he didnt agree with, he had no other options. He had to find a way to feed himself, clothe himself, and most importantly, free Emma. The sergeant filed the form and held out his hand. Isaiah shook it. The man smiled.

—Welcome to the United States Army, you poor fool.

He was given pants that were too large around the waist and an army tunic with sleeves that were too short. The stock of his rifle was beat up and covered with dried bloodstains that had seeped into the grain of the wood.

Isaiah managed the screaming and barking of the drill instructors far better than most recruits. To his surprise, they did not need to flog anyone in order to bend them to their will, even beatings were frowned upon. It wasnt long before he was intimately familiar with his Springfield rifle and with the bronze cannon assigned to his crew: a twelve-pounder, Napoleon Model 1857. It could rain hellfire more than a mile away.

The cannon's wheels often sank in the soft earth of Georgia's furrowed roads when being pulled by draft horses. Occasionally a wheel would get caught on a crevice or snap off the axle. His crew proved adept at fixing the wheels themselves rather than fighting for an overworked wheelsmith. The cannon became like a sort of child he had to constantly tend to.

Now he was marching back south, toward Atlanta. He was just one small element in a long column of men with a wagon train that stretched back some twenty-five miles. The men sang marching songs, and today they were singing his favorite hymn:

Old John Brown's body lies a mouldering in the grave,
While weep the sons of bondage whom he ventured
all to save,
But though he lost his life in struggling for the slave,
His truth is marching on.

They sang as they crossed the Chattahoochee River, the American Rubicon, for the die was cast and Atlanta would either surrender or bleed. Many complained about the regimentation of army life. Isaiah thought that was the easy part. It was the marching, the never-ending marching. He marched until his leather boots were worn thin and the flesh on the soles of his feet was raw.

The stream below was muddy: Peachtree Creek. Isaiah led the draft horses that pulled his crew's cannon across a wobbly pontoon bridge. There were two parts to the setup. The cannon was in front and the limber wagon, which held the ammunition chest, was in the rear. When traveling, the two pieces were joined to create a four-wheeled cart that could be pulled by horses.

Thousands of men below washed months of filth from their bodies on one side of the creek while hundreds more watered their horses on the other. Countless frogs and salamanders and whatever creature was capable of escaping the fouled waters made their way out and onto the riverbank. One of the fresh draft horses was spooked when the pontoon bridge tilted sharply to the side. The rear of the limber wagon slid to the edge of the narrow bridge. His sergeant proceeded to beat the horse over on the flanks and even over its eyes. It only frightened the animal, which pulled back on its reins as Isaiah tried to lead it. One of the wheels slid over the edge. The rest of Isaiah's crew ran over to try to pull the limber wagon back onto the bridge. He turned to his sergeant.

—Let me try to calm him.

The sergeant chided Isaiah for talking out of turn and continued beating the scared animal. The horse reared up. Isaiah took off his tunic and wrapped it over the horse's eyes and patted its muzzle, a trick he'd learned from Emma. It calmed down enough for him to lead it and the other horses to the other side. The sergeant called him an idiot anyway, but at least the situation was under control.

It took a lot of work, but eventually they got their cannon perched atop a small ridge. His crew was ordered to dig in. He heaved shovelfuls of red earth to the side to form a berm in front of their artillery piece. The Federal artillery crews formed a row along the tree line, their barrels aimed toward the clearing before them. When his crew was finished fortifying their position, they collapsed around their instrument of destruction, exhausted. Isaiah felt something was in the air.

It was a balmy Georgia day. Drums echoed far beyond the tree line as Isaiah and his crew stood erect. Some twenty thousand Confederate soldiers marched toward their position. One moment the birds were singing, and the next only the thunder of cannons. He loaded theirs and it fired and the earth trembled. He loaded it again. It fired. Over and over again.

It was exhilarating. He wanted to turn the whole field before him into a pool of Rebel blood. Now he had a weapon. Now he could fight back. Isaiah was so focused on the task at hand that he only got a glimpse of what was happening below. The Confederates were charging.

Load.

Fire.

Load.

Fire.

—Beaumont. Beaumont.

Isaiah could barely hear his sergeant screaming his name.

—Yes, Sergeant?

—Beaumont, I said grapeshot, damnit.

He turned his head and saw a small group of Rebels marching toward his position. He ran to the ammunition chest on the limber wagon and heaved the heavy round over to the cannon. He slid it down the barrel. A few of the Rebels knelt and fired upon his crew. Isaiah dove down behind the berm. Dirt kicked up around him as it was pelted with gunfire. Now the Rebels were only a few yards away.

—Fire, said his sergeant.

Grapeshot exploded out of the cannon. In one moment the Rebel soldiers were there and in the next they werent. There were only blood splatters on the trunks of trees and pieces of flesh and gray shards of cloth dangling from the branches. The sight of it pleased him. Then it sickened him. Then he wasnt sure exactly how he felt about it.

When daylight faded, the Confederates had been routed. Now they'd march upon Atlanta.

Chapter 19

ELMIRA

1864, Georgia

A soldier waved Elmira's carriage through a checkpoint. The entirety of Savannah was surrounded by earthworks and trenches. After she reached downtown, she got out of her carriage and sat alone upon a bench. She watched the Carolina parakeets hop from branch to branch in the trees of Oglethorpe Square. The Beaumonts and de Bellomontes had arrived with James Oglethorpe on a ship named *Anne* some 131 years prior to found the Georgia colony.

The story went that Miles' ancestors had been relegated to lands that the Yamacraw and colonists alike refused to settle upon. Some said a certain darkness hung over the grounds, while others said the red earth itself was tainted from some ancient tragedy lost to the ages. In any case, the Beaumonts saw an opportunity where others saw misfortune.

At first Elmira thought the claims were mere superstition of ignorant men. However, she noticed that the crops grown on their plantation grounds tasted peculiar. Everything had an aftertaste to it. As a result, she never ate anything that was grown on Beaumont Plantation and instead had all her food brought in from other sources.

Oglethorpe had co-founded the city with Tomochichi, Chief of the Yamacraw, in the hopes that it would be settled by yeomen farmers. Oglethorpe had envisioned a colony that would create agrarian equality and went about making the colony a home to Europe's wretched. In exchange for the land, Tomochichi desired the usual things: an alliance with King George II, trading rights, and goods. He was even granted an audience with the king. However, there was one thing she always thought peculiar: he desired education above all else. Or so the story went.

Oglethorpe outlawed slavery in the Georgia colony, though after he returned to Britain, the practice resumed. Now Savannah was a major Confederate city. History was a curious thing to her. Miles always liked to gloat that they were descended from Romans and had noble blood pulsing through their veins. Elmira wondered if he had misinterpreted his family history. Were they the descendants of the Romans, or their barbarian slaves?

Regardless, the founder had left, while the Beaumonts and de Bellomontes stayed. They were feuding before they even left the ship. The origins of their ancient quarrel had been lost to the mists of time in the Old World. And what did she, the sole matriarch of the Beaumont line, think? She didnt have the time to ponder such things. Only her son's well-being mattered to her.

The last letter she'd read had shaken her. Noah had been placed under the command of Ambrose de Bellomonte, now a general. It all seemed too convenient. She swore if Ambrose harmed a hair on her son's head, she'd have his.

Elmira got up and walked along President Street and into nearby Wright Square. She gazed upon the ruins of a small stone pyramid. The tomb of Tomochichi. She sat alone in the park and listened to the birds chirp. Miles was gone, as usual. He might as well have been dead. Her husband rarely sent letters or replied to hers. The best she could hope for was a terse message instructing her to be patient. Noah at least wrote letters four or five pages long. For a moment there was relief when they would arrive, but they often came in dirt-covered and crumpled envelopes. On a few occasions they had gotten wet and were unreadable by the time they reached her. Noah always said he was doing well. She didnt believe him. If his letters were in such a terrible state, what shape was her son in? She tossed dried bread to the squirrels.

—Elmira. It's been too long.

Elmira turned. Before her stood a tall man in a gray uniform: Pierce. He sat down next to her. Perhaps closer than he should have. She felt his leg against hers. She got up to move over but stopped and sat back down.

—Beautiful, said Pierce.

—It's my favorite park in the city.

—The park as well.

Her cheeks grew warm. The parakeets flew off. A luminescent feather fell from the flapping birds and slowly twisted and turned as it fell back to earth.

—Husband out of town?

—Always.

—That big old house must be lonely.

Out of the corner of her eye, Elmira could see Pierce gazing at her. He wasnt a modest man by any means. She continued looking forward.

—Why are you here? asked Elmira.

—I come here every day at noon. I'll be here tomorrow on this very bench.

They talked for a while and then parted ways.

Every day, Elmira made her way to the tranquil park, and every day, Pierce was there waiting for her. Miles was always away in Richmond, or so he said. There was, of course, the chance that she'd be recognized walking about with a man who wasnt her husband. She told anyone who asked that Peirce was a relative, which usually stopped the prying. With a parasol on her shoulder, Elmira walked with Pierce through the lush squares of Savannah. They dined at restaurants and admired the architecture of the city. He told her that he mostly built pontoon bridges and defenses for the army and preferred Shakespeare and natural philosophy to warfare, which in his words was *a terrible thing*. Oftentimes they would walk along River Street and watch paddleboats move up and down the murky waters of the Savannah River. Pierce would often ramble off some Shakespearean quote, no doubt in a pompous attempt to impress her, but she did not mind.

One afternoon, Elmira gazed at a steamer that had just pulled into the port. Its wooden hull was pockmarked with holes and singed black with smoke. She stared at it for some time.

—A blockade runner, said Pierce.

—Let us go someplace more pleasant.

—The theater then?

—I should head back.

—Nonsense. Meet me there tonight.

Elmira nodded. Pierce kissed her hand. The warmth of his lips against her flesh was like salve on a wound. He bowed slightly and returned to his duties.

That night they entered the theater and made their way to their box seats. The main show was *The Oresteia*. The inside of the theater was dark and warm from the heat of a full crowd. She had seen it all before. Still, it was a welcome distraction. Elmira caught herself chuckling at an absurd joke Pierce whispered to her and quickly covered her mouth with her hand. Pierce pulled it away.

—Is that a smile I see, Mrs. Beaumont? I dare say you're at risk of losing your reputation.

Her only response was another thin smile. Then she stiffened her back and resumed her steely demeanor. Pierce did not let go of her hand. The proper thing to do would have been to pull away from him—she was the matriarch of the Beaumont family, after all. She felt her fingers interlace with his. The touch of another person. Such a simple thing, yet it had remained elusive to her. Their hands remained intertwined, Elmira's heart pounding the entire time, until the show was over.

Gas lights flickered against the night sky. Pierce helped Elmira climb aboard her carriage. After she sat, she placed her handbag on the seat beside her and turned to say goodbye to Pierce. To her surprise, his face was mere inches from hers. His fingers slowly ran up the back of her slender neck and into her hair. She simply gazed back at him, frozen. His warm lips pressed against hers. Her reservations melted away, and one kiss turned into many.

At last she pulled away and he slipped out, smiling. The carriage lurched forward and the cabin filled with the sound of horseshoes clattering against cobblestone. Her head leaned against the back of her seat. She felt her eyes roll back into her head as her hand fell upon her flushed chest.

Chapter 20

NOAH

1864, Georgia

Noah's men had voted him on the Confederate roll of honor for his actions at Rocky Ridge. The highest decoration. It was the type of thing he'd dreamed about before the war. Now he felt indifferent toward it.

He was in Atlanta now. Darkness had hung over the city for the last several days as Sherman's army waited outside. They had come like a thunderstorm sweeping up everything in its path. Rail ties were torn out, heated, and wrapped around trees. Sherman bowties, they were called. Uncle Billy, as his men called him, was ruthlessly efficient. He didnt tie down his troops by ordering them to guard things, instead, they burned everything in their path.

Noah knew that Sherman believed that Southern opinions couldnt be changed, so he wanted to ensure they felt the cruelty of war firsthand. To Sherman, civilians were complicit in the war effort, for they had provided men and materiel for the Southern cause. Sherman said he wanted to make Georgia howl. Johnston was only able to slow him down. Now he was upon the gates of Atlanta.

Ambrose de Bellomonte tipped his desk over. Maps fell to the ground and glass inkwells shattered, leaving growing pools of sepia on the floor. Noah and the other staff officers stood at attention as their general threw whatever he could get his hands on across the room. Ambrose was none too happy about the recent turn of events.

—Jeff Davis is a moron. How could he replace Johnston with that reckless buffoon Hood? When Hannibal's at the gates, you dont fire Fabius. It's going to be Cannae all over again. Idiots. I'm surrounded by idiots. Doesnt anyone understand that Lincoln's Rottweiler is loose? They might as well just give Sherman my plantation, my home, and my four daughters on a silver platter.

Ambrose stopped pacing. He caught his breath and calmly righted his chair. Then he sat down in the most dignified manner, as if the antics they had just witnessed had never happened.

—Beaumont.

—Yes, sir?

—You are to oversee improvements to the city's defenses.

Noah saluted and left. He knew the other officers envied him for not having to stay in that room a minute longer.

Every tree in and around Atlanta had to be cut down. They needed them to make palisade walls and anti-cavalry barriers: *cheval de frise*. Noah's men chopped down trees in a park. Bark cracked and the falling trees gave a long, slow, creaking sound. It almost sounded like a scream. He thought about the old oak trees back home. His mother had made two swings on one of those trees. Old James used to push him in one of them. Isaiah sat in the other. Those old trees were ornaments upon Beaumont Plantation. He thought it a shame if they ever had to be cut down.

Smoke spiraled out of the tall brick stacks of industry. Atlanta was filled with factories, foundries, arsenals, and machine shops. It was the forge of the Confederate army. If it fell, all was lost. Its citizens worked around the clock to produce arms and other implements of war. Noah heard they were even considering arming the negroes. Such a thing used to be unthinkable. Atlanta also served as a nexus for several different railroads. The railways that flowed in and out of the city were the vessels that carried the lifeblood of industry to Atlanta's beating heart.

Now trains only left the city. They did not come in. Everyone knew it was only a matter of time before the rails would be ripped up by the Federals. The trains carried off war supplies and fleeing residents. Mostly women and children. Men caught trying to leave were drafted. Oftentimes they were deserters that had to be redrafted. One deserter was caught trying to sneak away wearing a dress and a powdered wig. The laughter was enough to make him plead to be shot like a man. He was simply given a rifle and ordered to the front while wearing the dress. All the while he was mocked at every street corner as he walked by. Even the black folks taunted him.

Women in brightly colored dresses, parasols in hand, had once walked up and down its main promenades. Now those streets were devoid of life. Stately yet empty mansions graced Atlanta's avenues. Even many of the bars and grog houses had shuttered their doors. Noah felt a twinge of guilt, for he was more worried about where he could fill his flask than anything else.

Noah had directed his soldiers to widen one of the trenches that zigzagged around the city. He needed to ensure that Atlanta was surrounded by a maze of continuous trenches and barriers. He walked along the perimeter defenses of the largely desolate city, now devoid of trees and anything of beauty. As he was walking over to one of the newly constructed earthen redoubts, he heard a familiar voice.

Ambrose.

It was highly unusual for the general to be out in such a desolate corner of the city rather than in his headquarters. Perhaps old Ambrose was checking up on him, or perhaps he merely wanted to assign him some awful task. Noah debated whether he should make his presence known to his commander. He began walking toward the sound of Ambrose's voice but stopped when he saw the general speaking to a lieutenant, a courier, so far as Noah could tell. He figured he ought to wait. Ambrose hated being interrupted. God knew there'd be retribution, and Noah would probably be digging latrines again.

Noah leaned behind an earthen wall of the redoubt and waited for Ambrose to finish conducting his business. He put a cigarette in his mouth and was about to light it when Ambrose's voice lowered to nearly a whisper. Noah could still hear him speak to the courier. His curiosity got the better of him and he tilted his head ever closer. His unlit cigarette fell from his mouth. He could hardly believe the words coming out of his commander's mouth. Ambrose finished with an order.

—Get my message to Sherman's lines.

Noah peered around the wall and saw him stuff several gold coins in the soldier's pocket. The courier saluted and took a rolled-up letter from the general. Sliding back out of sight, Noah felt his face grow hot with anger. He knew damn well what Ambrose was up to. The bastard was out to save his own neck. He had washed his hands of the Southern cause and was seeking to make a trade while he still had something to trade with. Everyone knew that Ambrose and Sherman had known one another before the war. In fact, it was one of the reasons Ambrose had been assigned to the Army of Tennessee to begin with: they figured he understood his enemy.

Noah hated the war. He didnt agree with his commanders, but he had vowed to see the war through to its end, or his end, whichever came first. The notion that Ambrose would betray the cause Walker had died for enraged him.

The courier saluted and left. Noah followed him and watched him mount a horse. After some distance had opened between them, Noah mounted a horse of his own and pursued. They passed through the gates of the city and out into a muddy hellscape. Beyond it lay the Federal forces, coiled around the city. Once out of sight from the other soldiers, Noah called out to the messenger.

—Lieutenant. Halt.

The lieutenant looked back at him with narrowed eyes. Then he dug his spurs into the flanks of the horse and snapped the reins. He galloped off at full speed and Noah pursued.

—You better stop. I'll shoot.

The messenger ignored him and continued toward the Federal lines. Noah had gotten the slower horse. With each second, the man pulled farther and farther away. He could now see blue kepi hats moving back and forth in the trench before him. Gunfire crackled, followed by laughter. Pot shots across the no-man's-land. The messenger pulled a white hankie and waved it high over his head. The shots stopped for a moment and then they fell upon Noah's location.

He unholstered his sidearm and aimed. The barrel of his revolver bobbed up and down as his horse galloped over boot-trodden earth. He closed one eye and slowly squeezed the trigger. There was a puff of gray smoke. The horse collapsed dead from beneath the messenger. The lieutenant slammed into the mud. The crack of gunfire continued from the Yankee trenches. Noah's horse fell over and he rolled onto the ground. The messenger climbed to his feet and ran on. A Yankee soldier motioned with his hand for the traitor to hurry.

—Come on, come on, the Yankee yelled.

Noah ran as fast as he could. He closed in on the traitor. He reached out, his fingers just inches away from grasping the man. But Noah was getting tired now and the courier was gaining ground.

He made one last effort, jumping forward. Noah's arms wrapped around the traitor's legs. They both tumbled into the muck. The lieutenant pulled out a revolver. Noah gripped the barrel. A shot. The hot barrel sent searing pain through his palm. He overrode his instinct to let go and squeezed tighter. Then he pulled the weapon free and threw it to the side. He seized the message from the courier's pocket.

Briefly there was blackness. He blinked it away. When his vision returned, the messenger had descended down into the Yankee trenches and was receiving pats on the back. His temple stung where the lieutenant had punched him. He looked to his hand. It still held the message. However, whatever information General de Bellomonte wanted to get to the other side was safe. They had the messenger, and the paper was a mere formality.

The Yankees continued to take potshots at him. He was forced to crawl on his hands and knees back to the defenses that ringed Atlanta. He collapsed into the trench covered in filth from head to toe and eventually returned to his quarters.

After cleaning up, he unrolled the message. He opened his diary and inked his pen. He was privy to Ambrose's cipher of choice and proceeded to unscramble the message. It offered to provide intelligence as well as assistance with the post-war effort in exchange for his property being left intact. The line that made Noah's blood boil: *The Southern cause is as good as lost.*

Ambrose was a traitor and a spy. He had joined the Southern cause to protect his plantation and further his family's reputation. Now that it appeared to be the losing side, he had changed his calculus. Noah had to report his newfound information to General Hood at once. He weaved through the narrow streets toward General Hood's headquarters. He was stopped by a soldier guarding the entrance.

—I need to speak to General Hood.

—Sir, no one sees the general unless called upon.

—It's of the utmost importance.

—No one sees the general.

—Let me in now. That's an order.

—No.

—There is treason within our ranks.

Noah held up the small paper and waved it before the guard. The guard seized it, then crumpled it up and tossed it into a muddy pool of water. Noah fell on his hands and knees and raked his fingers through the puddle. Every time he thought he felt it, he pulled up refuse or mud. After some time, he found it and unfolded it with the utmost care. The text's ink was largely washed away, the message garbled.

—What's the meaning of this?

Noah turned, his uniform covered in mud once more. He stood erect. It was General Hood.

—Sir, I have discovered treason in the ranks.

—Then shoot them, Major. Dismissed.

—Sir, it's one of your generals.

General Hood stroked his wiry beard for a moment before gesturing for Noah to step inside his quarters. He took a seat behind a desk and adjusted the straps on his wooden leg. Noah told him about the message and the effort he had made to secure it. Hood listened intently. His face gave no indication of surprise or interest. Noah continued to explain until the general put his hand up and stopped him.

—I am well aware of the feud between the Beaumonts and the de Bellomontes. But I did not expect that you'd sink to these depths to attack a fellow brother in arms.

—Sir, I have proof.

Noah placed the soggy paper upon General Hood's desk. He looked at it and raised an eyebrow.

—And it just so happens that it was destroyed?

—Sir, your guard took it from me and threw it in the mud.

—de Bellomonte told me you might pull a stunt like this, and quite frankly, given the history between you two, I'm not surprised. The only reason I'm not going to have you shot today is because I've had to deal with de Bellomonte's constant attempts to have you demoted or imprisoned. As far as I'm concerned, you two deserve each other.

—Sir, please.

—Dismissed.

Noah returned to his quarters. The personal items of his chest that weren't missing were scattered on the floor. The pages of his diary had been ripped apart and the pockets of his uniforms turned inside out. His mattress was cut open and the two soldiers who were digging through it stood up and looked at him. They unshouldered their rifles. Noah noticed that their bayonets were attached. He turned and found himself face-to-face with Ambrose de Bellomonte.

—I'll be watching you, Beaumont.

Chapter 21

EMMA

1864, Georgia

Emma buried a jug of milk in the cool earth. When the Confederate soldiers werent watching, she dug holes and put anything that wouldnt spoil within a few days inside. The soldiers were taking more and more food with each passing week.

Some of the ragged Rebel soldiers looked worse than their bony draft animals. The Edel family had quietly ordered the girls to hide away as much food as they could. At first, Mr. Edel was able to avoid the worst excesses of the Confederate army's needs with a bribe here and there. Now the bribes no longer worked. Confederate money was worth less than food. The best currency the Edel family had was whiskey, and they were in short supply of that. The Edels didnt have a single horse left. All of them had been taken into military service. The family was allowed to keep a few old mules and that was all.

One of the mules had gotten a slight limp. Emma lifted its hoof and found a nail wedged inside its foot. She pried it out and cleaned all four hooves. After that, she made sure the feed troughs were full and fresh straw had been laid. Emma returned to the farmhouse and was summarily whacked on the back of her neck with Nora's switch. She didnt flinch.

—What took you so long?

—One of the mules had a nail in its hoof.

She was whacked again. Before Nora could go on a diatribe, Emma caught another girl in her sights. The girl was being caned by Mr. Edel himself. The Edels rarely disciplined the girls directly, but the mere mention of the name Sherman resulted in harsh punishment.

A few of the dairy cows had even had to be slaughtered for food, and the ones that remained couldnt produce much milk. She noticed that the drummer boy had watched from a distance as her neck was tenderized by Nora's switch.

The boy sat next to her and watched her spread straw where the animal would bed down. Emma peered over her shoulder as she tried yet again to milk the cow. She gave the boy a sip of the milk and then took a sip for herself. It was rich and warm. She finished pouring the milk into milk cans and went to the hen house to collect eggs. The boy followed her.

—Dont you have a job to do? asked Emma.

—I'm supposed to watch you and make sure you're not hiding food from us.

—And how am I doin?

—Good, I think.

Inside the hen house was a clump of bloody feathers, once a chicken. Probably a weasel or a fox had gotten to it. She collected the eggs in a basket and slipped one into the boy's hand. His eyes darted from side to side as he slid the egg into his pocket.

—Your parents must miss you.

—My parents are in heaven. At least that's what my uncle told me before sendin me away.

—Then who takes care of you?

—The army.

A week came and went. It was odd. Emma hadnt seen the boy in quite some time. As she fed the chickens, Emma heard shouting. She crept toward the edge of the farmhouse and peered over the edge. Mr. Edel and the sergeant camped on his property were arguing. Mr. Edel tried to tell the sergeant that he didnt even have enough food to feed himself. The soldier reminded him that Mr. Edel had to comply with the law. Their voices rose and their necks turned bright red with anger like two roosters trying to out-crow one another. The soldier gripped the handle of his pistol. Emma shook her head. Pride would be the death of both of them. She ran between the men.

—Get in the house, Emma, said Mr. Edel.

Emma curtsied to the sergeant. It was an act of flamboyance she had learned from the Beaumonts.

—If it pleases you, Sergeant, where is the boy?

The red faded from the sergeant's neck and he released his grip from his pistol. He puffed out his chest and straightened his tunic.

—He's ill.

Her stomach tightened up in a knot. Before she could rationalize a reason as to why it was none of her concern, she spoke.

—If it pleases the sergeant, I would like to care for the boy.

The sergeant pointed to Mr. Edel and wagged his finger.

—That negress has got more sense than you do. Come with me.

The sergeant waved his hand. Emma followed him to their camp on the edge of the farm. She could see rice fields and swamps in the distance where the rolling pasture ended. The camp was a collection of dirty white tents filled with bearded men in tattered clothes.

She was led to the boy. His face was a deathly white pallor. His eyes were closed and his breath weak. He slept on a wool blanket placed on the mushy ground. The ends of the tent were open, allowing the cool winter breeze to pass over him. It seemed to her that none of the men had an ounce of common sense between them with regard to taking care of a sick child. Emma knelt down and felt the boy's forehead. He was burning up.

—I need to get em to the house. Now.

Her sharp tone seemed to surprise the sergeant. He crossed his arms and his untrusting eyes moved up and down her body, but he nodded to his men. They loaded the boy into the back of a wagon.

The wagon stopped in front of the Edels' house. Mr. Edel opened the door and seemed none too pleased that an army wagon was parked outside his front door. Mrs. Edel, their children, and Nora soon joined him to see what the commotion was. They all stood there on the front porch, appearing uneasy. Nora shook her head. Emma lifted the boy and carried him to the foot of the farmhouse steps. Nora blocked her path as Mr. and Mrs. Edel looked on.

—We dont have spare beds, said Nora.

—Then he can have mine. I'll sleep in the stables, said Emma.

The faces of the two soldiers accompanying the boy registered surprise. Mr. Edel placed his hand on Nora's shoulder. She scowled and then stood aside as he opened the door.

Chapter 22

ISAIAH

1864, Georgia

Atlanta was surrounded. The night sky lit up with hellfire as Isaiah's artillery crew opened fire. Cannonballs flew high into the purple sky before descending upon the city below.

Load.

Fire.

Load.

Fire.

It was night and they didnt need to aim well, they only needed to instill dread in the hostile population below. Between the bursts of cannon fire, his sergeant yelled out.

—Let's make some widows and orphans, boys. Widows and orphans.

He remembered each lash he had ever taken as he fed the beast with machine-like efficiency. They had been shelling the city with screaming iron for more than a month. From his vantage point he could not see where the cannonballs were landing. He only heard faint crashing sounds between the thunder of the cannons and felt the trembling earth.

His back throbbed and the tendons in his wrists were on fire after carrying the iron balls hour after hour, day after day. Then he felt the opiate of schadenfreude. The thought occurred to him that he was the one firing rather than the one being fired upon. He had once been relegated to powerlessness. Now it was he with the power, and now it was he who whipped men into submission. He doubled his efforts and loaded the balls even faster.

Load.
Fire.
Load.
Fire.

It was a cold night. He was wet from rain and shivered in his makeshift shelter. Everyone hated their leaky tents and had resorted to crafting their own structures whenever an opportunity presented itself. Usually these were made of mud and logs, though the wind always cut through the feeble attempts. His stomach groaned for food. It seemed he was given just enough food to stay alive yet not enough to have a full stomach. He was miserable until he thought of Emma. He reminded himself that the Federal army was her deliverance.

Isaiah felt a shockwave pulse through his body. He sat up to the sound of a terrible thunder. The dark, moonless night lit up with vermillion radiance. He crawled out of his tent and stood. Flames rose high above Atlanta. The first explosion was followed by another and another. The Federal cannons werent firing. The destruction was coming from within. It could only mean one thing—the Confederates were retreating.

After the smoke finally dissipated and the last of the skirmishes died out, Isaiah stepped foot inside Atlanta. It was devastation incarnate. It looked how Carthage must have after the Romans were through with it. Anything of military value had been destroyed. Several smokestacks still stood, but the buildings attached to them were gone. The landscape was covered in shattered bricks and debris. Unmoving arms and legs protruded from the rubble. The air smelled of sulfur and rotten meat. Bloated horses with stiff legs dotted the rubble-strewn streets. Masterless dogs wandered about. One of them, a brown dog with protruding ribs, followed him, begging for a morsel. He saw some fabric below his feet. It was a little green dress. A white porcelain doll. He picked it up. When he turned it over he realized his mistake. His hand shuddered and he instinctively let go. The dead infant fell to the ground. Then the brown dog sniffed at it. Isaiah kicked at the animal.

—Get, dog. Get.

The dog seized the infant in its jaws and ran off. He tried to chase it, but it was too fast.

The sight horrified him, yet he didnt consider himself responsible. After all, he didnt know how many of these people his artillery piece had killed, and he pushed the thought aside. In any case, he was just a simple loader, nothing more than a cog in the machine.

He was tempted to look inside the houses, despite their roofs being caved in, for something of value. He couldnt bring himself to do it after he saw the terrible creatures covered in gray dust wandering and moaning like the risen undead. They were the citizens of Atlanta who, by some terrible miracle, lived. The gaunt creatures held out their hands to any passing soldier. Pleading for food, water, medicine…anything the army could give them. Isaiah sneered and gave them nothing. He teased a few of them with morsels of food before snatching them away at the last minute.

Sherman ordered the city evacuated of all civilians, at bayonet point if need be. The general did not want to tie down his troops by making a great effort to hold the city. Instead, the plan was to ravage it and move southward and ravage the next one. Word around camp had it that the citizens had appealed for the general to let them stay and he'd replied that they *might as well appeal against a thunderstorm*. As far as Isaiah was concerned, they had reaped what they sowed, for the price of deliverance was paid in rivers of blood. He watched as a long line of the inhabitants were led out of the city to the muddy fields beyond.

As he returned to his camp he caught a terrible whiff of rot, then heard the buzzing of a great swarm of flies. He continued walking but the smell was so overwhelming he began to cough. He stumbled through the maze of rubble and came upon a massive pile.

Isaiah gasped. He had thought he had seen it all. Now thousands upon thousands of dead mules filled his entire field of vision. They were lumped atop each other in a macabre mound. The ones on the perimeter must have tried to run away in vain. He would later learn that the fleeing Confederate army had shot them all to prevent them from falling into the hands of the Federals. The ground was sticky with blood. A great flock of crows and carrion birds pecked at the mound of dead beasts. His pace quickened as he tried to leave the awful spectacle as soon as possible. Isaiah looked back and noticed a trail of red footprints behind him.

Sherman marched to the sea. The rumor was that they'd either take Savannah or annihilate it before the end of the year. Isaiah worried that Edel Farm would receive no quarter and be destroyed like Atlanta.

After a long rest, Sherman's army was on the march again. The general had informed the entirety of his forces by means of the chain of command that *war is cruelty, and you cannot refine it*. Then they were given orders to forage anything of military value and ravage the rest in a manner that each unit commander saw fit. Total war. The prospect of more vengeance excited Isaiah. His fellow soldiers sang as they marched south. It was another of Isaiah's favorites:

They will hang Jeff Davis from a tree.
They will hang Jeff Davis from a tree.
They will hang Jeff Davis from a tree.
Glory, glory hallelujah.

Isaiah found himself in the position of sinner and deliverer. Though he considered that God was imaginary, and whether he was a sinner or not mattered little. As Isaiah marched, one day he came across a farmer, his wife, and his two children. They cried and pleaded for him to stop. He smiled at them and stopped. He listened to their pleas for several minutes and patted the farmer on the back. Then he lit their cotton field alight. A great blaze spread out for hundreds of acres and filled the air with thick black smoke.

The Federal wagon train grew even more immense as tens of thousands of freedmen and women, not knowing where else to go, followed along in the rear. Together they were a great moving city. To the Southerners, they must have been like locusts devouring everything in their wake. For the most part he felt numb to the suffering around him. It was only the tear-filled eyes of the freed that stirred him.

Isaiah's socks were bloody and his feet raw. They marched hard, sometimes as many as ten or twelve miles a day. His back hurt and he felt more like a mule than a soldier. Each man had to carry five days of rations on his back. Yet he knew with each step, he was closer to Savannah, closer to Emma.

They tore up great stretches of railroad tracks, sawed down telegraph poles, and torched farmhouses. As far as Isaiah was concerned, it was a just war and the South had given them every right to conduct it in a way that ensured the locals who had supported the war would suffer its consequences. War was easy when far away. Hard when up close.

It was a fresh new morning when Isaiah had been assigned prisoner duty. He had requested this peculiar duty and was initially turned down. However, his persistence and annoyance of his captain paid off. He was to march the dozen or so barefoot Rebel soldiers to the next liaison point where they would be picked up by another unit. After the first five miles of marching, they stopped for a break. Isaiah pointed his bayonet at the group of prisoners. The poor bastards' faces were painted with fear as they tiptoed along the road. The Rebels had buried eight-inch shells with friction matches along the roadways as they retreated. A few Federal soldiers were killed, and Sherman retaliated by ordering Rebel prisoners to act as a picket line. If there was a shell buried somewhere, they'd set it off first. Isaiah took the means of retribution one step further.

—You all like slaves so much, so sing us some slave songs, he said.

The prisoners looked at him with fear and incredulity. He jabbed his bayonet in the air and screamed the order again.

—I said sing us some slave songs.

—Sir, we dont know any. Slaves are for rich people. We aint rich and we wouldnt treat you like this if you were in our position. It's without honor, said one prisoner.

—Well, you're slaves now.

Isaiah had heard of the walking corpses from Andersonville prison. Federal prisoners of war that were mere skin and bones. The whole army knew about it. Maybe they were telling the truth about not knowing any such songs, but he didnt care. Even if they didnt have slaves, they supported the man-stealers.

—We aint slaves, we're prisoners of war.

—Well, the strong do what they will, the weak suffer what they must. Now suffer.

One of the prisoners gave a look of dread and panic.

—Sir, please.

—I said sing, damnit, or I'll splatter your brains all over this here road.

He helped the prisoners along with a mangled rendition of O'er the Crossing, a song Isaiah knew by heart.

Bendin' knees a-aching, body racked with pain
I wish I was a child of God, I'd get home by and by...

The frightened Rebels' voices trembled as they sang while walking barefoot on the dirt road. His fellow Union soldiers laughed at the unique form of sadism he had implemented.

—That's the spirit, Beaumont.

What the Rebel prisoners didnt know was that there werent any more buried shells along the road. There hadnt been for miles. Isaiah had asked his captain if they could continue the charade for a few more miles, and the man had agreed.

Later, Isaiah patted the muzzle of one of the workhorses that pulled their artillery piece along the road. He was back in his artillery battery again. As they marched, he caught a remarkable sight. He saw General Sherman himself atop his mount. The grizzled man looked out at the desolate horizon around him.

As he was helping some soldiers pry up some railroad tracks, Isaiah felt a spatter against his face. He wiped it with his hand. His fingers were red. A corporal beside him collapsed with a hole in his torso. He was still alive, for now.

—Sharpshooter, cried an officer.

The men fell to their stomachs. A few rounds ricocheted around them and then stopped. A cavalry unit ran off toward the sound of the shots. Hours passed. The cavalry returned. They never found the sharpshooter. Isaiah found himself immediately promoted to corporal.

—Beaumont. We're going to destroy every barn and farmhouse within a five-mile radius. Is that understood? said his captain.

—With pleasure, sir.

A few hours later, they came across several Union soldiers from a different unit holding a family at gunpoint. The five children were crying. The mother was crying. The father was crying. Isaiah held his torch next to the modest farmhouse. For reasons unknown to him, he hesitated.

—Beaumont. What are you waiting for? Throw it in, shouted his commander.

He busted a window of the farmhouse with his hand and tossed the torch inside. It didnt take long before the entire structure was consumed by flames. That was the fourth house today he had set alight. The earth around him was black. It smelled of charcoal and death.

Days later, he found himself in a detachment from the main army. His battery of six artillery pieces halted. They camped when they reached Wolf's Head Creek. It was a quiet stream that flowed through what seemed like the middle of nowhere. His crew was ordered to dig in.

Chapter 23

ELMIRA

1864, Georgia

Elmira ran the bristles of her sable brush over coarse linen paper. The multitudes of watercolors bled together to form a deep brown, almost black stem below crimson rose petals. She studied the wilting rose in the vase next to her canvas. Then she mixed a hue as deep and as black as she could make it. She placed the brush down and picked up her finest-tipped brush. She dipped it in the red watercolor and allowed a few drops to drip in the black before rolling the bristles of her brush in the mixture.

After studying her painting for several seconds, she added long, sharp thorns to the stem. Elmira hung the finished painting on her studio wall with the hundreds of others she had painted over the years. All of them flowers from her gardens. The oldest ones were bright blues and yellows and pinks. The newest ones were dark purples and almost black shades of crimson. She sighed.

—I need to get out of the house.

Elmira sat alone in Oglethorpe Square. There werent many people in the city anymore. Several shops were boarded up, their owners having fled. Everyone knew that Sherman's hordes were burning everything in their wake, a trail of destruction that led straight toward beautiful Savannah. Elmira thought about leaving too. She had friends in Philadelphia, she had connections, and she had money. She could easily flee or bribe her way out of the Confederacy and into safety. Yet she stayed.

She looked longingly at the gorgeous city around her. She tried to commit to memory the graceful oak trees, the dignified architecture, the pleasant streets, and the beautiful scale of it all, for it was all about to share the fate of Atlanta. And what about Beaumont Plantation? It was a plot of land and a house. A family was more than a plot of land. A strong family could be an immortal thing. Above all, she knew the family must survive—Noah must survive.

She hadnt seen Pierce since that night at the theater. The war was nearly upon their doorstep and Pierce had to work around the clock to prepare for the upcoming siege. Most of the restaurants were closed and citizens were hoarding as much food as possible.

Elmira walked through the empty squares and along River Street. Only a single fishing boat bobbed atop the gentle waves. She walked past the theater and gazed at the spot where she and Pierce had kissed. Even now she could feel his lips against hers and the way her flesh had radiated. She hadnt felt that way since she'd first married Miles. He had grown bored of her rather quickly and his lust for her had all but disappeared. Still, fate had bound them together.

That afternoon, Elmira climbed aboard a carriage. It passed under the pillar like shadows of oak trunks and stopped at the front doors of Beaumont Hall. A servant wearing white gloves opened her carriage door and bowed. A silhouette stood at her doorway. She clutched her skirt and climbed the stairs. The man turned around. Pierce.

She wanted to embrace him but they weren't alone. Such a thing would be highly improper. A thin smile crept over her face. She tried to hide it, but such happiness was a rare thing.

—Mr. Westbrook. A pleasant surprise.

—Mrs. Beaumont.

—What brings you here?

—I'm afraid I have been ordered to Richmond to ensure their fortifications are in order.

The smile disappeared from Elmira's face. Part of her had known they would have to separate, yet for the longest time she had clung to a naive hope that he might stay. His simple response was all she needed to realize that Savannah's fate was sealed. The Confederate army was diverting resources to defend the capital. Her feelings were no doubt painted across her face. She only managed to utter a monosyllabic response.

—I see.

—I came to say goodbye.

Elmira was speechless for a very long time. She rubbed her hands together until she managed to mutter a response.

—Would you please come in? For tea perhaps?

Pierce gazed upward, his mouth agape, at the stained-glass ceiling of the foyer, the ornate wooden banisters, and the thick marble columns around him. He appeared breathless.

—My God. You live here?

—Come.

They entered her studio. She placed Pierce's flowers in a glass vase atop a small table. The wood-paneled room had several easels, marble busts, a drafting table, and a Tyrian purple fainting couch next to the window. Her watercolor paintings covered every surface. Elmira sat on her couch while Pierce slowly walked the room and studied them. It delighted her to see someone give her work so much attention. Her studio was where she translated her most intimate feelings into art. It was also where she read and stored all of Noah's letters. She rarely let anyone inside, not even servants.

—Why dont I see any of these paintings in the house?

—Miles doesnt care for them.

He took one of her paintings off the wall. It was a crimson rose with pointed petals—not the brightest painting in the room nor the darkest. She remembered how it had taken her months to perfect the color.

—This one. This is the one that reminds me of you the most: fierce and beautiful.

Elmira felt her face flush. Pierce turned to hang it back on the wall. She quickly rose from her seat. Taking the painting, she pushed it back into his hands.

—Take it with you, please.

—I will hang it in a heartfelt place within my home.

Such kindness was too much. Elmira's cheeks became wet. She caught herself whimpering. Pierce put the painting aside and embraced her. Elmira fell limp into his arms. She looked up at him and pressed her lips against his. Her bun unraveled and her long black hair fell upon her shoulders. They kissed with unrestrained passion. It was not long before the top of her dress was down around her waist and only her black pearl necklace graced her porcelain torso. Her eyes closed as her head fell backward.

The daylight was dying. Elmira and Peirce's bodies glistened with hours of passion atop the narrow confines of her fainting couch.

They talked. They talked about everything, but mostly family. He had talked to her more in the last twenty minutes than her husband had in twenty years.

—Do you love him? Miles?

Elmira's eyes shifted away from his. She gazed across the room at a large white rose she had painted years ago. The petals were delicate while the stem was dark green with dull thorns. It was her most tender painting.

—Yes.

—Why, if he treats you with such coldness?

—For Noah, for the family, until death do us part. It is my burden, my duty to the bloodline. I vowed to carry on the family legacy to his mother before she died. A vow I will stand by till the grave. She gave me the roses you see outside, after all. They're a special hybrid that has been handed down for generations. I tend to them like I tend to my family. Miles is a weaker, more spoiled man than his late father, so the reality is that the family now lives and dies through Noah's efforts. That is why I must do everything to protect my son and prepare him for the road that lies ahead.

—Elmira, you are so much more than meets the eye.

—What about you? You must miss your wife.

—I do. It was hard after the fever took her, but I've managed.

They talked a while longer, but the day was growing late. Peirce gazed at her as she finished tying up her hair and remarked how lovely she looked. They stood quietly together for quite some time before Elmira spoke.

—It is goodbye then.

—For now.

She leaned her head against Pierce's chest. She wanted to hear the thumping of his heart one last time.

Chapter 24

NOAH

1864, Georgia

Noah stood at attention. Ambrose de Bellomonte paced his command tent, re-reading his orders and muttering angrily under his breath. Ambrose had been ordered to take command of a cavalry corps—what was left of one, at least—and use it to delay Sherman's advance on Savannah. General Hood had taken the rest of the army and marched for Tennessee in the hopes that it would lure Sherman away. After learning of what had happened to Atlanta, Noah wasnt convinced that either effort would amount to much. But he told himself it wasnt his job to despair over such matters. It was his job to execute his orders. Ambrose balled up the orders and shoved the paper into the hands of a waiting staff officer. He turned to Noah.

—It looks like you get to be a cavalry officer again.

—Yes, sir.

—We are to wipe out a Federal detachment camped along Wolf's Head Creek. And, Beaumont?

—Yes, sir?

—You've been promoted to colonel. Dont fail me.

Noah's horse buckled when he mounted it. The steeds were as worn and ragged as the men who sat atop them. It was still dark and the sun had just begun to peek over the horizon when they rode out. Ambrose led the cavalry along the winding creek. Whether they rode out to seal the fate of the Yankees or their own, Noah did not know. He only knew he wished he'd had a chance to spend time with Ms. Caroline. His mother talked of the girl as if she was sent from heaven. It seemed to her that Caroline could do anything. In her letters she nagged him about the need for grandchildren and pleaded with him to be safe. She sent so many letters that he simply didnt have the time to respond to each one, but he saved every one he got. He wished for a warm bed, a hot meal, and of course, whiskey. He didnt have a God anymore, but at least he had the drink.

He could see trout finning in the clear waters of the creek. Such fish had been on his dinner plate more than once, but now he found himself admiring their freedom to swim where they pleased. A scout motioned for Noah. He rode ahead.

It was still morning when he reached a tree line that looked just like any other. He pulled his reins and his horse wheeled sideways. He held his hand over his brow and squinted. Noah could see the unmistakable green rust of Napoleon cannon barrels poking out from the wood line. There werent any other Confederate troops in the area. Noah rode back to the rest of the waiting cavalry.

He rode up to General de Bellomonte and informed him of the hidden Federal forces. Though he'd been unable to make out exactly how many troops were there, he had only counted six cannon barrels.

—Sir, we ought to scout the area further.

—We're overstretched as it is. We need the element of surprise. We need to attack now. What do you say?

Noah was taken aback. Ambrose had never bothered to ask his opinion on anything. Noah held his chin and thought it through.

—I think you are right, sir. Momentum and surprise is our best option.

—You know, Beaumont, I dare say that you're not half bad.

They watered and rested their horses. The suspense of the battle to come made Noah anxious. He wrung his hands and pulled out his pocket watch every other minute to check the time. He thought about taking a swig of whiskey but decided against it. Instead, he pulled out a small pocket mirror to trim his beard. The beard was streaked with gray and the bags under his eyes were almost purple. He didnt look like that eager young man who joined the army all those years ago. Now he wasnt even sure they were the same person.

Noah put the mirror down and shuffled through his haversack for his shears. He found them and held the mirror back up to his face. He blinked hard and his hand trembled. Instead of his own reflection, he saw a hazed-over eye and a dark, masculine face. He trembled and breathed heavily as James stared back at him. He dropped the mirror.

Noah stood up and crept backward away from the seemingly possessed object. He cradled himself with his own arms and looked from side to side. When he finally snapped out of it, he cautiously approached. He touched it and then pulled his hand back sharply. Noah gave a forced laugh and picked up the mirror. He took a deep breath and then gazed into the cracked pane. A single hazed-over eye gazed back at him.

He threw the mirror into the creek.

Ambrose called Noah forward and Noah rode up to him. The general wasnt wearing his usual flamboyant parade uniform. Instead, he wore something no different than any of the other officers.

—Beaumont, I want you to lead the assault.

—It would be my honor, sir.

What else could he say? Under normal circumstances, such a thing was indeed an honor, but he suspected that Ambrose had only granted him the privilege so that he, Ambrose, could *lead* from a relatively safer vantage point, for grapeshot did terrible things to a human body. Ambrose didnt want to die when the war itself was in its death throes.

No matter, duty called. Noah mounted his horse and unsheathed his saber. The blade wasnt pretty. It was notched and dented in several places along its length. Despite constant care, it still had creeping rust around the hilt and the leather handle was worn. The golden tassels that once hung there were long gone. Still, it was a tough old blade. He raised it high. Ambrose nodded and Noah shouted the order.

—Charge.

An all-too-familiar bugle call sounded. Noah dug his spurs into the flanks of his horse. They galloped into the tree line to flank the artillery.

The Yankees were caught unawares. He cut down the Federal soldiers before him, leaving a bloody trail of the dead and the dying clutching gaping wounds and moaning.

The Federal cannons turned toward Noah's cavalry. He was surprised by how fast the crews were able to heave the heavy weapons into place—then again, their lives depended on it. He noticed the unmistakable shape of a grapeshot canister being loaded into the cannon in front of him. He switched to his revolver. He could go neither left nor right in time, only forward. He dug his spurs in.

Noah shot one of the crew members before the round could be fired. The others fled. The loader ran behind the cannon and fired it. Right as Noah passed the threshold of the cannon, the grapeshot fired. He didnt dare look at his fellow men riding behind him. Noah could only exact vengeance upon the man who fired the cannon.

The Yankee raised his hands. Noah aimed his pistol at the man's head. He no longer believed in mercy. Yet when he caught a glimpse of the bastard's eyes, blue as lapis, his arm lowered. Noah recognized him. He did not believe in fate until that very moment. He might as well have been looking into the face of God.

He had seen men disappear into pink mist and fresh-faced boys get those fresh faces blown off. There was a cruel randomness to it all. It didnt matter how often a fellow prayed or how much he loved his family or how charitable he was. Some of the fresh recruits thought that if they could shoot sharp enough or grew strong enough, they could escape the merciless hammer of randomness. No. In one moment you were there and the next you werent. If it was your time, it was your time. Simple. Noah finally thought he had figured it all out. The Yankee called out to him.

—Noah?

—Isaiah.

Some men would have gloated about kill counts, for the higher the number the greater the honor. Noah had seen and personally slaughtered so many that he detested the act of killing, the sight of it, and the champions of it who had never personally bloodied their own hands. He looked to Isaiah and saw a sprig of life in the death around him. Noah climbed off his horse and held out the reins to Isaiah.

He took the reins. Hooves clattered behind Noah. Soon the Confederate cavalry would be upon them. He pointed.

—Run. That way.

—Come with me.

—Go on now.

Isaiah mounted Noah's horse and rode off. The Rebel cavalry galloping up behind Noah took potshots at Isaiah as he rode off. He was too far gone. A few of the cavalry soldiers had seen the whole thing. Noah had no regrets. Death had always hung over him.

The thin rope cut into his wrists. Noah had gotten word that all but one of the Federal troops that day had been annihilated. No quarter. No prisoners. It didnt stop Sherman though. Word had it that the general inched ever closer to Savannah. Noah knew the city was sure to fall. He only hoped his parents were safe.

The guards flanking him saluted. Ambrose de Bellomonte stood before him. He explained the situation to the general several times and Ambrose listened intently. Noah knew it wasnt because the man cared about getting the correct account of events. It was because he wanted to ensure the legality of the action he was about to take.

—Why again did you resort to treason?

—I didnt. He surrendered and was a lawful prisoner of war.

—Why, then, did you get off your horse?

—To take him prisoner.

—I was told you handed him the reins and pointed.

—I dont know what you were told, sir. I only know my reputation speaks for itself.

—Reputation? Oh, I'll see to it that your name is scrubbed from that roll of honor. In the past you've accused me of treason, yet it is you who aided and abetted the enemy, aint that right?

—No. I led the charge that seized Wolf's Head Creek.

—Wrong. I led the charge while you tried to run off with the Yankees.

—I only have the truth to give and nothin further.

Ambrose offered a mocking chortle.

—You've earned your sentence, Beaumont.

Noah stood in front of an oak tree not much different than the ones back home on the plantation. Moss hung delicately from the ancient, gnarled branches. His gray tunic had been stripped of all its accouterments. A few soldiers ruffled through his pockets. One of them took Noah's watch and slid it into his own pocket and another took his boots. He was also relieved of his cash and his flask of whiskey. He caught a glimpse of his saber, given to him by his grandfather, dangling from the hip of a young lieutenant.

Ambrose stood behind a row of twelve soldiers as they ramrodded lead down the barrels of their rifles. Noah's request to go without a blindfold was granted.

—Last words? asked Ambrose.

—For all have sinned and fall short of the glory of God. Glory to the South, said Noah.

The soldiers lifted their rifles. The holes in the barrels were black as night. The world around him fell into silence. He stood as erect as his war-beaten body would allow.

—Ready. Aim. Fire.

Chapter 25

EMMA

1864, Georgia

Emma was back to sleeping in the stables. But there were no horses. They had all died of glanders disease. Even the horses in the Rebel camp had succumbed to it. She had given the boy her bed and there simply wasnt any room for her. She was permitted to care for the boy so long as she did her chores first. She washed him and made a light soup for him every day. She didnt entirely understand why she was helping him other than some sort of deep maternal instinct. His fever had gone down and it seemed the worst had passed, but the boy was still bedridden.

Christmas was coming. Emma was working in the kitchen as the Edels were decorating. She overheard them talking about the desolation left in Sherman's wake and debated whether they should flee or not. Mr. Edel steadfastly refused. After she left the kitchen, she noticed a small toy with a bow on it.

There was a knocking on the front door of the farmhouse. Emma opened it and the Confederate sergeant stood before her.

—The boy needs to report to duty, said the sergeant.

—Sir, he can barely walk, she protested.

—We need to leave now. The Yankees are coming.

—He's still very ill. Please, let him stay.

—Get the boy now or I'll come in and get him.

Emma helped the boy dress in his ragged uniform, which the sergeant insisted that he wear. The boy's legs wobbled and he gasped for breath as she carried him down the stairs. Mr. Edel gave him his gift, a bright red top.

One of the soldiers slung the boy over his shoulder. The soldiers didnt bother to take down their camp or even bring along the goods piled up around it. They ran about, stuffing whatever they could fit into their pockets, while the sergeant barked for them to hurry up. Meanwhile he handed a long rifle to another soldier.

—Load the Whitworths. We're going to kill as many of the bastards as we can. No surrender.

Emma thought him mad. She ran up to him and made one last plea to let the boy stay. The sergeant shook his head. He said the boy was a son of the Confederacy and would live and die as a son of the Confederacy. Emma stood in front of the sergeant and again pressed him.

—I wont leave a man behind.

The sergeant pushed her aside.

After the rifle was loaded, the soldier handed it back to the sergeant. Then he began loading his own rifle along with the rest of the men of the camp. Once they were finished, they ran out into the fields.

The boy was gone.

Drums thundered in the distance. A great cloud of dust rose from the dirt road to the farm and came ever nearer. Faces of men emerged from the roll of dust. Men in matching blue uniforms immediately formed a perimeter around the farm. The Federals had come.

Emma found herself torn between elation and dread. It seemed Providence had deigned to free her on the one hand, yet she feared for the boy's well-being. Then there was the fear of the unknown. She watched from the relative safety of a barn. A few of the Federal soldiers looked in her direction but they seemed to have no interest in her.

There was a hard knock on the farmhouse door. Mr. Edel opened the door. Mrs. Edel and their children were huddled up around them. Emma couldnt make out what they were saying, but everyone in the house was soon corralled outside.

Several rounds popped off. The chickens scattered. More gunfire. The soldiers shot the dairy cows. They continued firing their weapons until all the livestock on the farm were dead. Every cow, every chicken, every pig. Nothing was left alive. To Emma's surprise, they didnt load up the poor beasts, simply left their carcasses there to rot.

Mrs. Edel fell to her knees and pleaded with the officer not to ransack their home or worse. The commander had a familiar expression upon his face, one that Emma knew all too well. It was the face of one who had seen too much suffering.

They were gathered around the officer. Emma crept forward from the barn and joined the group so that she could hear what was being said. The officer pulled a yellowed document with frayed edges from his pocket.

—The South has been liberated. The slaves are hereby granted freedom.

Emma's hands fell upon her heart. Her eyes welled up. She felt the embrace of her companions. Was it a dream? Her moment of elation was interrupted by Mr. Edel's pleas for mercy.

—You cant destroy our livelihood, said Mr. Edel.

The officer took a swig from a rusty flask and gave an incredulous laugh.

—I've lost three out of every four soldiers under my command because of the war you supported. To hell with your livelihood.

The officer gave a signal to his troops. The soldiers lit torches. They shattered the windows of the farmhouse and threw the torches inside. Emma and the other freed women stood nearby while Federal soldiers held Mr. and Mrs. Edel back as they cried out from the relative safety of the pasture. Anything on the farm that was cable of burning was set alight. It didnt take long before the entire property was consumed with flames. Thick black smoke billowed toward the heavens.

A shot echoed from the nearby grove. A soldier was hit in the leg. Another shot followed. Now she saw an officer clutching his bleeding neck. He fell to his knees and gave a gurgled cry for help.

Everyone crouched down. Several of the soldiers began shouting orders. As she lay on her stomach, she saw the fallen Federal soldier before her. She wanted to close her eyes, to turn away, but she couldnt take her eyes off the blood slowly pooling around the man. His lusterless eyes remained open and he gazed upward toward the sky. The officer motioned for his cavalry to head toward the surrounding swampland. They thundered toward it with pistols drawn.

As stretcher bearers carried away the fallen, Emma saw several familiar faces. The five Confederate soldiers had their hands bound and were being pulled behind the Federal horses. The boy was slumped over the back of one of the horses.

The five Rebels were lined up in a row with the burning farmhouse not far behind them. The boy was dumped beside them. The air grew colder.

—We're prisoners of war. Where's the judge advocate? demanded the Rebel sergeant.

—You just shot the judge advocate, replied the Federal officer.

—You cant just shoot us like this.

—When you get to the other side, you can take it up with the judge advocate. There's actually only one of you we need to deal with right here and now. Which of you fashions yourself to be a sharpshooter?

The Rebels remained tightlipped. Even in their precarious situation, they refused to sell one another out. The Federal officer paced back and forth.

—One of you needs to man up or I'll have to shoot you all.

The men said nothing. The officer threw up his hands and sighed.

—You killed one of my boys, and one more will probably die from the amputation. Nothing?

Still, the Rebels did not speak.

—Have it your way.

The small band of soldiers were lined up against the collapsed hulk of the burning farmhouse. The boy was among them.

—What about the boy, sir? asked a Federal soldier.

—Hell, he's already about dead. Might as well put him out of his misery. It's the kindest thing we can do.

A group of Federals lined up and began loading their rifles. The men gave no last words. The boy coughed as he clutched the painted top the Edels had given him. The officer raised his sword high in the air.

Emma stood at the edge of the formation. She looked to the boy and then looked at the rifles. The boy looked around, confused as to what was happening. Emma shook her head as her eyes welled up. She knew what she was supposed to do. No one needed to tell her. Still, she shook her head and muttered to herself:

—Why does it have to be me, Lord? Why me? She knew the answer.

The Federal soldiers had finished tamping down their rounds. The officer paced in front of his men, looking each one dead in the eyes, then stopped when he reached the end of the line and raised his saber.

—Ready.

The soldiers pointed the rifles at the five Rebel prisoners and the boy, who struggled to stand. Emma's heart pounded and she breathed heavily. She told herself not to be a fool. The officer yelled his next command.

—Aim.

Emma ran forward. She embraced the boy and shielded him with her body.

—He's a child, she cried out.

The Rebel sergeant standing next to the boy looked at her with a combination of incredulity and reverence. He started to speak several times but was unable to talk until finally a singular word slipped from his mouth.

—Why?

Before she could even attempt to answer his question, two soldiers seized her arms and pried her off the boy. He reached out to her. As she was dragged away, the Rebel sergeant spoke to her with wide unbelieving eyes.

—Young lady, you walk with God.

The man looked to the ground. She could tell his mind was working a mile a minute. In the short time she had known him, he had never exhibited a single emotion other than anger. Until the tears began to stream down his face, she hadnt thought he was capable of anything besides rage. The sergeant cleared his throat.

—I alone fired the shot, he said. These men are innocent.

—Finally, some integrity, said the Federal officer.

He motioned to his soldiers. The boy and the other Rebel soldiers were pulled out of the lineup. The sergeant stood alone. As soon as Emma was let go, she ran to the boy and held him.

—Fire.

Emma covered the boy's eyes as she cradled his head. Smoke burst out of the barrels of the rifles. The Rebel sergeant slumped to the earth.

The Federal soldiers ended up having to stay the night. They told her that Fort McAllister had been taken and that Savannah was surrounded. Despite the danger, the only place she could think of to go was Beaumont Plantation. After all, Isaiah might still be there.

While the other Rebels were taken prisoner, they let Emma look after the boy. Emma wrapped the boy in a blanket and had him sit next to one of the campfires. She had unfinished business to attend to.

Emma scoured the farm. She couldnt find Nora. Just as she was about to give up, she caught the outhouse atop a hill in the corner of her eye. She climbed the hill and pulled open the door to find Nora sitting there upon her throne.

—Bitch, close the door, said Nora.

Emma thrust her foot into the woman's chest. Nora fell over backward and her weight knocked over the flimsy outhouse. Her thick legs tumbled skyward. Nora's dress draped over her face while her bare ass bounced down the hillside.

Nora came to a stop at the bottom of the hill and tried to push her dress back down. The freed women watched with their hands over their mouths and bulging eyes. The Federal soldiers watched with amused indifference. Emma dusted off her palms.

She noticed a large herd of confiscated pack animals that followed the soldiers. Half-joking, she asked for a mule from the Federal troops, but to her surprise she was given one. She had witnessed very little of the war but she had seen enough that she prayed Savannah be spared the fate of Atlanta.

The following morning, she put the boy on top of the mule and walked toward Beaumont Plantation.

Chapter 26

ISAIAH

1864 to 1865, Georgia

The smoke cleared. Isaiah watched from a distance as Noah collapsed. A man who could only be Ambrose de Bellomonte walked up to the corpse. He removed his revolver and fired a bullet into Noah's head. Isaiah held his hands tight over his mouth and turned away.

His old battery was all but wiped out. On the one hand, he had his life. On the other hand, his superiors had questions regarding how he'd managed to get out alive while acquiring a branded Rebel horse. A few accused him of being a coward or a deserter based on the heresy spouted by his accuser. He was ushered up the chain of command until he came face to face with a colonel.

How he made it up so high, he wasnt sure. He figured his story was too far-fetched to be believed, yet too intriguing not to share with the other officers. The colonel was a stern man with a severe countenance and intelligent eyes. He seemed far more interested in the makeup of the Rebel forces and their means of attack than Isaiah's unlikely escape. The man asked the same questions over and over, squeezing him like a lemon until the most minute detail was revealed. When they returned to Isaiah's story, he explained once again to the colonel that his brother fought on the other side and had given him the horse and was subsequently executed because of it. The colonel nodded and didnt give any indication of whether he believed Isaiah one way or the other.

—Your name is Beaumont? asked the colonel.

—Yes, sir.

—As in the Beaumonts and the de Bellomontes? Congressman Beaumont? Those Beaumonts?

Isaiah hesitated. He knew if he got caught in a big lie he'd be in a world of trouble, yet if he told the colonel of his heritage he worried where he might end up. Now that they were in Savannah, there was a risk of his identity being revealed. He needed to get to Emma. He was almost there. She was surely free by now.

—Yes, sir.

—So you're rich?

—No, sir.

The colonel crossed his arms and studied Isaiah quietly. He stood there, sweating, in dead silence for what seemed like an eternity.

—They say you're half-Indian, is that right?

—Yes, sir.

—Didnt know they had Indians on Beaumont Plantation. What kind?

—Sir?

—Awfully curly hair you got for an Indian. And your so-called brother. Is he half-Indian?

—No, sir.

—Interesting. You know, I fought in the Seminole War. I know a few Indians. Anyway, your intelligence has been most useful. I see no evidence of any wrongdoing. Dismissed.

While he was being assigned to a new artillery battery, he was told that several Federal soldiers had captured the capital building in Georgia and held a mock legislature and repealed the state's secession. He wanted to share in their laughter, but his mind was elsewhere.

Within days of resuming their march, the trenches and earthworks that surrounded Savannah came into view. They had destroyed some two hundred miles of rails and burned great swaths of Georgia on their march to the sea. Thousands upon thousands of freed blacks marched behind the army beside a vast array of seized livestock, a nomadic city in and of itself. Isaiah had no idea what they could do with them all.

The only means to reach Savannah was through a series of narrow causeways that crossed swamps, marshes, and flooded rice fields. No doubt Sherman would sooner level the city than expose his men to fire upon those causeways. Isaiah knew all the mills and surrounding farms had been taken.

Isaiah's artillery piece was trained on the beautiful city in the distance. If the inhabitants inside weren't annihilated with cannon fire, then they would be starved to death. He stood ready to turn its pleasant promenades and lovely squares into rubble and ash. One city had already been destroyed with Sherman's fire and brimstone, and Savannah now awaited its inevitable fate. The men around him were ready to create a new ruin and sow the earth with salt.

Ten days and ten nights passed. Everyone in Isaiah's artillery battery was itching to fire their cannons. To his shame, even he was caught up in the excitement. It seemed to him that men's desire for violence was an unquenchable thirst, a bottomless cup, that could never be filled with enough blood. Tomorrow they'd rain hellfire upon the city.

Isaiah watched from his vantage point as a delegation emerged from the city. A man in a suit and a top hat walked across the causeway. He soon learned that General Hardee's Confederate troops had built a pontoon bridge across the Savannah River at night and fled. Savannah's mayor had met with General Sherman himself and surrendered. There would be no fire and brimstone.

Federal troops buzzed in and out of Savannah's shops. All the Rebel flags were put in a great pile in the street and set alight. The residents stood on the sidewalks and looked on with dread.

Isaiah figured the city must have swollen tenfold thanks to the influx of troops and refugees. Sherman settled himself in Mr. Charles Green's coral-colored Gothic Revival mansion. Isaiah had passed the home's manicured gardens a few times during his childhood when he traveled to the city with Elmira and Noah. He was frustrated he hadnt gotten leave yet. He needed to find Emma. For now, he could only content himself to sit outside Sherman's headquarters and wait.

Twenty black citizens had gone inside to meet with Sherman. When they came out, a crowd was waiting for them. They ran toward them and pestered them for details of the meeting. Isaiah learned that Sherman had issued Special Field Order 15. The order confiscated coastland from Charleston to the St. John's River in Florida and redistributed it to freed slaves, forty acres per family. Forty acres and a mule, they called it. Beaumont Plantation was going to be chopped up.

Isaiah's request for leave was finally granted. He needed to get to the Edels' farm. He needed to find Emma. The farm was close. He knew he should conserve his strength, but he ran anyway. Emma would be there waiting for him. When the smell of charred wood and rotten meat filled his nostrils, he stopped. He knew it was just over the hill in front of him. His stomach tightened at the thought of what he might find on the other side.

Isaiah climbed the hill and fell to his knees at the sight of the charred remains of Edel Farm. Dead creatures littered the landscape. As he heaved aside blackened boards in search of any sign of Emma, he felt a sharp smack against his neck.

—What you think you're doing diggin round here?

Isaiah turned around to find a large black woman holding a switch. He took several steps back and nearly tripped into the smoldering rubble behind him. Melted gold jewelry dangled out of her bulging pockets. Behind her was a square of old cloth filled with whatever trinkets the woman had been able to scrounge from the rubble. She whacked Isaiah again with her switch.

—I said get.

Isaiah held up his hands as she pelted him on the head with her stick. He grabbed the stick from her hands and snapped it.

—Where's Emma?

—That bitch?

Isaiah's eyes widened. The large woman stepped back and crossed her arms. A broad smile of yellowed teeth appeared across her face.

—I dont know where she is.

He knew damn well that she knew. It seemed obvious that Emma hadnt been on the best terms with this woman, whoever she was. He could see thousands of footprints and the remains of a Federal camp. She must have waited until they left and come back to scrounge. Isaiah stood straight and returned her smile with one of his own.

—I guess I cant dig up that box I was told about.

—Dig up what box?

Isaiah began to walk away.

—I've said too much. I need to go.

The woman ran around in front of him and blocked his path.

—Where's this box? What's in it?

—That's why I came here. To ask Emma. She knows where it is.

The woman crossed her chubby arms.

—You lie.

—You're right. I'm lying. Stupid to think the Edels would bury a box of their most precious things right before the war came.

Isaiah stepped around the woman and climbed the hill that bordered the farm. He was just about to head down the other side when he heard heavy breathing behind him. The woman was sluggishly climbing after him. She held her chest and panted heavily as she reached the top.

—I'll tell you where she went. But I want half.

Part of him didnt want to push his luck, but his confidence got the better of him.

—No. I'll find Emma myself.

The woman grabbed his sleeve.

—Please. I can help you dig.

—I can help you out, but I can only give you 10 percent.

—Young man, help an old woman out.

—Fine. One fifth.

—Please. I'm a kind old woman. Everybody tells me so.

—Well. I can give you one third, but…

—But?

—I need to make sure you're not trying to trick me. I dont want to be sent in the wrong direction. Toward the Rebel army.

—A trick? No. I promise. Nora always keep her word.

—Then you wouldnt mind lending me some of that loot as a token of your sincerity? Only until I get back, of course.

She studied his face for several seconds. Then she plunged her meaty hand between her breasts and pulled out a half-melted gold coin. She tossed it to Isaiah.

—Beaumont Plantation. She's goin there.

Chapter 27

ELMIRA

1864 to 1865 Georgia

Four dark horses pulled a shiny black lacquered wagon under the agony of the midday sun. Miles stood on his doorstep as the dull creaking sound of wagon wheels against furrowed earth came to a stop. A simple pine coffin lay bare in the back, unadorned with the honors of the flag. A soldier dismounted from the wagon and saluted and spoke to Miles.

She hadnt believed the awful news until that very moment. Elmira ran over and climbed atop the wagon and embraced the coffin as she cried out. Her wails were so loud that everyone hid in their cabins and the dogs in their kennels. Elmira sobbed and screamed and wildly pounded the top of the coffin with her fists.

—I'll find who hurt you and follow them to the gates of hell, she cried.

Her servants approached and gently pried her from the coffin and led her off the wagon and up the stairs of her home. After she climbed the stairs, she tried to embrace Miles. He sidestepped her, wiped his tears away, turned, and went inside. She heard his office door slam.

She stood beside a table in an empty room. The only thing inside was Noah's body atop the table. Her son's flesh was discolored and his body bloated. She figured he must have lain out in the open for some time. When she'd gotten the letter telling of his death, she had paid to have his body immediately placed in a cask of rum and shipped to Beaumont Hall. He'd been moved into a casket shortly before he arrived. Her precious boy's face was still recognizable and there was no pain in his countenance.

Elmira took off his bloodied tunic pierced with bullet holes. After she removed all his rum-soaked clothes, she dipped a rag in a basin full of water and proceeded to wash her son's body with care. Her servants had offered to help but she felt it was a duty too important to allow anyone else to do. After she finished washing her son, she dressed him in his best suit, fixed his hair, and lovingly adjusted his cravat until it was just so. Then, with tears streaming down her cheeks, she kissed Noah's pallid lips.

Elmira's black umbrella shielded her from the pouring rain. She spent her time sitting upon a small wooden stool next to Noah's grave. She'd had him buried in the red earth of Beaumont Plantation next to his grandparents.

Elmira had insisted that his headstone be made of hard granite. Miles had wanted marble, yet marble was soft and easy to weather. She didnt want Noah's name to be erased by the wind and the rain. It was only after she threatened to hurl herself out a window that Miles relented.

She stroked the cold gray headstone. Elmira placed her umbrella to the side and climbed off her little stool. She hugged the headstone and fell into a fit of sobbing.

—Please come back to me. Tell the Lord in heaven that I need you back.

Her wet hair was glued to her shoulders and her soaking black dress clung to her skin. Her fingernails left trails of white residue on the granite as she dug into the headstone.

—I will make everything right, my dearest Noah.

Elmira paced her room. She no longer bothered to curl her hair or even tie it up. She managed to get dressed every day, but she only wore her black mourning dress. She had learned that Noah was shot for treason. He had aided some unknown Yankee spy, or so the story went. Ambrose de Bellomonte had penned her a letter stating that he had nothing to do with her son's execution, that it was an officer below him that carried out the act. She didnt believe a word of it.

The Federals were coming and Miles had fled. She refused to go with him. She would live and die at Beaumont Hall. Now Elmira's only company was the lifeless walls of her mansion. She held her ear up to the silk wallpaper. She could almost hear the laughter of Noah's childhood. Elmira would chase him as he'd run and play throughout the halls. Through Noah's childhood, she had relived her own, and she'd liked it better the second time around. He'd put his little feet atop hers and they'd dance and they'd both laugh. They always had the grandest Easter egg hunts on the plantation grounds. Elmira never told Noah that she had enjoyed them more than he did. She wiped her eyes.

A day came when Noah didnt want to play in the halls, or go on Easter egg hunts, or dance with her. The house had become lonely again when he went off to the academy. Miles was as warm as a winter's day. She had put her hopes in Noah getting married. She could have grandchildren. Beautiful grandchildren. The laughter would return, the dancing and Easter egg hunts. Then Ambrose de Bellomonte stole it from her.

Elmira sat on her porch alone. Her teacup vibrated from the click-clack of hooves. She knew who was coming and she didnt care. As the hoof clops drew closer, she heard shouting. Cavalry troops poured onto her property followed by a caravan of foot soldiers and empty wagons. The Yankees had arrived. Soon, several hundred were on the plantation grounds. Elmira sat calmly as a Federal officer walked up to her. She knew they wouldnt kill her. No. She couldnt die until she had fulfilled her purpose.

—Detain her, said the officer.

—Who are you?

—Forgive my rudeness, ma'am, I am Colonel Evans. We'll be using this fine establishment in service of the Union.

Colonel Evans tilted his head and nodded in the direction of Beaumont Hall. Several soldiers dismounted from their horses and walked inside the mansion. Elmira's heart sank. They would track mud all over her fine carpets. She took one last sip of her tea before she stood. Two Federal soldiers placed her in shackles. They were cold to the touch and cut into the flesh of her small wrists.

—I've brought someone here to keep you company. He should be here any minute.

An army wagon pulled up. A group of tied-up men rode on the back. When the wagon pulled into view, she saw General Willard and a handful of Confederate soldiers sitting upon it. Her husband sat among them. Miles wore sloppily applied rouge, his face was powered white, and a pointed dunce cap sat atop his head.

The colonel redirected his attention toward Miles.

—Nice place, Congressman. May we borrow it?

Miles tried to speak but the gag stuffed in his mouth muffled his voice.

—Why thank you. I do appreciate that.

The soldiers carried out expensive furniture, carpets, sculptures, anything they could get their hands on. They loaded it onto their wagons. They took her fine dining room carpet and placed it in the middle of the grounds. Her mahogany table and chairs were placed atop it with plundered food and barrels of wine in the center.

The slaves gathered around. Some cheered and others burst into song. Colonel Evans unrolled a scroll of parchment. With his cigar still in his mouth, he read from it. The Emancipation Proclamation.

> *...And by virtue of the power, and for the purpose aforesaid, I do order and declare that all persons held as slaves within said designated States, and parts of States, are, and henceforward shall be free, and that the Executive government of the United States, including the military and naval authorities thereof, will recognize and maintain the freedom of said persons...*

Some cheered. Some sobbed. Others were quiet and hesitant. Perhaps a few thought it was a trick. Elmira watched as soldiers loaded up her fine things in wagons. Several army wagons full of her belongings disappeared down the dirt road. The soldiers sat upon her Persian carpet and drank her wine.

—You, black folks, what are you standing around for? Join us. There's lots to eat, said Colonel Evans.

They took a cautious seat, their faces still unsure if what was happening was real, as if they feared the lure of happiness. Elmira's blood boiled.

—You do such terrible things to a lady before Christmas, she said.

—You misunderstand, ma'am. I've already given you a Christmas gift.

—By stealing my family's things and ransacking our home?

—By forbidding my men to burn your house to the ground. Merry Christmas.

Elmira spent the rest of the day locked in one of Beaumont Hall's rooms. She could hear the chatter of Yankee soldiers and the shatter of glass.

Several days later, the door opened. Colonel Evans stood before her.

—You're free to go.

—What about my husband?

—He's coming with us.

Stepping outside, she saw that they had cut General Willard free. The Federals tried to send him on his way, but the rotund general puffed out his chest and demanded to be taken prisoner with his congressman. The Yankee soldiers explained to the general that the camps were full and that they were only keeping high-profile prisoners. That angered the general all the more, much to the amusement of the Federal soldiers, and it was only when they threatened to shoot him that he acquiesced.

General Willard approached her and apologized to Elmira for her son's death. He then complained that he had lost a promotion due to Ambrose de Bellomonte and told Elmira that Ambrose had signed an instrument of surrender to General Sherman surprisingly early. When she asked if Ambrose was responsible for her son's death, he said he didnt know but opined that Ambrose was a snake and he wouldnt put it past him. Elmira asked the general to stay in touch. General Willard said that he still served the South, unlike de Bellomonte, and promised he would make himself available in any way necessary should she need him.

They watched as the wagon that carried Miles disappeared down the road.

The inside of her home was bare, her gardens trampled by horses. Only a few paintings of Miles' family remained, all of them vandalized. What the soldiers hadnt taken, they'd destroyed. Her servants shuffled past her. They didnt make eye contact as they meekly left the plantation grounds.

The Yankee soldiers used her home as their barracks. She was allowed to sleep inside but had to contend with the taunts and catcalls of the soldiers every time she made her way back to her room. Her studio was ransacked, her paintings burned or stepped on.

She watched from her window as the Yankees milled about on her property. Most of the black folks were gone, but a few stayed for reasons unknown to her.

Federal surveyors measured the plantation grounds.

Chapter 28

EMMA

1865 Georgia

The nearest road to Beaumont Plantation cut through an unfamiliar woodland. It was a different route than she'd arrived by, but it seemed like the fastest way back. Emma, the mule, and the boy atop it walked along a stretch of narrow road surrounded by the black waters of the swamp.

The daylight began to fade and the old trees creaked and groaned against the wind. She could have simply spent the night with the large caravan of freed men and women following the Federal army, but she was pulled toward Beaumont Plantation.

As they walked along, Emma heard hissing. She stood still. Her head swiveled but she could not make out where the noise was coming from. As she walked along the narrow path that cut through the swamp, she noticed that the hissing came from her right side. She turned and saw pink flesh. It was only after she blinked a few times that yellow teeth came into view. An alligator sat atop a dead log. It snapped its jaws shut and then opened them again. The mule tried to pull away. She took the reins and pulled the animal forward as quickly as she could.

Her feet were tired and the mule's must have been too, for it grew more ornery with each step. She found a dry patch of land off the trail and began to construct a lean-to out of branches and large leaves. She took the boy off the mule and crawled inside the modest structure she had created. The boy's face had lost all color and his breaths were growing shallower with each passing hour. She closed her eyes.

She awoke to a sharp breeze. It cut through her clothes and caused the hairs on her limbs to rise. She rubbed her arms with her hands and pulled the sick boy close. The breeze grew colder. A single light glowed outside her lean-to. As she sat up, the yellow light grew closer.

Emma stepped outside. She picked up a stick and gripped it tight with both hands. The light continued to move toward her. Through the fog of darkness, she made out a hand wrapped around the thin metal handle of a lantern. White eyes and a face returned her gaze.

Emma held the stick out in front of her, ready to strike whoever or whatever was coming toward her.

—Get back. I dont want any trouble, she said.

—I know you dont, Emma.

The person holding the lantern stepped forward. It was a black woman who looked about sixty years old. She wore an impossibly white dress with an intricate burnt-orange pattern around the wide neckline. It wasnt like any dress Emma had seen before, it was loose and flowing and she wore a matching headwrap. The odd woman spoke. Emma didnt understand a word of what she was saying, a language she had never heard before. Perhaps the woman was one of the Geechee people, but she wasnt sure.

—I dont understand, said Emma.

In an instant, the woman spoke English, clear as day.

—I said, it is cold out. Please come to our home.

In a normal situation, Emma would have declined the woman's offer. However, her current situation wasnt normal. It seemed as if the entire world had turned upside down. Everything was in a state of great upheaval, the boy was near death, and before her stood a woman who had appeared out of nowhere in the middle of a swamp and knew her name.

The woman lived in a one-room cabin that stood on stilts about two feet off the ground. It was sheathed in uneven boards and had a shake roof. The door was painted blue. Inside it glowed a radiant yellow from a wood stove. The warmth felt heavenly.

—Why are you carryin around this white child? asked the odd woman.

—He is sick and has got no parents. They were goin to shoot him.

The woman placed a hand on the boy's forehead and turned his head to one side as she studied his face. Then she turned her back to Emma and began mixing something together with a mortar and pestle.

The walls were decorated with brightly colored paintings and long faces carved of wood. Several candles flickered on a table full of talismans, a crucifix, and other trinkets adjacent to her. In a few moments, the woman held a concoction to the boy's mouth. He drank it and fell back asleep. She served Emma a wooden bowl of shrimp and grits. There was an uncomfortable silence in the cabin once they both finished their meals. Emma decided to try to talk to her.

—How do you know my name?

—I know all kinds of things. Things from the past and things to come.

Emma wasnt sure if the woman was some sort of witch or soothsayer or simply a mad hermit.

—I see. So, do you live alone out here?

—No.

The answer surprised her. It had been a rhetorical question to get a conversation going, for there was only one bed in the cabin and no indication that anyone else lived there. Emma looked around again to make sure she hadnt missed anything.

—With who?

—The rivers, the trees, the earth, they are all living.

Not knowing what else to say, Emma simply nodded. The odd woman still refused to answer how she had come to know Emma's name.

The next morning, Emma was about to put on her headwrap when her strange but hospitable host invited her outside. She put the yellow headwrap atop the mat she had slept on and walked outside. The woman said that she had to communicate with the holy spirit.

There was a small fire there. The woman began to circle it, pounding sticks together and singing in an unknown tongue. Emma gasped as the woman collapsed and began to shake and mumble. Her eyes rolled back up into her head, filling her sockets with white. Emma rushed over to help her. As soon as her hand made contact, the woman sat up. Her eyes rolled back down and she turned toward Emma and pointed her long, crooked finger at her.

—You are part of an endless loop, and it is reborn within you.

Emma stepped back. She'd already been uneasy, and now she was downright frightened. The woman must be mad. Perhaps she had spent too much time alone in the swamp. Her kindness was welcome but her bizarre antics were not. Emma needed to leave.

—I really must get going, she said.

The woman held out her palm and pointed it toward the soggy dirt road.

—Beaumont Plantation is that way.

—But I didnt tell you where I was going.

The odd woman gave a broad smile.

Emma found her mule and put the boy on top. His color had returned and he was beginning to talk once more. She walked down the road while the cabin disappeared in the mist behind her.

She was quite some distance away when she placed her hand on her head and realized that she had forgotten to put on her head wrap. Emma sighed. She turned around and walked back into the mist, toward the cabin.

She walked up and down the road several times, certain she'd reached where the cabin had been. She figured she had simply gotten lost. Then she saw a flash of yellow wafting in the dank breeze. It was her headwrap, hanging from the crooked branch of a dead tree. Her blood ran cold as she cautiously reached out and took it.

Savannah appeared once she crested the hill. Its earthen fortifications were dotted with men in blue. The Federals had taken it. She entered the city and found it bustling with activity. Emma had never seen the city so crowded and busy. Federal troops were everywhere, as were the refugees who trailed the army. Mobile shops operated out of covered wagons as well as mobile brothels with their red lamps flickering away.

As Emma guided the mule through the city streets, she received a few odd looks and probing questions she refused to answer. There were lines pouring out of the churches as people sought whatever charity could be found. She spent the entire day seeking out anyone who could help her. There were so many wretched souls in need of care that the problem seemed insurmountable. Emma became increasingly frustrated, angry even. Her feet were tired from walking what felt like every street in the city. Seemingly out of options, she sat on the curb of a street and began to cry.

She gritted her teeth and wiped away her tears.

The boy wasnt alone. Thousands of children had become orphaned during the course of the war. She eventually found an army chaplain who directed her to a newly established orphanage in Savannah run by nuns. She embraced the boy one last time and then they parted ways. By nightfall she saw a great stone edifice atop a lonely hill—she had reached Beaumont Hall.

Chapter 29

ISAIAH

1865, Georgia and South Carolina

Isaiah arrived at Beaumont Plantation. He was surprised that it hadnt been destroyed, given Miles' infamy. It crawled with Federal troops. The fields were empty and the horses were all gone. Most of the black folks had left. While many of the plantation owners had fled, Elmira had stayed. That didnt surprise him.

He rushed to his mother. She weaved a round basket made of sweet grass and behaved as if the momentous events of the last few weeks hadnt happened. He embraced her. She grunted. She took one look at him with her yellow eyes and resumed weaving her basket with her knotted hands. His blue military uniform and sudden appearance after being gone for so long werent of the slightest interest to her. Isaiah put his hand on her shoulder and tried to make eye contact.

—Ma, why havent you left?

—Where else am I gonna go?

His eyes caught a fresh mound of red earth under the oldest tree on the plantation. A silhouette in a flowing black dress was hunched over next to it. As he grew nearer, he could hear the faint whimpers of the woman in black. She clutched Noah's dark gray granite headstone with both hands and sobbed quietly.

Isaiah thought about telling Elmira the real reason for her son's sacrifice. He hesitated. The wound was still too raw and tender. He knew he didnt need to explain or rationalize her son's qualities as a man, for a mother already knows such things.

He wanted to hate her for the way she clapped her hands for service, for the way she lorded over others, for the cruelties she profited from. He wasnt sure what emotion he felt toward the woman, but he found he couldnt bring himself to hate her. He walked up to her and, not knowing what else to do, did the only humane thing he could think of. He held her, for he knew no one else would.

It began to rain. He took Elmira's hand. She refused to let go of the tombstone. As he pulled her away, she clung to the slab until her grip came loose. She collapsed in the red mud and wailed. Isaiah picked her up. The other Yankee soldiers gave him sideways glances as he carried her inside the house. He later came back outside and stood before Noah's grave in the pouring rain, alone. He stood silently for quite some time and then put his hand on the cold granite. He left a single bloodred rose upon the mounded earth and then he went outside to sleep in his old cabin.

The following morning, he awoke to someone knocking on his cabin door. He assumed it was Elmira. Yet when he opened the door, Emma stood in the threshold. Despite his certainty that his mind was toying with him, she was still there, as demure and lovely as she had ever been.

His fatigue and worries melted away as they fell into one another's arms. There were no words, only their mutual embrace. Neither seemed to believe that the other was real.

As they were catching up and eating lunch inside the cabin, there was a knocking on the door. He opened it. In the doorway stood Elmira in black clothes. She lifted her chin and glared at Emma, then turned to him.

—Can I have a word with you?

Isaiah nodded. He stepped outside and Emma followed him. Elmira narrowed her eyes at her.

—Alone. If you please.

Isaiah looked to Emma. She gave a slight nod of affirmation and he followed Elmira inside Beaumont Hall. They walked through the empty halls of the mansion. Elmira told him that they planned to chop up the property per Special Field Order No. 15.

—I no longer care, she said.

—Where will you go?

Elmira shrugged. She placed a cigarette in an ivory holder and lit it. She took a deep puff.

—First, I will free Miles. He could tell she was trying to muster the courage to say something to him. She turned to him and took one of his hands.

—Stay with me, Isaiah. I can provide for you. I can find you a wife and you can have children. I can help look after them. Wont it be wonderful? Isaiah pulled his hand away.

—What about Emma?

—Let her marry someone of her station.

—I am of her station.

—Nonsense, Isaiah. You can read and write. You've been trained in etiquette and philosophy and arithmetic and so many other things that I've taught you. I've given you the best life I could, under the circumstances.

—Circumstances I am at war with.

He tried to walk away. Elmira blocked his path.

—Why are you being so stubborn?

Isaiah took the woman by the shoulders and kissed her forehead. Tears streamed down her porcelain cheeks.

—Goodbye, Elmira.

He stood at Emma's side outside the little chapel she always attended. There was a small crowd of freedmen and women in attendance. Isaiah wore the nicest thing he owned, his uniform. Emma wore the only dress she had. She held a bouquet of wildflowers picked from the countryside. They exchanged vows and kissed and Emma became Mrs. Emma Beaumont.

As they cheered, Isaiah caught a glimpse of crimson inside a black carriage waiting in the distance. He struggled to make out the woman's face, but he already knew who it was. Before he could approach, the woman inside motioned for the driver to move along.

He awoke the next morning. Emma lay beside him upon some blankets they had laid on the floor of his old cabin. Usually the bells would ring at this time of day to call the slaves to labor. Now the bells were silent. Beaumont Plantation was a peculiar place. He couldnt quite put his finger on it. It seemed to have a gravity of its own that pulled people toward it. It seemed as if he were living a dream for he realized his leave was about to be over. He was required to report to duty tomorrow. Emma slid into her dress. She tied her hair up and wrapped her arms around him.

—Do you need to leave?

—They'll shoot me if I dont.

Emma whimpered as he gently pried her fingers loose from his hand. He kissed her once more before the wagon he sat in jerked forward with Elmira watching from the balcony. His mother stood at Emma's side and merely gazed vacantly at the horizon.

Sherman's army burned its way toward the capital of South Carolina, the cradle of secession. Massive columns of blue surrounded the city of Columbia. It was the alpha and it would become the omega.

It was more of a town than a city. The army outside easily outnumbered the inhabitants several times over. Smoke rose from within it and the smell of charred cotton filled the air. The Rebels had destroyed what they couldnt take with them and the city surrendered without a fight.

The stores in the warehouses were already smoking heaps but the flames began to spread and consume the nearby buildings. The Federal soldiers grumbled that their vengeance had been taken from them.

Troops fanned out throughout the burning city. The first places to be seized were the bars and general stores. Soldiers drunkenly wandered the streets as flames climbed toward the night sky. Isaiah joined the other members of his battery as they scavenged the city for loot. They kicked down the doors of a home. A woman held her two crying children as they sifted through her belongings. She was relieved of her jewelry, even her wedding ring, and anything else they could find of value.

After they robbed the woman, they went to the neighboring house. It had already been cleaned out, so they kicked down the doors of a church. A pastor kneeled before a large cross and kept his eyes glued to his Bible. He couldnt count how many times he'd had his back torn open with the lash under the evocation of God's will. He knew their game and they couldnt hide behind their clerical attire from him.

—Burn it. Burn it all, he cried.

Brutality had to be met with brutality. Everything had to be destroyed. Isaiah threw a torch. The preacher ran toward the torch. Before he could pick it up, Isaiah jammed the butt of his rifle into the pastor's gut. The man reeled over in pain.

The other soldiers fled as the church became consumed by the flames. Isaiah pulled back the hammer of his rifle and aimed it at the pastor. He felt the cold steel of the trigger against his finger. The pastor looked up at him from his knees.

—I forgive you and I hope you find your peace, young man.

—I dont require your forgiveness.

The pastor held up his hands in prayer and closed his eyes. Isaiah's hands trembled. He commanded his finger to pull the trigger, but he could not. He lowered the rifle and he and the pastor fled the church. Minutes later, the flaming steeple collapsed into the nave.

On one side of the city, Federal soldiers lit fires, and on the other they tried to put them out. He went into an alleyway and sat down against a brick wall. There he uncapped a bottle of stolen rum and drank what was left in a single sitting. Everything around him faded into darkness.

—Isaiah, a familiar voice called.

His nostrils filled with the sharp stink of rot.

—Isaiah, said the voice. Louder now.

He felt the patter of rainwater against his face. The brick wall he sat against was still warm from the fire.

—Isaiah, commanded the voice.

His eyes shot open. Thunder cracked as a bolt of lightning illuminated the dark night sky. He sat up. He could make out a large silhouette standing at the end of the rubble-strewn alleyway under the purple luminance. Then the alley became dark again as the lightning disappeared. Another bolt ripped across the night sky. The silhouette's face lit up. Isaiah's eyes widened. He tried to scream but nothing came out. He tried to crawl away as a giant man walked toward him.

—James?

As he lay on the ground, James' immense, scarred torso stood over him. His wounds were still open and his face was gray and decomposed.

—James, you're dead…

Everything went dark again. He was gone. He gave a sigh of relief and sat back up. Then another sharp quake of thunder followed by purple illuminance. He was now face-to-face with James. Both of the man's eyes were completely white and Isaiah could smell the rot of his old friend's flesh. He slid backward hard against the brick wall, unable to escape.

—Have you forgotten?

Isaiah trembled as he shook his head.

—No, James… I havent forgotten.

Then he blinked and James was gone.

The bright white moon had peeked out from beneath the black clouds. Isaiah noticed a hand. And then an arm and part of a leg, sticking out of a pile of bricks. He narrowed his eyes and made out a face. A dead man. He looked to be in his thirties. One of the residents.

Isaiah wondered if anyone had ever cared about this anonymous man turned corpse. Surely he had a mother, a family. Now he was rat food. Isaiah gazed at the dead man's contorted and stiff fingers, then looked at his own and moved them. On the outside he knew he was alive. It was the inside he wasnt too sure about. He felt numb. He held a knife and studied the blade. He tapped the tip with his finger. Isaiah held his finger to his face and gazed upon the globule of blood that formed at the tip. Then he rubbed the warm, sticky blood between his thumb and forefinger until the bright red hue gave way to a dull ochre. He could feel the pressure, but he could not feel the pain.

—Is this all there is?

He closed his eyes and tried to remember Emma's face. His mind was working against him. He opened his eyes briefly, took a breath, and then squeezed them shut tighter. He tried to remember the smell of her hair and the softness of her skin. He tried to remember her smile. Emma didnt smile very often, but when she did the entire world lit up. The light was fading, he was losing her. Just then a young woman peered into the alleyway.

—Father. Father, the young woman cried out.

He ignored her. Then three drunken soldiers stumbled up to the woman. She tried to walk around them but they stood in her path. She backpedaled into the alley.

—Have you seen a tall older man with brown hair and…

—We only see you, the drunk lieutenant interrupted.

The young woman tried to dart off to the side but one of the men grabbed her arm and slammed her back against a brick wall. She gasped for air as the three soldiers dragged her deep into the alley, adjacent to the pile of rubble where Isaiah was sitting. She was forced onto the ground. The woman's eyes met with his as he tried to crouch farther out of view.

—Help, she screamed.

The largest soldier unbuckled his pants, the lieutenant. Isaiah slowly stood up from behind the debris pile. The lieutenant grabbed the woman's chin in his hand and leaned his rifle against the trash cans. Then he ripped open her blouse.

—I found her. I ought to go first, protested one of the soldiers.

—I outrank you. You'll get your turn when I'm finished.

Isaiah found himself in a familiar situation. Only this time, he found himself in the company of the predators rather than the prey. A dark part of his damaged soul wanted him to relish in the pain of that girl. He clutched his head as a thousand uncomfortable memories flooded his mind. He tried to forget, but he couldnt.

Isaiah took a few steps back. No, it was not in his power to stop her destiny. God had determined his fate, why shouldnt he let God determine hers? He couldnt allow himself to become soft-hearted, for the world was not forgiving to the weak. If he helped her, he'd be striking a superior officer, a death sentence during wartime. Then he'd never see Emma again. Then again, the thought occurred to him that he might not deserve Emma. For the briefest of moments, he was angry. Angry at everyone who had shown him kindness for forcing him to question his actions, or lack thereof.

The drunken lieutenant lifted up the young woman's dress. She tried to push it down. Another soldier grabbed her delicate wrists and held them above her head. The lieutenant fondled her and tried to kiss her. She bit his lip. He wiped the blood from his mouth, studied his bloodied fingers, and spat the blood at her face.

—Somebody help me, please.

Isaiah turned away, unable to watch. His palms were sweaty. He wanted nothing more than to leave, but shame burned inside him like a hot coal.

Isaiah's trembling hand grabbed the large lieutenant's blood-stained rifle. The lieutenant turned his head, his pupils dilated as the butt of the rifle collided with his face. Before the other two soldiers could react, Isaiah swung the rifle and struck one over the back of the head. The stock of the rifle cracked and split as he hit the other across the stomach. He tossed aside the damaged weapon and held out his hand to the young woman.

—We need to run. Now.

She staggered to her feet and took his hand.

They ran.

Chapter 30

ELMIRA

1865, Georgia

The Federals had left. Elmira wondered if they were going to hang her husband as she sat alone on her cold marble floor and sulked next to the squares of dust where her furniture had once been. A broken marble bust lay at her feet. She was dismayed by how fast the soldiers were able to clear out all seventy-five rooms of Beaumont Hall. Elmira rubbed her arms as a sharp breeze whistled through one of her shattered windows. The books that remained in her once magnificent library lay scattered on the floor.

Elmira cracked open her door and peered outside. Most of the negroes were gone, but to her surprise several remained. The Yankee devils had left her alone with them. Why were they loitering about? Shouldnt they be on the parcels Sherman carved out for them? She began to breathe heavily.

—The windows are shattered. They can easily walk right in, she said to herself.

Elmira closed the wooden shutters on every window. She locked every door. Soon the interior of Beaumont Hall was dark. The pantry was cleaned out. There were only a few cans of food, a pile of flour on the floor, and some hardtack the Yankee soldiers had discarded. The wash basin was full of dirty water. Elmira cupped the water in her hand and drank it. She wasnt going to step outside and risk getting lynched.

How many days had she been cooped up inside? It didnt matter. Every time she sucked up the courage to wander outside, there was a rapping on the door. They wanted blood. *Her* blood. Elmira gazed into the shattered panes of her mirror. There were bags under her eyes. Her frazzled hair hung loose and her cheeks had grown hollow.

Someone was whispering. She moved to another room. More whispering. It was faint. Very faint. She couldnt make out the words, but she could hear the voice.

—Who are you? What do you want?

Elmira ran from room to room. The whispers followed. She huddled up in the corner of the pantry. Mice squeaked. Mice were everywhere. She couldnt see them, but she could hear them behind the walls. She climbed inside one of her cupboards with a pillow and slammed the cupboard door shut.

—Safe. It's safe here.

Elmira awoke hours later and climbed out of the cupboard. Glimmers of light beamed through the shutter slats. Was it daytime? Surely, the angry negroes had held up lanterns to the windows to give the appearance of daylight. It was a trick. Yes. They wanted her to come outside. Then they'd torture her. Elmira walked up to one of the windows. The warm rays shone upon her face.

—You're not going to trick me, she yelled.

More whispers. At first, Elmira was afraid of them. But she had been hearing them for so long, she had gotten used to them.

—Someone is trying to communicate with me. Yes. Someone from beyond.

Elmira wandered the house with unkept hair and white undergarments. She placed her ear against the wall.

—The voice is coming from beneath the wallpaper.

Elmira tore off the yellow silk wallpaper. There was yellow wallpaper everywhere in the mansion. She hated wallpaper. She pressed her ear against the wall again.

—No. I was wrong. The voice is coming from beneath the plaster.

Elmira pounded the plaster with her fist and clawed at it to no avail. She wandered the house again and found a broken chair leg. Returning to the wall, she bashed the chair leg against the plaster wall until it broke apart and only wooden strips remained. Elmira placed her ear against the wooden strips.

—The voice is just under these.

She pried them apart. When they broke away, she tore them off the wall with her hands. Elmira peered into the dark hollow of the wall.

—Noah? Is that you?

Elmira held her ear next to the hollow.

—Noah, please answer me.

She put her head completely in the void.

—Noah, I miss you dearly. Why wont you talk to me?

Nothing.

—Noah. Noah?

She cried and pounded the wall until her knuckles began to bleed. Then she collapsed upon the ground.

Elmira awoke hours later. Or at least that was how much time she thought had passed. Her stomach ached with hunger. She had eaten all the hardtack. The large basin of filthy water was empty. She'd have to go outside for more.

Rising, she stumbled across a container of her rouge lying on the floor. She picked it up, took off the lid, and smeared it upon her face haphazardly. She studied her reflection in the mirror.

—Beautiful.

She stumbled into the library. One of the shelves had only a single book left upon it. Elmira began to laugh. She laughed so hard her eyes watered. She stumbled to the bookshelf and knocked on it. When there was no reply, she held her ear to the bookshelf.

—Hello. Is anybody in there?

When there was no answer, she laughed some more. Elmira pulled on the bookshelf, but it did not budge. She paused to laugh. Then she pulled again. A puff of dust filled the air. The bookshelf pulled open. A hidden door.

Behind the door was a passage that led to a winding staircase. The Yankee soldiers had cut open mattresses. They had taken sledgehammers to her marble floors and a few of her walls in search of hidden wealth. Elmira was surprised they hadnt found the passage. Too obvious, perhaps? She climbed down the narrow stone steps and stepped inside the chamber that mostly served as a wine cellar. Hundreds of bottles of fine vintages. Elmira laughed.

—I had almost forgotten. I suppose I didnt even need to drink that dirty water.

She laughed some more. Then she slid one of the wine racks to the side. Behind it stood a very large iron safe. She entered the combination. Next to a tall stack of gold bars lay a little toy horse. She picked it up as if it were the most precious thing in the world and held it to her chest. Noah's favorite toy from when he was a boy. Miles had thrown it away when Noah left for the academy. Elmira had dug it out of the trash and placed it in the safe. Better that the Yankee soldiers had taken the furniture, the art, even the gold than the little wooden horse.

Inside the safe she also found several rifles, ammunition, some jewelry, and various documents. She loaded one of the rifles, a lever action Henry rifle, and took some gold double eagle coins before she closed the heavy door of the safe.

Elmira shuffled to the kitchen clutching her Henry rifle. She checked the stove. There was still enough wood for a fire. She peered inside her barren cabinets. A small victory. She found a box of matches, struck one, and tried to light the stove. The brief flame died. She tried again. The flame grew larger but then died out. She gritted her teeth and threw the matches to the ground. Elmira pounded the iron stove with her fist and let out a sharp cry.

An hour later, she dug the matchbox out of the pile of flour and tried to light the stove again. She went through three more matches. All failures. This had been so easy when she was a girl—second nature. When her mother died, her father had depended on her to cook while he worked the press. Was she really so useless after all these years?

—Please.

The stove lit up and Elmira breathed a sigh of relief. She searched for some water but of course there was none. She got a bucket to take to the well. She cracked open one of her front doors and peeked outside and then slammed it shut.

As she crouched against the door, she hugged her rifle. Elmira sat there for several hours. She was sure any minute now the doors would crash open. A mob of angry freedmen and women clutching torches and farm implements would barge in and exact vengeance upon her.

Glass shattered. Of course, why come in through the heavy door when the mob could bash through the shutters and windows? Elmira's hands trembled. The sweat from her hands made the wooden stock of her rifle glisten. Her head swiveled to the nearest window. But no one was coming in. There was a fresh pile of broken glass on the floor. Perhaps a loose shard had merely given way to gravity.

Thunk. Thunk. Thunk. Three powerful blows against her front door.

How many could she kill before she had to reload? Sixteen if she aimed well, but she figured there must be dozens of negroes outside.

Thunk. Thunk. Thunk. Her heart raced. Sweat accumulated in the pit of her neck. She could run to the third-floor balcony. Yes. She figured she could take them out from high above. It would give her time to reload and kill a few more before they managed to get to the third floor. But what then? Would they retreat? Or would they realize their superior numbers, take their losses, and overpower her? Her mind shifted to thoughts of being captured alive. What horrible things would they do to her? She didnt have a vivid imagination in that regard, but she did remember clearly the punishments exacted by Jed at her husband's orders, even her own orders on occasion.

Perhaps she could hide in the wine cellar. How long could one survive on wine alone? Should she spend the day in the cellar and sneak out at night? Would any of the freedmen and women be up that late? Even if she got past them, she might have to contend with Federal soldiers roaming about the countryside. Elmira whimpered as she turned the gun around and held it to her forehead.

—I cant live like this.

Her finger touched the cold steel trigger. She thought of Noah. All she had to do was squeeze it, and she would be reunited with her son, for all eternity. Wouldnt God forgive her?

Thunk. Thunk. Thunk. The terrible noise from the door reverberated throughout the entire house. Would Noah be happy to see her? Of course he would. Why wouldnt he? Elmira thought about Miles. Her boy would be upset if she left his father to rot in some cell. She lowered the rifle.

She rose to her feet and walked toward the front door, her cheeks dry, her shoulders pushed back. *Thunk. Thunk.* Before the third blow could connect, she heaved open the heavy wooden door with one hand, took a few steps back, and raised the rifle to eye level.

—Mistress, please dont shoot, said a middle-aged freedman with his hands raised.

About a dozen of her freed men and women surrounded him, all of them with their hands raised. They appeared confused. Several widened their eyes as her face came into the light. To her surprise, there was no log, no battering ram, no makeshift weapons. There was only a group of now freed men and women staring at her and blinking.

—So, you've finally come to torture and rape me. Well, I choose death, yelled Elmira.

The middle-aged freedman waved his upraised arms.

—Woah. Woah. Ma'am, we just wanted to ask you if you had jobs for us? That's it. I swear.

—You just want jobs? As in paid labor?

The group all nodded.

—Oh, I suppose I didnt think of that. Do you mean to trick me, gain my trust, and then make me your slave? Do you think I dont know what you're up to. Is that it?

—Aint slavery illegal now, ma'am?

—Illegal? Oh, yes, I suppose it is. We'll see how well the Feds enforce it. Fine. Just know I'll be watching you. Elmira lowered the rifle. With her free hand she took a fistful of double eagles from her pocket and placed them in the freedman's hand.

—Divide it amongst yourselves. Do…whatever it is you normally do.

The group gazed at the mound of precious coins in awe. The crowd dispersed and the freed men and women began to work. Elmira slung the rifle over her shoulder and grabbed a bucket. She carried it to the well. The group appeared surprised when she heaved the water up herself.

Back inside the kitchen, she took some of the flour piled on the floor and began to make dough. She slid it into the oven. Her mouth watered as the room filled with the crisp smell of fresh bread. It was burned slightly, but it still tasted like heaven. A tingle of satisfaction ran up her spine as she finished eating. Why had she allowed herself to become so dependent on others? Someone pounded on the door.

—I already paid them. What do they want now?

Elmira leaned her rifle against the wall and walked toward the door without it. Halfway down the hall, she stopped. She returned to the kitchen and grabbed the weapon.

She flung open the door, annoyed. A tall and gaunt man with a square jaw, wearing a fine suit, stood before her. He had a self-assured grin across his face. It took Elmira a few moments to recognize him: Ambrose de Bellomonte.

—Good afternoon, Mrs. Beaumont.

—How dare you.

—Such a shame. It looks like they took everything. I suppose I was one of the lucky ones, to escape such terrors.

Her hands shook with rage. She had her Henry rifle. She could end him right now. Just one easy pull of the trigger. No. Death was just one ingredient in her recipe for retribution. Elmira was going to bake a lovely cake of vengeance and de Bellomonte's blood would be the icing on top. She licked her lips. She could almost taste what was coming to him. Taking a deep breath, she managed her composure.

—I swear to God in heaven that I will follow you to the gates of hell.

—You wound me, Ms. Beaumont. One of my commanders found your son guilty of treason and exacted the lawful punishment. I had nothing to do with it, truly. If it is any consolation, I would have intervened. I am so very sorry for your loss and that your family's reputation has been tarnished in such a way.

Elmira knew it was a lie. Did he think she couldnt read a newspaper? The papers said he'd been the highest-ranking officer present when her son was executed. She almost pitied Ambrose at that moment. The poor fool thought she was a simpleton. He had no idea of the impending hurricane before him.

—Get off my property.

Ambrose gave a courteous nod and began to walk away. He stopped midstep and turned.

—I can save your husband.

—What do you want?

—To free your husband. Of course.

—What do you really want?

—A fair and mutually beneficial transaction. Because you have suffered, Madam Elmira. I would like to lend you a helping hand. I will purchase Beaumont Hall from you at a very fair price. You and Miles can buy yourselves a nice home far away from such terrible memories. Out in the frontier.

—And if I refuse?

—You're free to do as you please, but I cant guarantee that your husband will be spared from the hangman's noose. I went to West Point with the Yankee commander holding him. A commander who owes me a favor. My old friend, and temporary enemy, was willing to pull some strings to spare your husband the noose. I did you both the kindest favor. I ensured your husband was sent somewhere…humane. Believe me. The Yankees arent happy with him. Miles couldnt stop bleating about how he was given the honor of firing off the first shot at Fort Sumter.

Ambrose gave a curt smile and walked away. An attendant opened the door to his carriage and he took his seat inside. Just as the carriage was about to depart, Elmira ran up.

—I must see him. My husband.

—Of course, Madam Elmira. You'll find that I'm a very reasonable person. Not the caricature your husband vilified during his campaign. I'll arrange for you to see him. Do consider my offer in the meantime. By the way, the Federals have allowed local elections to continue for the time being. Because I can bring about reconciliation after this war is over, I am running for mayor. Your father's support in the papers would be most welcome. He handed Elmira a poster. It was emblazoned with Ambrose's image and read *DE BELLOMONTE FOR MAYOR*.

Elmira smelled that something was amiss. He was a Confederate general. How had he acquired a pardon so quickly? Nearly every person of status caught in the North's grip had been squeezed out of any wealth they had left. Why was de Bellomonte doing so well? His carriage disappeared down the dirt road. Elmira crumpled the paper.

She went to Savannah and did something she hadnt done in a long time. She entered a Catholic church. Though she had never stepped inside the church before, it immediately felt familiar and comforting to her. She had nothing against her husband's church. It was a fine church, it just wasnt hers.

She sat next to the priest behind the screen.

—Bless me, Father, for I have sinned.

—When was your last confession?

—Twenty-seven years ago. The night before I was married.

—Please go on.

She told the priest everything. She confessed her adultery and numerous other sins. She asked numerous times if she was taking up too much of his time, and every time he asked her to continue. After she finished, he gave her a long but kind lecture and assigned her an act of penance—never to see Pierce again, among other things—and then absolved her of her sins.

Then there was another long silence.

—Anything else, my lady?

Elmira decided to make another confession.

—Bless me, Father, for I am about to sin.

—My lady, it does not work that way.

—I've found the person responsible for my son's death and I'm going to exact terrible vengeance upon him.

—My lady, I urge you not to go through with whatever it is you're planning to do. All who take up the sword shall perish by the sword.

—Oh, Father, I wont use a sword. Please pray for my son Noah, and if you can find it in your heart, for me.

With that, she got up and left.

Chapter 31

EMMA

1865, Georgia

Emma poured some stew into Mary's wooden bowl. Mary slurped it loudly. It was hard to imagine that Isaiah's mother had ever been the famed beauty everyone said she was. Her eyes were an unusual and brilliant copper color, but somehow the light inside them was gone. Emma could make out her high cheekbones and balanced features that must have been pleasing to the eye in youth but were now ravaged by time and the harshness of her life.

—Is it good? Emma asked.

—It's alright.

That was about as much conversation as she could squeeze out of her. The others had said she used to be very talkative in her earlier years, charming even. Emma wanted to ask her what had happened inside Beaumont Hall to change her so, but she couldnt bring herself to do it.

Emma didnt ask permission to stay at Beaumont Plantation. There was so much chaos about that it made no difference. The master of the house was gone and the mistress was in a state of inconsolable grief. Emma made a little money selling baskets and whatever labor she could offer to anyone who needed it.

Still, she was happy to be reunited with her congregation. A few had fled north, but many familiar faces remained. Sunday was the one time of the week she actually looked forward to. She even managed to get Mary to start going along with her. The disgruntled woman grouched the whole way there every Sunday.

—Let me sleep, woman, Mary would say.

Emma would gently cajole her and tug her toward the waiting wagon full of congregants. She'd tug at her sleeves while smiling and speaking in a soft voice, almost the way one would deal with a child. Today was no exception.

—Come on, Ms. Mary. I'll bake you somethin nice for you when we get back.

—I said I dont wanna go.

—I have some sweet potato pie with your name on it.

Emma gently pulled her along. Mary tugged her arm away sharply.

—Fine, damnit.

Then Mary would mutter and curse under her breath the whole way. The other congregants covered their mouths to hide their laughter. It was a sort of game to them. Sometimes they'd count how many swear words the woman would use on the way there and see if she had broken her previous record. To Emma's surprise, the rugged, ill-mannered woman became unusually quiet inside the little chapel. The pastor was able to help Emma read the words she didnt understand and he also helped her write letters to Isaiah. Though it worried her that she wasnt getting any letters in return.

A family of her fellow parishioners had received an allotment of forty acres from the Union army. They said they needed a hand to work the rice paddy and offered Emma a place to stay if she helped out. It wasnt terribly far from her church or Beaumont Plantation should Isaiah return, so she agreed to stay with them.

As she was packing the few things she had, Emma caught a flash of crimson.

—Where are you going, dear Emma? asked Elmira.

—My friends have been allotted some land. I'm going there.

—Where, might I ask?

—Once the land of a man by the name of Mr. Meyers.

—Be careful, Mr. Meyers isnt known for his hospitality. I suspect that the Yankees will come to realize that they actually have to govern the people they've conquered. I assure you that rescinding property rights isnt going to go over well with the locals. I doubt they'll want an insurgency that will drag on for years. I would stay here, if I were you. My rent is affordable.

—Well…well, things have changed, mistress.

Emma's loud words didnt so much as raise an eyebrow from Elmira. Her expression was apathetic and she left as Emma finished packing her things. Emma knelt down next to Mary.

—Come with me, Ms. Mary.

—I was born here and I'm gonna die here.

—But you're free now.

—Look in the damn mirror. You aint free.

Emma didnt understand. Mary grumbled and cursed to herself and began weaving a new basket. Her house was full of beautiful, unused baskets. She made far more than she could use or sell, and it was the only activity she was interested in.

So she climbed aboard the wagon with Sarah, Jacob, and Lizzy. Sarah was a widow about thirty years of age, and her son Jacob was about fifteen. Lizzy was Sarah's younger sister and was about the same age as Emma.

They soon arrived at their cabin. It was next to a rice paddy. It wasnt a large home, but it was sturdy and had a wood stove on the inside. There was more than enough room for the four of them to stretch their legs out at night. Sarah said that they caught catfish in the paddy when the water was high and that they never had a short supply of pork thanks to the feral hogs roaming the area.

Emma began to learn the ins and outs of growing rice. Sarah's family had grown rice for generations. Emma slapped her neck. She wiped off the crushed insect in her palm. The buzz of mosquitos was terrible. Sarah laughed.

—They're a curse and a blessing, said Sarah.

—A blessing? asked Emma.

—Not many people want to work this land.

Emma smashed a trio of mosquitos on her arm.

—I think I understand why.

—It's good land though. Good land.

Mr. Meyers had officially owned the land before the Federals came and forced him to divide it up. Within days of the order, Sarah, Jacob, and Lizzy had built a cabin while gun-toting soldiers held Mr. Meyers and the locals at bay.

A few weeks passed. and the Federal soldiers stopped patrolling the area. Emma didnt want to get her dress wet, so she had to wade into the murky water in her underwear. Her bare shoulders were a feast for the mosquitos, but at least her clothes were dry.

Sarah, Jacob, and Lizzy began to check their fish traps. She felt a moment of elation as she gazed upon the wriggling catfish inside. By the time she got to her last trap, she had enough to feed the four of them and then some. They soaked them in brine and then cooked them over an open fire. With full stomachs, they all went to bed.

She awoke to a cracking sound. She peered out the window and saw flashes of yellow flame. Emma wasnt sure what it was until she heard men's voices.

—Get on out of there, one shouted.

Taunts were followed by gunfire. The four of them huddled together and peered out the window. Six men approached. One held a lantern in one hand and a rifle in the other. The rest carried torches with rifles slung on their backs.

—This aint your land, said one of the men.

They backed away from the window. It shattered. Several torches were tossed inside. They all tried to stamp out the flames, but it was no use. The flames began to consume the wood cabin. Emma could hear bullets ricochet off its thick wood exterior. She and the others flung open the door and ran.

Bullets pinged around them as they fled into the swamp. She could hear the men hoot and holler and bellow with laughter as the little cabin was devoured by the flames. The men pursued them until they reached the water line. Then they stopped and reloaded. They fired into the darkness. The water was up to Emma's neck now. She couldnt see anything around her. Only fear of being shot or lynched or worse kept her legs moving. Her toes struggled to touch the muddy bottom. She took another step. Her foot sank calf-deep into the mud. Her head went under the black water. Then a hand clenched around her arm and pulled her up. She coughed and gagged as the putrid water made its way out of her lungs.

—Jacob, Sarah, Lizzy? Was that you?

—Shush, was the only reply.

As she trekked through the water, she felt something slither over one ankle and behind another. She felt her eyes bulge and goosebumps crawl up her flesh. She could still hear gunfire in the distance.

Something fell from a tree and splashed in the water behind her. Out of instinct. she looked over her shoulder, but she couldnt even see her hand in front of her let alone what was behind her. She could only make out shapes. Was the thing in front of her a log or an alligator? She did not know. She only knew she feared men more than animals.

The void in her vision filled with sounds and thoughts. She heard wolves and coyotes howling. The wind cut through the trees around her. Her feet made a sucking sound with every step in the muck below. Only the whispers among her party gave her comfort.

Hours went by. Her wet clothes were heavy as she pulled herself out of the water and onto a muddy bank. Candlelight glowed from a cabin window. A hand fell upon her shoulder—it was Jacob. She turned and looked longingly at the cabin door. It would be warm inside.

—Should we ask for help? asked Emma.

—Help? No one's goin to help us, he said.

As a group, they decided to avoid asking. They quietly made their way away from the property. A dog barked. Then another started, and another. A man came out of the cabin with a lantern in one hand and a shotgun in the other. He aimed it at them.

—Who's there? said the man.

—Just passing through, said Jacob.

The man placed the lantern at his feet and held the shotgun with both hands. The light caught three more figures around him. Each of them had a gun pointed at them.

—This is our land, said the man.

Emma fell to her knees and held out her arms. Perhaps it was wisest to consider those people in the cabin enemies and to keep them on a need-to-know basis. Still, she pleaded for mercy.

—Our cabin was set ablaze, said Emma.

The three figures lowered the barrels of their guns. They huddled together and talked amongst themselves. The man held his lantern up to her face and studied it. Rather than turn away, she decided to look up at him. Though she could not see him, she knew their eyes had met.

They were allowed to sleep in the barn. The straw was fresh and as good a place as any to sleep on. The farm was owned by the Wolfe family. An old woman with a copper face covered in hard lines handed her a hot cup of some unfamiliar tea. It felt good going down her throat and it lifted her spirits as the warmth filled her stomach.

Grace was about Emma's age. She wrung out Emma's wet dress for her and hung it out to dry. Grace had a wide face and dark brown, almost black, hair. The man who had spoken to her was a white man named John. He was strongly built and had a cropped, dark red beard. The other two men were Grace's cousins. There was no mother.

The following afternoon, their clothes were still damp. They did not wish to push the boundaries of the Wolfe family's hospitality and set off to leave. Mr. Wolfe insisted they stay one day longer. At least until their clothes were dry.

Grace had a warm smile and a contagious laugh. Like Emma, she had no parents. John was her uncle. Grace was as talkative as Emma was quiet. She opened the darkest corners of her heart to the world and had a way of sucking Emma into her life. Even though they had just met, Emma felt like she had known her for years. What did Emma have in common with a half-Scottish, half-native woman who had grown up under completely different circumstances? Nothing and everything.

Emma prayed with her little congregation for the last time. Her pastor, Sarah, Lizzy, and Jacob would be departing from the port of Savannah to Pittsburgh. Between them they had enough money to get Emma a one-way ticket. She declined the offer. None of them knew anything about city life, but they were willing to take their chances. Emma turned to the pastor.

—Have any letters come for me?

He shook his head no and apologized. She hadnt gotten a letter from Isaiah since they had gotten married. She had overheard someone say that four out of every ten men who'd fallen in battle were never identified. All she could do was wave as the wagon disappeared down the forked road.

Chapter 32

ISAIAH

1865, South Carolina

He pulled her arm, hard. They jumped over a collapsed light post and weaved between piles of brick interspersed with bloated dead horses. Dirt from the streets clung to the soles of his boots, still sticky with the price of victory. The interiors of the collapsed buildings around them glowed an unnatural red. Hell had risen to the surface. Black smoke spiraled upward out of the windows, making its way to the heavens only to trickle down silver ash upon them like tears from God.

The girl's golden hair came loose and fluttered in the hot wind. Isaiah's legs cramped and his lungs cried for air. He looked behind him. The lieutenant and his accomplices appeared, their faces bloodied from Isaiah's blows. If they caught them without any witnesses, they'd kill them both. Just two more bodies among many in a devastated city—questions need not be asked.

He feared for her more than himself, for his death would be quick—hers wouldnt. He had to get to the camp. If there was one thing the army loved more than blood, it was bureaucracy. They'd ask the proper questions, fill out the proper forms, file a report, give him a trial, and then shoot him in the prescribed fashion, but the girl would be safe.

They turned down a narrow street. It was blocked with rubble. Again, he looked over his shoulder. The lieutenant and his soldiers were gaining on him. He wanted to catch his breath, but if he did it would be his last. They continued on and passed by a group of Federal soldiers digging through the rubble of a general store. The soldiers pocketed what trinkets they could fit in their pockets. They paused and looked up as Isaiah ran past. The lieutenant caught up to them and pointed in his direction.

—He's a deserter. A deserter. Get him. That's an order.

The soldiers dropped the bricks in their hands and ran toward them. The Federal camp was about one hundred yards beyond a maze of caved-in buildings and smoldering debris. They climbed through a glassless window of a partially destroyed building. They crawled over and under charred beams and warm piles of shattered brick. The soldiers pursued them. Isaiah and the woman reached another window. Rubble was piled high against it and there was only enough room to crawl on one's belly through the narrow opening. The charred beams cracked and groaned. The sound of bricks tumbling down from the ruined walls echoed in the room that smelled of burnt flesh.

—You go first, said Isaiah.

The young woman shook her head. It was total blackness on the other side of the window. Death was coming from one direction, and the unknown was on the other.

—If you dont crawl in there, we die.

The young woman crawled into the narrow space. Her feet disappeared into the darkness. Isaiah followed her. The sharp bricks cut his elbows as he pulled himself through the space. His shoulders rubbed against the edges of the confines with no light in sight. He wondered if he had already saved his would-be killers the trouble of burying him.

Light. The fires of the Federal camp appeared in the distance, just outside the city. The young woman pulled his arm and helped him to his feet. There were no streets. Only walls and debris. They climbed through windows and over piles of brick until they cleared the city.

As they ran into the scorched fields, he heard shouting behind him and saw several silhouettes chasing them. Isaiah squeezed the young woman's hand tight. The Federal camp was almost upon them.

They crossed into the crowded camp, which had a population greater than Columbia. He told the girl to be on her way. She didnt want to leave his side, but he told her she still wasnt safe and that she should find the provost marshal and speak to him. The girl nodded and began to walk away. She stopped and turned.

—I'll pray for you, she said.

—Dont bother, nobody's up there.

The girl walked back and placed her hand on his cheek. She looked up at him with tender eyes as if to suggest he was somehow injured.

—I know there is a God because He sent you.

The words shook him. Before he could think of something to say, the girl disappeared into the crowded camp. Isaiah met with the highest-ranking officer he could find. The major listened with annoyance as he described the incident in detail.

A few moments later, the lieutenant and his soldiers ran up behind him, their uniforms powdered gray with ash. The lieutenant threw his hat to the ground and pointed a crooked finger at Isaiah.

—He struck a superior officer. He tried to desert. He's a traitor.

The major sipped his coffee.

—All three charges?

—Yes, sir. I have witnesses.

—So you want me to kill him three times?

The major crossed his arms and listened as the lieutenant gave his version of the story. Then he looked to his men, who all confirmed that Isaiah had tried to desert and struck the lieutenant when he tried to apprehend him. The major threw his arms up.

—Court-martial him. I dont have time for this shit.

Isaiah found himself in shackles once more. He was kept in a group of other detained soldiers awaiting a verdict from the judge advocate general. Most of them were deserters, drunkards, and insubordinates. A guard appeared and directed them all to the court.

He stood in a long line of the accused. The court-martial was held under the shade of a chestnut tree. The judge, a colonel, sat behind a simple table with a gavel atop it. Witnesses and spectators sat in looted wooden chairs and on tree stumps. When called, each defendant stood before the judge and gave his version of events. There was some rapid back-and-forth with the prosecution. Occasionally the judge would ask questions. Then he'd slam his gavel down and issue a verdict. Each trial took about ten minutes and all of them were found guilty.

—Corporal Isaiah Beaumont, called a voice.

Isaiah stood before the judge. He was an older man, bald, with baggy eyes. He was hunched over his table and took one quick glance at Isaiah before returning his eyes to the documents before him. He mumbled the charges under his breath while reading: striking a superior officer and desertion.

—How do you plead? asked the judge.

—Not guilty.

Isaiah told the judge what had happened. As he told his version of the events, the judge cut him off midsentence and demanded clarification on one matter and then another before letting him continue on. He turned to the lieutenant, who had about fourteen men sitting behind him. Isaiah recognized two of them as the attempted rapists and the others as the looters who'd pursued him several nights prior. He looked for allies in the crowd and found no one. The young woman wasnt present.

The right side of the lieutenant's face was purple and his eye was swollen shut. His arm was in a sling. The lieutenant accused Isaiah of attempting to desert and explained that Isaiah had struck him. The judge asked the witnesses, who all agreed that Isaiah was a deserter and had done so. One of them even went so far as to accuse him of being a Rebel spy. The judge listened intently before he turned his head toward Isaiah.

—You struck him, yes?

—Yes.

—Looks like you got him pretty good.

There was a chuckle from the crowd. The lieutenant wasnt amused. The judge rapped his fingers against the table as if in thought. He looked at Isaiah and then looked at the lieutenant once more. He gripped his gavel and raised it.

—Wait, said a voice.

The young woman ran up to the stand. Isaiah hadnt had a chance to see her in daylight. She couldnt have been older than fifteen. Her hair was the color of straw and her face possessed a youthful innocence. She pointed to the lieutenant as she struggled to catch her breath. Two soldiers ran up behind her and tried to seize her arms.

—He tried to rape me, said the young woman, pointing.

The judge held up his hand to stop her from talking, but she continued to point and retell the events of that night. The judge pounded his gavel against the table until the young woman stopped speaking. He then went on a long monologue about military court etiquette and gave everyone in the area a ten-minute civics lesson on how the court system worked. When he was finished, another person ran up. The judge sighed and rolled his eyes.

Isaiah's heart sank.

It was the preacher. The preacher whose church he had torched. The preacher he had hit with the butt of his rifle while looting the house of God. The preacher wore a fine black suit and a white collar. Such symbols must have made an impression on the judge, for he was far more patient with the preacher than with the young woman. The preacher identified himself in a drawl as thick as molasses. He said he was a witness and asked to give testimony. The judge agreed. The preacher adjusted his collar and stood straight. He pointed at Isaiah.

—This man.

The preacher paused. The only sound was the birds chirping and the breeze passing through the branches of the chestnut tree. He turned to Isaiah and their eyes met.

—I can attest that the man who stands before you is not only a man of honor but a man of the highest character. He should be given a medal, not chains. He saved my one and only, my lovely daughter Annamarie. I swear to God in heaven that every word is true.

Everything in his life had taught Isaiah that cruelty was the bedrock of human society. If he'd been in the preacher's position, he'd have exacted vengeance and delighted in it. It was too much to bear. He felt tears streaming down his cheeks. He didnt understand the preacher's motivations. He was part of an army that had destroyed the preacher's home, his church, and his city. He didnt understand why a man he had treated so cruelly would defend him. Even now he found himself struggling to believe the preacher's intentions.

The judge leaned back in his chair. The crowd of onlookers had grown tenfold. Isaiah could hear the creaking of the wooden chair as the judge leaned forward once more. He pounded his gavel against the table.

—I find you not guilty of the charge of desertion.

Isaiah's heart rose in his chest.

—Guilty of the charge of striking a superior officer.

His heart sank as dread filled his veins.

—You are to be confined to hard labor with a twenty-four-pound ball and chain attached to your leg, upon such works as the commanding general may direct, from the date of the approval of this sentence until January 1, 1866, and forfeit to the United States all pay and allowances now due or that may become due to you.

Isaiah lowered his head. Part of him was elated he wasnt going to be going to the firing squad. The other part dreaded that he would have to be away from Emma even longer. Just as the war was coming to a close, he found himself a slave once more. As he turned to leave, the judge spoke.

—Son, you struck an officer, my hands are tied. I've done all I can do for you. Godspeed.

Before Isaiah was led away, the preacher embraced him and Annamarie kissed him on the cheek. He was pulled away and an iron clamp was closed around his ankle.

Chapter 33

ELMIRA

1865 Georgia

Elmira made her way across the dead waters of the moat by way of a creaky wooden bridge. The thick redbrick walls of Fort Pulaski were pockmarked by cannon fire and the stars and stripes fluttered high above. Expressionless Union soldiers stood erect at the point of entry.

A stone-faced Federal guard dug through her things while a female attendant aggressively patted her down. The woman's clammy hands ran up and down her legs and between her breasts. Elmira would never have tolerated such humiliation in the past, but she needed to see Miles. A rusty-barred gate screeched open as she was led through a musky corridor lined with prison cells. Only a few high-profile prisoners were kept inside. The rest overflowed into the central courtyard. Prisoners of war. Their faces were gaunt and their eyes had sunk deep in their sockets. The whole wretched place reeked of death.

Elmira barely recognized the naked man. He was huddled up in the fetal position inside a humid cell that smelled of stale urine and mold. He had lost weight. His fingernails were long and yellow while his beard had become white and scraggly. When she stepped inside, her husband didnt even acknowledge her presence. She wrapped her arms around him then pulled back and gazed into his eyes. They were glazed over, more beast than man. He neither embraced her nor bothered to look in her direction.

—It's me, Miles. Your wife, Elmira. You remember me, dont you?

Miles moaned.

—What did you animals do to him?

—He was treated no different than anyone else. Some have stronger minds than others.

Miles gave off a series of low moans.

—These conditions are squalid. How dare you keep him like this?

—At least we fed him. You should have seen how you kept our boys at Andersonville.

Elmira stood in the cramped quarters of the fort's commander. She tried to explain that her husband's mind was gone and that he should be allowed to live under house arrest instead. The commander was unmoved. He explained that Miles was too important a prisoner to let out of his sight, even if his mind was gone. The commander stood and opened his office door to let her out.

—I must say that the legends are true.

—Legends?

—Of Mrs. Beaumont's beauty. You're well known amongst my men.

Elmira cocked her head to the side and smirked.

—Of course they're true.

She pretended to stumble as she moved to the door. The commander caught her, just as she knew he would. She pressed her breasts firmly against his rotund torso. Elmira's eyes met with his for several moments. The commander hesitated before he gently pushed himself away, as a gentleman should. Then he awkwardly helped Elmira dust herself off.

—Forgive me, I can be so clumsy sometimes.

—No apology required, ma'am.

Crocodile tears worked their way down Elmira's high cheekbones. She pressed her face against the commander's chest, who seemed taken aback at her forwardness.

—Now that Miles has gone mad, I'm all alone in my extravagant home with no one to share my fortune with.

—No one?

Elmira sighed.

—My chambers are so very cold at night.

—They are?

She stood back. The commander pulled a neatly folded handkerchief from his pocket and dabbed her wet cheeks. Elmira let her overcoat slip to the floor. She just so happened to be wearing an off-the-shoulder dress with a low-cut scoop neck. The commander's eyes worked their way down her face and stopped at her chest. She tilted her chin up and gave him a judgmental look, the kind a schoolmarm would give to a naughty student, albeit with a slight smile.

—What are you looking at, Commander?

The commander cleared his throat.

—Your black pearl necklace.

—Of course. Elmira reached behind her neck and purposely fumbled with the clasp. Oh, Commander, can you help me with this?

The man's hand trembled slightly as he undid the clasp and held the necklace. It slipped off her neck and the commander held it out with two hands, clearly not knowing what to do next.

—It's very rare. From Tahiti. It's worth more than most people's homes and manors.

The commander's eyes widened as he gazed upon the necklace in his hands. He felt the individual pearls as if checking to see if they were real. Elmira stepped forward until her face was mere inches from his. He could no doubt smell her lavender perfume emanating from her chest. She touched the commander's hand and closed his fingers around the pearl necklace.

—A gift, for your wife.

—Ma'am, I cannot.

—I've lost a son in this war. Call it an emblem toward reconciliation.

The commander began to lean forward with his lips parted. Elmira turned, picked up her overcoat, and closed the door behind her.

Sometime later, Elmira stood under her colonnaded porch as a boxy carriage made of riveted steel pulled up. Two guards climbed down and opened the back doors. Miles was lowered into a wheelchair. He wore the same torn and disheveled clothes he had worn the night he was seized. Miles didnt say any words, he merely grumbled nonsense. Elmira embraced him. Her petition for Miles to be placed under house arrest had been granted.

—Come inside, my dear Miles. Everything will be alright. I wont allow that snake, Ambrose, to hurt you anymore. He's going to pay for what he's done to this family. I promise you.

Freedmen had begun building cabins on her property, which had been divided amongst them. There was a rapping against her front doors. Once again, several of her former house slaves stood on the porch and stared back at her.

—We were hoping we could work for you again? asked one of them.

—Why would you come back here?

—Of course, we all miss our mistress.

Elmira raised an eyebrow and they read her skepticism.

—There aint any jobs.

—I am willing to take you back, even though you left me in my moment of need, but I can only pay you a month from now. Times are tough, you understand.

The women gave a mutual nod of resignation.

—At your service, mistress.

—Excellent. Now clean up this mess.

Soon, the mansion was sparkling clean. The freedmen occupying the plantation grounds agreed to repair the damage inside for a modest amount of coin. She also had them bring the furniture she had ordered in Savannah. And now that the city port was open once more, she was able to order more furnishings from Europe. Her new dining room table was divine. She was sure Miles would love it. Elmira hung several of her new watercolor paintings of roses throughout the house. It was the first time her art had ever been displayed so unapologetically in the open.

It was another sunny afternoon as she wheeled her husband to the dinner table. A servant brought a tray full of food. Elmira sat beside her husband and spooned soup into Miles' mouth as she caressed his cheek. He had cleaned up nicely, with a fresh bath and a shave, but he seemed oblivious of his surroundings. She wasnt sure if he realized he was home or not. It didnt matter to her. She rather liked her husband in his current state. Before, Miles had never bothered to acknowledge her importance to him or her contributions to the family. He'd never uttered a single word of affection since they'd been married. His independence was her solitude. Now, she finally had his undivided attention he was completely dependent on her. Elmira shoved the empty soup bowl into a waiting servant's hand and then cracked open a book. She read it aloud to Miles. Every few pages, she'd look up and smile at her beloved as he grunted and stared off blankly into space.

Elmira kissed Miles' forehead. She went upstairs and dug through what was left of her wardrobe. She took off her black clothes and put on a flowing crimson dress and curled her black hair. Elmira held up a new silver hand mirror as she applied her makeup.

Miles' condition was steadily improving. He had begun using simple sentences again, although he was still confined to a wheelchair and probably would be for life. He'd also begun to lean away from her caresses and attempted to wheel away when she tried to have a conversation with him.

She sat on the bench in the shade of Liberty Square. Soldiers in blue continued to mill about in Savannah. She gritted her teeth when she saw mayoral posters for Ambrose de Bellomonte nailed to the trees, tarnishing the lovely scenery around her. Former Confederate General Willard had tipped her off regarding some rumors surrounding Ambrose. The old general had suggested she enquire with officers from Sherman's army about the so-called rumors.

A Federal officer sat next to her. He lit his pipe, took a few puffs, and read a pamphlet. Elmira fumbled with her purse full of gold double eagles and dropped it between the two of them. It easily contained a workingman's three-year salary. Elmira held up her hands in mock surprise.

—Oops. I'm so careless.

The Federal officer peered over the edge of his pamphlet at the purse and then resumed his reading.

—It's true. He's in league with Sherman. They were close before the war, he said.

He took a deep puff of his pipe and didnt take his eyes off his reading material as he spoke. Elmira held a small mirror and dusted her face with powder as she spoke.

—How is he in league with Sherman?

—He knew he was fighting a losing battle. He agreed to provide intelligence and surrender his forces at the predetermined time in exchange for a secret pardon and protection of his property.

—The bastard.

—Indeed.

—I need proof.

The officer dropped a large brown envelope tied shut with a twine next to the coin purse. They both reached down. The officer took the coin purse while Elmira took the envelope. After the officer put the coin purse in his pocket, he removed his pocket watch. He flicked open the cover and checked the time.

—Look at the time. I must get going.

The officer stood and tipped his hat toward Elmira. She bid him good day and he departed. She opened the envelope and sifted through the documents. Her hands shook with rage as she read several pieces of correspondence between de Bellomonte and Sherman. Then she found proof of what she already knew. It was Ambrose's signed order that executed her son.

Many weeks had passed, and while Miles remained a little more forgetful than he used to be, he had recovered most of his capacities. It was morning as he ate his breakfast and read a newspaper. Elmira leaned in to kiss him. Miles leaned away. She cast her eyes toward the floor. However, she refused to feel sad, and her eyes perked back up with renewed excitement.

—Darling, dont you want to ask how I managed to free you?

Miles shrugged and grunted. Elmira scooted closer to her husband and placed a hand on his shoulder. He brushed it aside. He turned and looked at one of her rose paintings on the wall.

—Keep that tripe in your studio where it belongs.

As Elmira sipped her coffee, she caught a glimpse of her sad reflection before circular waves began to appear in her drink. She wiped her watering eyes and cleared her throat.

—Do you like the new furniture? she asked.

Miles rapped his knuckles against the dining room table.

—This is cherry. Our last table was Cuban mahogany.

Elmira kept her eyes cast downward toward her plate. Miles didnt even bother to glance at her as he turned the page of his newspaper.

—Miles, what happened inside the prison?

—I dont remember.

Elmira struggled to bury a dark thought that crept forward. She knew she should feel happy about her husband's unexpected recovery, but as much as she hated herself for the thought, she realized she missed him the way he was.

Miles wheeled over to the window and peered outside.

—When this war is over and the Yankees allow us to have elections again, I will run for governor.

—You? You helped start a war against the Union. They'll never allow you to run. You're lucky they didnt hang you in front of a baying mob.

—I have the support of the people.

—You're delusional.

His hand trembled. Spit foamed up in the corners of his mouth like it always did when he was furious. He swung his open palm down toward her face. Before it could make contact, she seized his wrist. He tried to pull his hand free, but she would not let go. He was too frail and damaged to overpower her. He balled his free hand up in a fist. Her eyes met with his, daring him to do it.

—Now it is I who is stronger.

—Know your place, woman.

There was panic in his voice and his eyes were wide with disbelief. He looked to the nearby servants, who refused to look at him and quietly left the room. His eyes darted around the perimeter of the room in a futile search for allies. Elmira leaned in close.

—My place? My place is as mistress of this plantation. It was I who petitioned on your behalf and freed you from prison, and it was I who restored Beaumont Hall. I expect— No, I demand that you show your dutiful wife some gratitude for once.

She flung his withered arm free from her grasp and stood over him, her eyes blazing. All Miles could do was cower before her.

Two days later, her servant called her to the front door. She was greeted by a tall, skeletal-looking man with dark deep-set eyes and hollowed cheeks.

—Greetings, Mrs. Beaumont. May I meet with you outside, please?

Elmira rolled her eyes and followed the man outside. Once she crossed the threshold of the door, two men in white uniforms grabbed her arms. The gaunt man tilted his head toward the open doors of a waiting paddy wagon. The men in white forced Elmira inside.

Through the bars of the wagon, she could make out the silhouette of a tall stone building atop a misty hill. Its ornate spirals and turrets speared into the dreary sky. As the stone building grew closer, Elmira read the wrought iron letters above the gate: *SAVANNAH INSANE ASYLUM.*

She was pulled from the paddy wagon. She kicked and shouted commands as she was dragged under the pointed stone arch of the intimidating doorway.

—Let me go. Do you know who I am?

When her protests went unheard, she resorted to screaming. She bit one of the orderlies' hands. The man responded by grabbing a handful of her black hair and pulling it until her jaw relaxed its grip. The male orderlies pushed her into an uncomfortable wooden chair. They stood before her with their muscular arms crossed. An unsmiling woman with thinning hair and a large, fleshy mole on her cheek tossed a stack of papers into her lap.

—Fill those out, barked the woman.

Black tears stained with eyeliner dripped onto the papers. Elmira tried not to give them the satisfaction, but her emotions had gotten the better of her. The pen in her hand trembled as she filled out the forms. She handed them to the orderly, who directed her to a small room with cracked plaster walls. It smelled stale. A single lamp flickered on an old oak desk inside. Elmira hesitated at the threshold. She didnt want to step inside. The orderly gave her a push, stepped in with her, and slammed the door behind them.

—Take off your clothes, said the orderly.

—Excuse me?

—Lady, I aint got all day. We cant have anyone bringin in contraband.

—I most certainly will not. Why am I here? I have done no wrong. This is pretrial punishment. I demand my attorney.

The guard rolled her eyes and opened the door to shout into the hall.

—Edna? Assistance, now.

Another female orderly nearly thrice Elmira's weight and with twice as many chins entered the room.

—Clothes off, barked Edna.

—I am Elmira Beaumont. My husband was a congressman and my son a war hero. I am a property owner and I have rights.

The female orderlies slammed Elmira against the wall. Plaster pieces crumbled into her hair. The smaller orderly pressed her forearm against Elmira's neck. Her throat closed shut. Only when the room began to fade to black did that orderly release the pressure. Elmira gasped for air.

—Should have cooperated.

A blade appeared in Edna's hand. Elmira tried to fight back. She pushed and screamed. Edna sliced through the shoulder straps of her dress and pulled it down to her ankles. Her undergarments followed. The greasy hands of the orderly ran up and down her body. She shrieked when the orderly jammed a chubby finger inside her. When Elmira thought she was finished, she did so again, this time in a different orifice. Edna smiled, revealing a missing front tooth, and slapped Elmira's backside.

—No contraband.

The other orderly let Elmira go. She huddled up into a ball and sobbed upon the moist floor. They tossed a ratty gray asylum gown down beside her feet.

Chapter 34

EMMA

1865, Georgia

Grace held Emma's hair as she threw up into the toilet trough. When Emma caught a whiff of what was below, she vomited again. She only stopped when her stomach was empty. Grace wiped her mouth with a damp cloth and brushed her hair away from her face, then guided her toward her bunk.

—Did you eat some bad food? she asked.

—I just have been feeling tired lately.

Emma collapsed into her bed. Her shift would start in four hours and she needed to sleep. They had secured jobs as washer-women in Savannah. They lived in a crowded communal dorm and were entitled to stay there so long as they remained employed.

As soon as she fell asleep, it was time to wake up. A new day. Another fifteen hours. Emma wiped the sweat off her brow with the back of her hand. The inside of the washroom was hot and sticky from the blazing furnaces, which sat beneath copper boilers filled with laundry. Her wheelbarrow tipped over and all the firewood she had collected spilled out. The other laundresses didnt bat an eye. They were too busy with their own chores to acknowledge her plight.

The copper boilers' appetite for firewood was insatiable. By the time she had lugged firewood from one end of the building to the other, the logs were already consumed by the blaze and she would have to go back and get more.

—Quit wastin time. Get it under the boilers, barked her boss, Mr. Taylor.

She tossed the firewood back into the wheelbarrow and pushed it next to the boilers. Emma coughed from the thick smoke as she heaved the wood onto the hungry flames. Another woman stood on a platform above and stirred the clothes with a long wooden paddle as they boiled. The new girls were always assigned nonstop firewood duty.

With Grace's help, she had forwarded Isaiah her most recent address but hadnt gotten any letters from him. The thought that he might be among the thousands of nameless rotting in far-flung battlefields kept bothering her.

After the first seven hours of her shift were over, Emma stacked her plate high with food. She grabbed twice as many crackers as she would normally take. Grace sat down next to her. Emma stuffed as much as she could into her mouth within moments.

—Are you sure you should be eating all that? asked Grace.

—I'm hungry.

—You were throwing up all night.

—I'm just really hungry.

—Does anything else bother you?

Emma's eyes darted from side to side and she pointed to her breasts.

—They're sore.

—Are you…pregnant?

She choked on her food. Her eyes drifted to the floor as they began to well up. She ran out of the dining hall, placed her forearm against a tree, and buried her head into her elbow and told herself not to cry, it was no use. Grace touched her back.

Every day, after Emma finished her fifteen-hour shift, she left the laundry to read the casualty lists posted on a board downtown. One night her heart stopped for a moment when she came across one of the few names she could spell: Beaumont. She began to whimper but stopped herself. The first name was smudged and she tried to tell herself it was another Beaumont, that it couldnt be Isaiah. She repeated it to herself over and over again all the way back to her bunk.

She retired to her communal room and then spent the next hour removing wood splinters from her hands with a pair of rusty tweezers. After she was done, she wiped herself down with a wet rag and climbed into her bunk.

Emma stared blankly into the darkness, her eyes glazed over in deep thought. The boardinghouse was for company women only—single women. Once she gave birth, she would be fired. Mr. Taylor had his choice of displaced Southerners hungry for work.

How could she possibly provide for a child when she could barely take care of herself? It seemed like only yesterday she was playing with little dolls made of bound straw and scraps of fabric. She didnt want to wake her friend, but she needed her. She shook Grace's shoulder and the woman's heavy lids opened.

—What should I do?

—You have to decide whether you want to keep the baby or not.

—Or not?

—There is an elixir you can get from the apothecary. If you drink it, then you wont be pregnant anymore. You wouldnt be the first laundress here to drink it. Even I have drank it.

—You were pregnant?

Before she could squeeze an answer out of Grace, her friend was sound asleep again. Emma wrung her hands. How could she raise a child alone? If only Isaiah was alive, she could have the baby. It wouldnt be easy, but they'd have each other. Was he really dead? She pushed the painful thoughts of happiness out of her mind. Here there were no dreams, only the aches and pains of her labor and the constant reminder of how things were and not how they could have been. She shook Grace awake once more. Her friend opened her eyes halfway.

—I want to buy the elixir.

Graced nodded and fell back asleep.

It was Sunday. Her only day off. Grace handed her a paper bag. The sparkle in Grace's light brown eyes was no longer there. It was the first time she had behaved in such a somber fashion.

—It's painless, she promised.

Emma took the bag and locked herself in a closet full of cleaning supplies. It was the only privacy she could find in the boardinghouse. Inside, the rusty-capped glasses of chemicals caught the light of a yellow candleflame. Opening the bag, she pulled out a glass vial that contained a cloudy liquid. With a twist, she snapped off the top of the vial. The smell of minty pennyroyal mingled with the harsh scent of an unknown chemical, rising from the open bottle. She gagged as the odor filled her nostrils. Her hand quivered as she brought the vial to her mouth. One sip and all her worries would be gone. She pressed the cold glass against her lips. She held it there for several seconds as her eyes welled up.

Why did Isaiah have to die? They were going to spend their days together and get a home of their own. Enough thinking. She resolved to swallow the liquid and be done with it. Her hand refused to move. Her lips would not comply. Emma's breaths became shallow and erratic. Her heartbeat quickened as a thousand thoughts went through her mind. One of those thoughts made her heart rise up inside her chest.

The only thing left of Isaiah is inside me.

Isaiah lived within her, and at this very moment she was about to snuff that out. Emma lowered the vial. A roaring flame filled her soul. It was an instinct, a primal power. She held the concoction in her trembling hand for several moments, gazing at the instrument of her freedom. Then she threw it against the wall. It shattered. It left a thick trail of liquid that trickled down the rough brick wall. It was love that had given her a baby, and love couldnt be a mistake. Her unborn child was now the only thing left for her.

Emma opened the closet door. Isaiah lived through that child. A child she would offer everything her soul had to give. An immense weight lifted off her shoulders. Emma realized she no longer had to live for herself. Now she would live for her child, or die if she must. The clucking rumors of the other women and the impending loss of her job now seemed to matter little in comparison. Emma had found her truth. She found Grace standing outside, holding her wrist.

—I didnt do it.

Grace embraced her.

Emma was elated to be relieved of firewood duty. Now she had to empty and fill the boilers with fresh water. She would heave out buckets of dirty water from the boilers and dump them outside. and then carry buckets of fresh water back. The hardest part wasnt carrying the water but climbing the rickety steps that led to the boilers.

It had taken quite some time, but she had filled all the boilers with water. Now she was carrying her last heavy bucket of water to the final boiler when she slipped. She rolled down the steps and crashed into a pile of firewood. The filthy water of the boiler soaked her.

Emma wrung out her skirt while Grace filled her buckets for her.

—Get back to work, Grace. She's a big girl and can help herself. Now get, said Mr. Taylor.

Grace flashed her contagious smile. It was all Emma needed to get through the day. She spent the rest of the day bent over a basin full of gray water, scrubbing clothes against a washboard. Her hands were soon raw. She hated bleaching the most. The ammonia burned her fingers when they touched the stinky, urine-based concoction used to bleach clothes. Mr. Taylor picked up a soggy garment.

—You scrubbed too hard and ruined this dress.

—It was already like that, Emma retorted.

—I'm goin to take it out of your pay.

Before she could respond, Mr. Taylor had turned around and begun berating one of the other girls. Grace whispered to her.

—Mr. Taylor is brainless and ugly as a toad. God must have taken the day off when he was born.

Emma laughed.

—Your insults are gettin better.

—It's not an insult. It's an honest description.

—It's for the best. Giving him a brain would be too cruel.

Laughter was the only medicine that kept her mind off Isaiah's fate. The girls' serious expressions returned when Mr. Taylor approached to check up on them. As soon as he walked away, they burst back out into laughter. Grace's cheerfulness seemed inextinguishable by the harsh winds of life.

Months went by. In the middle of one endless week, Emma was scrubbing a faded blue shirt against her washboard. Although her hands hurt and her knees were sore, she had a feeling of comfort. Grace was working at the basin beside to her.

Mr. Taylor walked up and eyeballed her. Usually when he did that he was fishing for an excuse to dock pay. He pointed at her waistline.

—Is there a problem there?

Emma froze. She and Grace had sworn to keep her pregnancy a secret for as long as they could. She had even made larger, looser clothing to try to hide her growing bump. Thus far she had managed to hide her protruding stomach, but Mr. Taylor's eye was too sharp. Grace stood in front of Emma.

—Mr. Taylor, she's just a fatty, that's all. Cant stop stuffin her face.

—Girl, I dont care what you do away from this place. Once that thing comes out, you cant stay here.

Mr. Taylor walked away and proceeded to dock the pay of the new girls who were loading wood under the copper boilers. Apparently, their wheelbarrows of firewood werent full enough. Emma hung up the faded blue shirt and pulled another from the heap of laundry next to her. As she scrubbed, drops fell from her eyes and formed tiny circular waves in the murky water.

Emma and Grace and several other washerwomen huddled over a newspaper. General Lee had surrendered. The war was over now, but she didnt feel excited, for she had heard nothing from Isaiah. That is, aside from a name in a newspaper that she prayed wasnt his.

With each passing day, her stomach grew a little larger. Mr. Taylor kept a close eye on her, his eyes almost pleading for her to slow down so that he could replace her sooner. She worked even harder.

Almost a week passed. Emma was walking across the street to buy some fabric to patch her dress when she saw that a crowd had gathered around a boy. A paper boy. She joined the throng and heard someone say the news aloud: Lincoln had been shot.

Chapter 35

ISAIAH

1865, South Carolina

To his surprise, none of the deserters had been execut-ed. He didnt know if they were left alive out of mercy or because they were more useful as laborers. In any case, deserters and drunkards made up the majority of his company in the prison camp.

He and the other prisoners finished digging a hole. It was so large it looked as if a fireball from the heavens had torn a great gaping crater into the face of the earth. They had been at it all day. When they were done, he and his fellow prisoners began trying to crawl out of the hole. Such seemingly simple tasks were exac-erbated by the twenty-four-pound iron ball Isaiah had to pick up and carry around with him. The guards stood around the edge of the hole with their arms crossed and watched with amusement as the prisoners held their iron balls and struggled to climb out.

Their feet often slipped on the loose earth and slid back down the steep edges. Isaiah was the first to make it, after four attempts.

—Hurry up, Beaumont, shouted a guard.

He went to a row of wheelbarrows and placed his iron ball inside. He and the other prisoners wheeled over to hospital tents. The terrible moans emanating from within made his stomach lurch and the smell of rotten flesh destroyed his appetite. He picked up amputated arms and legs and carefully placed them in his wheelbarrow, atop his ball. Isaiah wheeled his macabre payload to the pit and dumped the limbs inside. Then he went back and repeated the process.

As he pushed the wheelbarrow toward the pit once more, he tripped over his chain. He fell on his face and the wheelbarrow tipped over and his iron ball and the limbs spilled out. He stood and tried to lift his ball. It slipped out of his hand. He used some nearby leaves to wipe the wet surface and then was able to get a good grip. He picked up the limbs and put them back in the wheelbarrow. When he reached the pit, he tossed them inside. It was just another Monday.

Isaiah stood before a soldier who was standing sentry outside the prisoners' tents. He asked if he could write a letter. Of course, neither his mother nor his wife could read, so he hoped to send it by way of the church so the preacher would read it to them.

—No. You cant write a letter. Write when you get out, said the guard.

Every time they rotated guards, he'd ask the new one in the hopes that one of them would show mercy, yet every time he was denied. He understood what was going on in their minds. As far as they were concerned, he was the scum of the earth. They didnt care about the circumstances of his imprisonment. The guards probably thought he was a deserter, a traitor, and Lucifer himself all rolled into one.

Isaiah wasnt quite sure how much of his sentence had passed. He only knew it was suppertime for the prisoners. A young soldier, a fresh-faced corporal, handed him his dinner in a dented tin bowl. He couldnt have been older than seventeen. Isaiah thanked the guard and reached out to take it. Then the guard dumped the contents into the trampled mud before him and then dropped the bowl.

—You dont deserve to eat like a man, so eat like a pig.

What could he do? If he didnt eat, he would grow weak and get disease and die. He wouldnt see Emma again. If it wasnt for her, he figured he'd simply refuse to eat and let the night take him. He got on his knees and picked up the boiled potatoes and pieces of stale bread caked in mud and ate them.

Isaiah knew the innocent-looking boys often had the biggest penchant for cruelty. Isaiah received special attention in their desire to inflict suffering. Everyone at the camp, soldier and prisoner alike, knew he was reputed to have saved a woman from rape at great cost. It had become a sort of lore amongst the unit. Most of the other prisoners and even a few of the guards admired him for it.

Isaiah understood all too well that they couldnt allow themselves to believe that they might be maltreating not only an innocent man, but one who had a shred of integrity as well. The thought probably horrified them. Far more comforting to think that he deserved to be in his current situation, to dismiss the heroic stories surrounding him as mere lies. It was like putting a hood on a man condemned to die. It was for the executioner's sake, not the condemned's. It was so they didnt have the opportunity to look past the condemned's eyes and into their soul. Such a thing could cause a lifelong shudder in even the hardest of hearts.

Today was not unlike any other day. As he spit out the little rocks and pieces of grit from his mud-caked food, the guard gave him a sharp kick in the side.

—I know you were the one who tried to rape the girl.

Isaiah said nothing and continued picking bits of his bread out of the mud. This annoyed the young guard, who was clearly hoping to get a rise out of him. He smashed the last of the chopped potatoes with his boot.

—So do you admit it?

Isaiah stood and stared directly into the guard's eyes. That offended the young corporal greatly. The chatter of the prison camp gave way to silence. A few curious guards and soldiers passing by paused and meandered closer to watch the commotion. Isaiah said nothing.

—Answer me.

The youth revealed a strap of leather. Isaiah wasnt sure that it was something officially sanctioned by the army, but the guards were expected to keep order, and so long as that was done, no questions were asked.

He said nothing. His eyes teared up something fierce after the first blow of the leather strap fell across his nose. His left eye was blotted out with another blow and he felt warm blood drizzle down the side of his neck after yet another struck his ear—it must have split open.

—Kneel, demanded the guard.

—I only kneel before God.

Isaiah lifted off his shirt and dropped it beside him. The layered webs of scar tissue on his back were now on display for all to see. The eyes of the young corporal before him widened with incredulity. Then he gritted his teeth and swung the leather strap down upon Isaiah. The leather made a clapping sound as it struck his bare torso. The strap fell across his shoulders, his chest, his face, and his arms. He merely stood there quietly and took the blows without flinching. This made the guard even angrier. The crowd grew larger.

Isaiah knew that fear was a form of power. He had known this most of his life. He stood unafraid and the guard doubled down on his efforts to impose dread upon him. As the leather strap fell upon his torso again and again, Isaiah felt a sense of peace. His pride seemed of no concern to him. He let everything go. Meanwhile, the corporal's face was flush and tears flowed from his eyes as he yelled obscenities and struck him again and again.

A lone prisoner stood up.

—Mercy, he yelled.

Another prisoner stood.

—Mercy, have mercy.

Within a few moments, all the inmates were on their feet. The silence of the camp gave way to the cries for mercy. Soon the cries were coming from the other end of the camp too. Now even the Federal soldiers watching the spectacle began to cry out. The ones who had been there the longest were the first to speak up. Isaiah figured they were tired of blood and suffering.

A first sergeant pushed through the crowd. He walked up to the corporal and yanked the leather strap from his hands and shoved him to the side. He aggressively motioned to another sentinel to take the corporal's place. The sulking young man was directed to guard another part of the camp. Then the first sergeant pointed to Isaiah.

—Stop causing trouble.

The prisoners and the soldiers erupted into applause. The first sergeant elbowed his way into the crowd of clapping onlookers. He looked over his shoulder at Isaiah and narrowed his eyes. Then he looked around at the still growing crowd.

—All of you, get back to work.

The first sergeant glanced at the food mashed into the mud and then left. A few moments later, he returned and shoved a tray of food into Isaiah's hands. Isaiah thanked the man, who stormed off. Everyone could hear him loudly berating the young corporal.

Isaiah wiped the rill of blood from his neck with his hand. He put his shirt back on and sat on a muddy log and ate his food. A fellow prisoner sat on the log beside him. The man looked from side to side and pulled out a beat-up canteen. He poured the contents into a tin cup and handed it to Isaiah.

He held the tin cup to his mouth, expecting water, but the pungent smell of whiskey filled his nostrils. The prisoner gave a broad smile, revealing seven teeth in total. Isaiah raised the tin cup and thanked the man for sharing his contraband with him. He drank it all in one gulp. The whiskey seemed to take the enamel off his teeth, but Lord knew he was grateful for it.

He lay back and let the fog take him.

Chapter 36

ELMIRA

1865, Georgia

Elmira stood in a long line of patients. They all wore the same clothes and shuffled aimlessly. Some moaned. Others wailed continuously. A few laughed. Their behavior was tolerated to some extent, but when they got too far out of line they were dragged away and locked in a special room.

—Patient 2821, step forward, said the orderly.

—I have a name, said Elmira.

—2821, you will speak when spoken to. Stand against that wall.

Elmira grudgingly did as ordered.

—Straighter. Stand straighter.

A flashbulb went off.

—Turn to the side.

Another flash. The orderly read from a clipboard.

—Special orders. Send 2821 to the room.

There was no light inside the padded room. The fabric walls smelled of urine and an indescribable must. The tile beneath her was cold and hard. She heard the muffled screams of a woman in the cell adjacent to hers. Elmira peered through the bars of her enclosure and saw a man wandering outside in the dank hallway. He wore a shirt but no pants and was having a conversation with his sister, who wasnt there. How was he out there while she was locked away? After what felt like an eternity, the heavy door slid open.

—Lunchtime, barked an orderly.

Elmira soon stood in a line as an oatmeal-like slop was ladled onto their wooden trays. She sat in a wooden dining room chair but quickly stood back up when she felt warm liquid against her backside.

—Disgusting.

She found another seat. The man eating across from her laughed hysterically. He'd take a bite of gruel and laugh again. It was almost more of a scream than a laugh. He didnt have a single tooth left in his mouth. Elmira took a small taste of her meal and gagged. The man across from her laughed.

Her eyes caught a woman's flowing hair, dark as night. The woman sat in the corner naked with her arms wrapped around her bony body. Her mouth was agape in a perpetual scream, yet only gurgling moans emanated from within. Elmira began to think the padded cell wasnt so bad after all. She caught a pair of bright blue ribbons in the corner of her eye.

A little girl in a spotless dress was sitting there upon a bench. Her dark brown pigtails graced an otherwise pale, round face. Only her amber eyes had any color at all. Elmira walked over to the girl and sat next to her.

—Why hello there. What's your name?

The girl didnt answer. She simply stared blankly at the wall.

—I didnt know they kept little ones in such a frightening place.

She said nothing. Elmira realized her awkward attempts to get through had failed.

—I'll be on my way then.

The little girl sharply turned her head. Her amber eyes locked onto Elmira's.

—Noah misses you, the girl whispered.

Elmira's eyes bulged and she held her hand against her heart. She got up and backed away, trapped all the while in that amber gaze. A hand seized her arm. She turned to the side. It was the orderly.

—Lunch is over. Time to get back in your room.

The little girl waved.

Elmira struggled to put the odor of urine and sweat emanating from the off-white padded walls out of her mind. The room was cold. So very cold. She huddled in a corner and brought her knees up to her chest. Her body wanted to sleep. Her mind couldnt. She rose from the corner and hammered her fist against her cell door.

—When am I going to meet the one who runs this awful establishment? The doctor?

The orderlies outside were conversing with one another. They briefly looked her way and then continued their conversation. Elmira hammered the door again.

—I wish to see the doctor at once.

One of the orderlies rolled her eyes and turned her back toward Elmira.

—What are they paying you worthless wretches for?

The orderlies gave a slight chuckle. Elmira's cell door slid open. One of the orderlies held her hands behind her back while the other grabbed her chin.

—You'll see the doctor when we say you'll see the doctor. The orderly shook a dark brown glass bottle. Open wide.

Elmira tried to turn away. What terrible concoction was in the bottle? The female orderly pressed her thick fingers into the sides of Elmira's cheeks, forcing her mouth open. She struggled but soon found the bitter liquid running down the back of her throat. The orderlies shoved her against the padded wall of her cell and slammed the door shut.

She wiped the yellowish substance off her chin and her chest. Elmira crawled to her chamber pot and stuck her finger down her throat in an attempt to puke out whatever poison they had given her. It was no use. She had already begun to feel dizzy. The walls began to close in around her.

She huddled back into the corner of the room with her knees against her chest. The walls pulsed in and out with every beat of her heart. The moans and wails of the other patients were drowned out by the beating. She was tired. Very tired. Part of her wanted to relax and forget the world existed. It wanted her to forget and submit. She began to see patterns in the walls. Emira squinted her eyes to sharpen her blurry vision. Faces. She recognized one of the faces.

—Noah, is that you?

She crawled to the other side and caressed the wall.

—No. Dont leave me.

Elmira kissed the wall and then lay on her side. She began to sob. The overwhelming urge to relax, to forget, seeped through her consciousness. There was a sense that all she needed to do was let the medicine take her.

—No. I wont forget. I'll never forget.

Elmira wasnt sure how much time had passed. Was it days, or weeks? The orderlies let the nonviolent patients pursue hobbies at least, and Elmira was given some materials to paint with. Naturally, she had to pull some strings and pay for them herself. She passed the time creating watercolor paintings in the large communal room.

As she was painting, she heard the ever-elusive Dr. Russel berating one of the orderlies about some linen that wasnt folded to his exacting specifications. He yelled at the young woman at the top of his lungs. The other orderlies in the room disappeared. Then Dr. Russel picked up the linens and tossed them to the filthy floor and commanded her to rewash them. After he disappeared down a hallway, Elmira put down her brush and walked over to the orderly. She proceeded to help pick up the linens as the woman tried to hold back her tears.

—Such a difficult job you have, said Elmira.

—I dont want any help, replied the sniffling orderly.

Elmira pretended that she didnt hear and continued picking up the linens. The orderly sobbed as she placed them in a basket.

—You know, Dr. Russel is cruel to me too, Elmira said.

—He's cruel to everyone.

—I have a letter I've been meaning to get out to my dear hus-band, but he refuses to send it.

—Sounds like something he'd do. No matter how hard I try, he's always demeaning.

—Ladies like us must stick together.

—But you're an asylum patient. You're a crazy person.

—Do you know who I am?

—Everyone knows who you are.

—Then you know I'm very rich and I might be able to help someone like yourself. If you help me. Perhaps you could send out my letter for me?

The orderly gave a mocking laugh. She reminded Elmira that she was committed against her will and had no power within the walls of the asylum. After putting the remaining linens in the basket, she began to walk off. Elmira grabbed the woman's forearm with a vise-like grip. The stunned orderly stopped and looked up at her.

—Send my letter and I'll see to it that you never have to work again.

The frightened woman pulled her arm free and ran off with her basket of soiled linen.

That night, Elmira's cell door slid open. A diminutive figure stood in the dark threshold, holding a single candle. As she stepped forward, Elmira made out the familiar features.

—Give me your letter.

She had one already prepared. Of course, it wasnt really going to Miles, it was going to her close friend, Judge Foster.

Elmira figured a week had passed when she was taken by both arms and led through the narrow corridors of the asylum. While the orderlies unlocked the barred door, Elmira saw her reflection in a mirror hanging on the wall. Her flesh had grown pallid. The skin around her eyes was dark. Her black hair had lost its shine and was brittle and unkempt. Worst of all was the ratty gray hospital gown they forced her to wear. The color just wouldnt do. She was led to another door.

—Dr. Russel will see you now.

Elmira entered a grand office. The gaunt man she had met earlier sat behind a sumptuous rosewood desk. The wall behind him was festooned with framed degrees, certificates, and all manner of awards. In the corner of the office, Elmira observed an upside down *VOTE FOR DE BELLOMONTE* sign behind the doctor's briefcase. Dr. Russel gestured to a wooden chair in front of the desk.

—Please have a seat, Mrs. Beaumont.

The cold chair sent a shiver up her spine as it touched her bare legs. They had been force-feeding her medicine every day. Everything was still a haze, even though Elmira took every opportunity to vomit as much of the substance out as possible.

—I demand to know why I'm here.

—You're in no position to demand anything, Mrs. Beaumont. Relax. We're just here to help you.

Elmira considered herself a quick judge of high-society types. She could tell that the doctor's condescension was only matched by his pretension. A man who took himself far too seriously. Elmira blinked hard. She tried to will away the effects of the medicine.

—Help? By locking me in a filthy room? By having your sloppy attendants run their disgusting hands all over my body and poison me? I would much appreciate it if you stopped giving me your so-called help.

—You shouldnt mock the generous people who are trying to take care of you.

—Why am I here?

—You're a very ill woman. We've gotten anonymous reports that you've not been well. When we interviewed a few of your servants, they said you had torn apart some walls to… Dr. Russel adjusted his monocle as he read a report. Speak to your dead son. Is that right?

Elmira held her tongue. She knew the only way out of her present circumstances was how well she used it. She took a deep breath.

—Of course I speak to him.

Elated, the doctor adjusted his monocle and held his pen up

to a notepad. —Really?

—Oh yes. Through prayer. It's the Christian thing to do.

—Why are you running off from your husband and cooping yourself up in a hotel?

—Run off? I would never do such a thing.

—Your husband said you were very angry with him. Your actions contradict your words.

—Like everyone else, we lost much in the war. Miles is still in bad health because of his brutal treatment by the Yankees. It's true, I was angry with him. He has these outbursts from time to time. From terrible memories, I suspect. He needs my help. Therefore, I must get back.

—Is that so? What about these reports about you tearing off all the wallpaper in your home?

—Is not liking wallpaper a sign of insanity, dear doctor?

The doctor gave a huff and threw down his notepad. He picked up a stack of the watercolors she had painted in the asylum and sifted through them.

—Flowers, yes?

—Yes.

—They're not very pretty flowers. Some of them are dark and others are decayed. In a few cases, you've painted only stems devoid of petals. Why not paint something pretty?

—Is life always pretty, Doctor?

—Disturbing images for a disturbed mind.

—Art, corrected Elmira.

—I dont believe a word out of your mouth, Mrs. Beaumont. I'm afraid you're going to have to stay here for quite some time, until you're willing to be honest with me. I'm here to help you. But in order to help you, you have to be truthful with me. That will be all for today.

—Wait. You're right. I wasnt being completely truthful with you.

The doctor picked up his notepad and smirked.

—I'm glad you've come to your senses. Continue.

—The truth is, if you dont let me out of here, I'll see to it that you and this entire squalid establishment are buried in trouble. I assure you I have friends in both very high and low, *very* low, places. I wont stop until I take everything from you.

The doctor gave a forced laugh.

—You have no power here, Mrs. Beaumont.

—Oh, but I do, and I have arranged for you to meet someone.

The gaunt doctor's face went from its natural gray hue to red. His lower jaw trembled as he snapped his pen in two with his thumb.

—Nurse. Get Mrs. Beaumont out of my sight.

She was dragged outside and into her cell.

The following afternoon, Elmira's door opened. The light was so bright she had to cover her eyes with her arm. After a few moments of adjustment, she made out a blurry figure in the doorway. She blinked a few times until the figure came into focus. It was Dr. Russel.

—I just spoke to your attorney and even to Judge Foster, of all people.

—Why, what a surprise.

—And one of my orderlies has just retired at an unusually young age.

—That is indeed unusual.

Dr. Russel spoke through clenched teeth.

—It has been strongly suggested to me, in more ways than

one, that you may have been institutionalized here wrongfully. I have also been strongly advised that I owe you an apology. So, my apologies.

Early the next morning, Elmira was shoved out of the asylum paddy wagon in front of her home. A servant ran out of the front doors toward her.

—Mistress, thank heavens you're safe. I was told you were locked away in the madhouse.

—Just visiting, said Elmira.

She entered her home barefoot. She still wore her ratty, urine-soaked asylum uniform. Her black hair was matted and wild. The first thing she noticed was that all her watercolor paintings were gone. As she entered the home, Miles' eyes widened and his mouth hung agape.

—You're back? How?

—You. You sent me, your dutiful wife, to that awful hell.

—You're just a poor pathetic creature in need of help, so I helped you.

—I know of your affairs, Miles. I've always known, and I'm afraid my patience for you has run out.

Her utterly calm and collected tone seemed to frighten him. He wheeled away to an adjacent room. Elmira pursued. Then he wheeled himself into his chambers and she heard the lock click on his door. She turned and went to Miles' study and sat at his desk. It was the ugliest piece of furniture in the house. Perhaps that was why the Yankees hadnt taken it.

From the chair she could gaze upward at the only remaining portrait painting of Noah. The rest had been burned in their bonfire. He stood proud in his uniform, though he wore a somber expression. With one brush of her arm, the items atop Miles' desk were cast to the floor. She flung open his desk drawers and dumped the contents as well. Then she flung the drawers against the wall. Most of them were empty.

There was a rustling sound in one of the drawers when she shook it. There was nothing inside. She shook it again. Again, she heard the noise. Something was definitely in there. At the very back of the drawer she found a small, finger-thick notch. She pulled on it to reveal a fake bottom. Inside the thin space was a collection of letters. She had long known that he had hidden his correspondence in the desk somewhere, but could never bring herself to seek it out and read it. Instead she had chosen ignorance over the pain of knowing.

She began reading. Her heart sank when she got to the third letter:

> *My dearest Miles,*
>
> *I do so hope you are well. Have you gotten rid of her yet? You have no need to be with that lunatic woman your parents implored you to marry. Her father's fortune is already yours for all intents and purposes. What are you waiting for? As you have told me so many times before, you hold no affection toward her. I know your son's death is a heavy burden upon your heart and I am here for your comfort. I anxiously await to read the good news.*
> *Love,*
> *Catherine*

Elmira unlocked Miles' chamber room door and kicked it open. He wheeled himself into the corner. She stepped toward him clutching the letter in her hand. In a futile attempt to escape, he climbed out of his wheelchair. Elmira followed him at a leisurely pace as he tried to crawl away.

—There are going to be some changes, my dear Miles.

Chapter 37

EMMA

1865, Georgia

Emma struggled to keep up. Mr. Taylor took every opportunity to dock her pay to the point where she was almost
working for free. It was hard to lean over the wash basin
with the added weight of her growing baby. She ignored her ach-
ing back and swollen ankles. Her body commanded her to rest,
but she disobeyed. She needed the money. Mr. Taylor stood over
her as she worked, his eyes never leaving her.

—Hurry up, Emma. Those clothes aint going to wash
themselves.

That was the third time he had chastised her that morning.
The larger her belly grew, the harder Mr. Taylor pushed her.
Emma had told herself that if it was endurable, she had to endure
it, and she vowed to earn every scrap she could. After Mr. Taylor
left, Grace rushed over and helped her fold the clothes.

Later that day, Emma hung the garments on the clothesline. It was very important to take down the clotheslines at night and reinstall them in the morning lest the soot from the nearby factory stain the thin rope. Emma remembered how one girl had forgotten to do so. She'd ruined the clothes of twelve separate customers. Mr. Taylor had fired the girl and kept her entire paycheck for himself.

Girls were always coming and going. Sometimes they were fired. Most quit.

Mostly, Emma scrubbed officers' uniforms. The Federal army's presence was a boon for business. Emma's hands had turned the same gray color as the water. Most of the other laundresses assumed she was a war widow and took pity on her, others simply didnt care. However, a few sought to amuse themselves at her expense. Amelia was one such woman.

Amelia's breath reeked something fierce. Every time she opened her mouth to talk, Emma held her breath. Rumor had it that she had relations with Mr. Taylor, relations in his office, relations in the supply closet, relations in the alleyway, but Emma considered that none of her business. Perhaps that was why the woman thought herself a queen. Amelia tapped Emma's shoulder.

—Who's the daddy, and how much did he pay you?

Emma was too tired to fight back. Even standing and walking proved to be exhausting. No matter what abuse she faced, she was determined to hold true to herself. Others could not damage her soul. She ignored the woman as she hung up her pile of clothes. Amelia yanked it out of her hand and tossed it on the filthy floor. Now she'd have to rewash it.

—I asked you a question.

Grace picked up a bucket of filthy water. Amelia shrieked as Grace poured it over her head. She attempted to retaliate but slipped on the wet floor and fell against a clothesline, bringing all the hanging laundry down with her. Mr. Taylor walked over.

—Amelia, quit playing around. Emma, you have caused too much trouble, you're fired.

—But I didnt do anything, she insisted.

—I pushed her in, said Grace.

—Get out, now.

Emma climbed to her feet and waddled toward the doorway, holding her stomach. The other women kept their lips tight and their eyes on their wash basins. None of them dared upset Mr. Taylor. They all feared being cut loose. Grace walked after Emma.

—Grace, you can stay. You're a good worker, said Mr. Taylor.

She ignored him and continued to walk away. His tune changed as they walked closer to the doorway.

—I will give you a raise.

Grace held open the door. Emma's eyes met with those of a young woman, about her age, clutching a handbag. Behind her stood another woman and another and another. The line of people seeking employment spilled over into the street. Grace looked to Emma and took her hand and slammed the door shut behind them.

As they walked away from the laundry, a wave of contractions overcame Emma. She just about collapsed on the sidewalk. They didnt have time to make it to Grace's family in the countryside. She stumbled into an alleyway. The pain was such that she was no longer able to stand on her feet.

Night soon fell upon them. Emma could see her breath. She rubbed her arms under a lean-to Grace had fashioned from scrap wood covered with layers of burlap before leaving to search for help. Her friend returned empty-handed. It seemed the war had drained the city of every resource and sucked out every ounce of compassion. The churches overflowed with destitute people with outstretched hands seeking anything the ministers could spare, be it food or even a glimmer of hope. Emma closed her eyes.

A warm hand wrapped around hers. She turned her head and saw two eyes, a haunting shade of blue, staring back at her—Isaiah. He smiled and wrapped his arm around her. A dark thought interrupted her happiness.

—Isaiah, you're dead.

He gave a broad smile. His teeth came into view. They were yellow, and several were missing. Her chest rose and fell faster than before. Maggots spilled out of his eye sockets. The gray flesh from his face began falling off in chunks. She backed up and bumped into a brick wall. He gave a wicked grin and punched her hard in the stomach.

Emma's eyes opened. She screamed as she clutched her belly. Cold rain drizzled through the leaky roof of the lean-to and onto her head. Grace rose from her makeshift bed and patted her forehead with a rag.

Hours later, the silence of the alley was filled with the sharp wail of an infant. Emma held the baby against her sweaty chest. Grace brushed Emma's sticky hair away from her face.

—It's a boy, said Grace.

Emma kissed the top of the infant's head. She gazed into her son's trusting eyes. He hadnt asked to be born into the cold, unforgiving world. She couldnt promise him comfort or wealth. She could only promise that she'd work her fingers to the bone to give him his chance at life.

She named him Isaiah James Beaumont.

Grace returned early the next morning. She wore a new white and tangerine dress and carried two boxes and grinned as she tore one of them open. Grace tossed the lid aside and pulled out a new dress.

—I got it for you, Emma.

Emma was surprised to see such extravagance. The only dresses she had owned were the ones she'd made. To buy such a thing she could craft herself seemed like a wasteful luxury.

—Grace, you shouldnt steal such things.

—Steal? I got a job as a hostess.

Emma loved the dress, but she couldnt bring herself to tell Grace lest her friend decide to keep the expensive garment. After all, she was happy with the dress she had. It just needed some patching and a deep cleaning.

—You shouldnt waste your money.

—Your clothes are worn out, and besides, they've still got baby gunk all over them. Try it on.

Her eyes widened as Grace held out the blue dress. Emma had only worn white, gray, or yellow dresses made of secondhand fabric. She reached for the dress and then pulled her hand back slightly, almost afraid her hand would pass through it and then she'd wake up disappointed.

It was real. The fabric was soft to the touch. Then there was the color. A brilliant, deep blue. She had never held a fabric so richly dyed. It was something she had only watched the mistresses and well-to-do freewomen wear from a distance now she held such luxury in her own hands.

She slipped out of her ragged dress and slipped into the dark blue dress. It was soft against her skin and fit perfectly. For a moment, she no longer felt dirty or impoverished.

Grace held out a small hand mirror. When Emma caught her reflection, she broke down. She hardly recognized the woman in fine clothes looking back at her. Never had she dared to imagine such affluence. She wiped her eyes and the moment passed. She had to push such dangerous thoughts aside. The dream was over and Emma began to lift the dress off, but Grace grabbed her wrist.

—You need to wear it. I've found us a place to live and we need to look presentable.

A landlord with a permanent scowl paused to light his pipe before he turned his key. The door to apartment No. 6 creaked open. They stepped inside. A cast-iron stove took up much of the space. The walls were of crumbling plaster and the single window had a crack in the pane. Emma peered out.

—Do you like it? asked Grace.

—I love it, but it's just a dream, Grace.

The old landlord grumbled something to Grace between puffs of his pipe and tossed a set of keys to her. He disappeared down the hallway.

—It's ours.

—How?

—I told you. I got a good job. Now we can both be spinsters together.

The apartment filled up with secondhand furniture. While Grace worked, Emma stayed in the apartment and cooked food, washed clothes, and ensured Grace kept her spending habits in check so that she saved enough for rent. Grace had a thing for nice clothes. It seemed that she brought home a new dress every week. What time Emma had left over, she spent hawking bakery goods and steamed yams on the nearby street corner—a basket in one hand and her baby in the other.

Emma began to wonder how Grace could afford to spend so much. Finally, one morning, she pretended to sleep as Grace rose from bed and did her hair. When the apartment door slammed shut, Emma quickly put her clothes on and put her baby in her back sling. She locked the door and followed her.

She tried to keep as much distance between them as possible. But then Grace disappeared in the crowd. Emma picked up her pace and caught a glimpse of her tangerine dress fluttering between the throngs of people as she entered a modest three-story brick building. Its windows glowed red from oil lamps.

Grace reappeared to sit on a second-floor windowsill. A long line of Federal soldiers wrapped around the side of the building. It was the most infamous building in town: the Lion's Den, the largest brothel in the city. Guilt came over her as she watched Grace kiss a man before she closed the drapes of her window. Emma returned home. She removed her blue dress and threw it to the ground. She collapsed onto the floor and sobbed.

That evening, Grace returned with her usual infectious smile. Emma wanted to smile back, but she couldnt bring herself to do it. She debated how she would let her friend know she had discovered her secret. Emma decided to simply tell her directly and hope for the best.

—I know you work at the Lion's Den.

Grace's smile faded.

—You followed me?

—You dont have to work there. We dont need to live in such a nice place.

—I make more in one day at the Lion's Den than we both made in two weeks at the laundry.

—I'll find a better job. You dont have to do such work.

—There's not enough work here.

She knew Grace was right. Everyone was out of work, and now that the discharged Confederate soldiers were returning home, there would be even less. As Elmira had predicted, Special Field Order No. 15 was rescinded by President Johnson—forty acres and a mule was stillborn. Grace wiped her face with the back of her hand.

—I know what we can do.

—What?

—Move.

—To where?

Grace's eyes lit up and her usual smile returned.

—Up north.

Emma remembered what her father had said. They were going to go north, to the Free States. Now she had a chance to make her father's dream come true.

Emma wrung her hands. The thought of moving both frightened and excited her. The war was over and Isaiah was gone. Part of her wanted to cling to the hope that he was still part of the occupying army, that he just hadnt been discharged yet. Emma had sent numerous letters and always updated her address as they moved around in the hopes that Isaiah would find her easily. Yet she never got a reply back. Not for months. She had to choose between the immediate needs of her son and sitting and waiting for a ghost while starving. Emma looked down at little Isaiah.

—Let's go.

It was hard, but Emma and Grace managed to save enough money for their move north. Neither of them knew what to suspect in the big city, so they simply saved as much as they could. Soon it was time to leave.

Emma walked under the avenue of oaks that led to Beaumont Hall. The place was much quieter than it had been in the past. There were sharecroppers working the land, but they were far fewer in number than the slaves who had once occupied it. The house and the cabins looked more or less as they had before the war, and the plantation still seemed to exude a gravity that pulled her toward it. However, things felt different.

Emma knocked on Mary's door. It opened. Mary seemed indifferent to her sudden appearance and merely grunted hello. She asked Mary if she had gotten any word from Isaiah. Emma feared that he had likely died in the war.

Mary looked to the floor and shook her head. Emma held out her baby and told Mary that it was her grandson. The woman looked at the baby stone-faced for a long time before clearing her throat.

—Looks like him, she said.

She resumed stirring her pot full of stew. Emma thought she saw tears rolling down the cheeks of the woman's weathered face, but she couldnt tell inside the dark cabin. Emma told her she had to leave, to go north. She implored Mary to come with her, and promised Mary that she would find a way to look over her.

Mary refused.

Emma didnt understand. Why would the woman wish to stay in an awful place that had taken a beautiful and energetic young woman, broken her, and turned her into the creature she now was? Emma thought it madness. But Mary was a freewoman and she had to respect her wishes. She left a basket of goods and bid her farewell.

Emma was back in Savannah. She knocked on a door. A woman with a steely expression cracked it open and peered out.

—Yes?

Emma explained that she was there to see the boy. The woman at the orphanage seemed unamused at this inconvenience but soon relented. The door widened and Emma found herself in the boy's arms. Her cheeks were wet by the time she let go.

The boy was taller and much plumper. His hair was neatly combed and he wore clean clothes. He said he worked as a newspaper boy and had learned to read and write. Emma told him that she was there to say goodbye. She would be leaving for the north in a few days.

—Dont leave. Isnt it nice here?

—It's a right pretty place alright, but I have to go. But maybe I'll stroll through Forsyth Park one last time, said Emma.

The boy wiped his face. He did his best to hold back his tears, as a young soldier should. They embraced a final time before Emma said farewell.

Chapter 38

ISAIAH

1866 South Carolina & Georgia

The iron clamp creaked open, revealing his raw and blood-tied ankle. The top of his foot had been swollen for months from the metal shackle shifting up and down upon his foot as he walked. Yet none of those annoyances bothered him. The guard took the ball and chain and placed it in the back of a wagon and turned to Isaiah.

—You're free to go, he said.

His legs felt as light as air. He stumbled as he tried to walk away, his feet unused to regular movement. He took several steps and then stopped, realizing he was penniless and didnt have any means of returning to Georgia aside from his own two feet. He was still in South Carolina, on the outskirts of the ruins of Columbia. As a prisoner, he had continued to do hard labor for the occupying Federal army known as Military District 2, which covered North and South Carolina.

He contemplated trying to find work so that he might buy a train ticket. Then he dismissed the idea. Despite the devastation around him, the jobs were being filled with returning Rebel veterans and freedmen and women. Still, he thought he would have as good a chance at getting work as anyone. The problem was that Emma didnt know if he was alive or dead. He couldnt afford a telegram and he figured he could get to Savannah faster than a letter. Still, he wrote one and sent it to her in case he got hung up on the way.

His legs had carried him across Georgia and South Carolina as part of Sherman's army, and they'd carry him back from whence he came. He ate the last meal he was entitled to and packed a knapsack full of discarded hardtack and salt pork and whatever other provisions he could acquire. Then he set out south toward Georgia.

He trudged over the wagon wheel-furrowed road through the landscape he had helped ravage. He walked past blackened piles of charred lumber, once barns and houses, that he'd passed on his way toward Savannah. He passed several covered wagons filled with families returning to the homes they had fled. He knew many of them would come home to their farms only to find ashes. Yet the birds sang and there were sprouts of green life in the mired fields.

That day, he walked until nightfall, then started a fire and set up camp in some woods off the side of the main road. He figured he could be back in Savannah in two, maybe three more days. He lay back and listened to the red wolves sing to the moon and closed his eyes.

There was a sharp prod against his belly. He felt it again. He opened his eyes and saw several silhouettes standing over him against the morning sun. Blinking hard, he made out the grizzled face of a bearded man pointing a rifle at him. Two younger men stood at his side. The bearded man jabbed him again with the rifle: a Pattern 1853 Enfield, a favorite among the Rebels. He spit a stream of tobacco-stained spit and spoke.

—Yer on my land.

—Apologies. I'll be on my way.

Isaiah tried to stand up. The man jabbed the rifle barrel hard into his shoulder.

—Hold it.

—I got nothin of value.

—Where'd you get that canteen?

Isaiah looked down at his canteen. He realized his stupidity. Its side was emblazoned with thick black letters that said *US*.

—I found it in the field.

—Pa, he looks like a Yankee to me, said one of the boys.

—That true, you a Yankee?

—I served with the South.

—What unit?

His mind raced as he tried to think of the opposing armies he had fought. He figured the man before him was fishing for an excuse to take out his misery on someone, for he was wearing Federal-issued boots he had likely stolen from a fallen soldier.

—Army of Tennessee. Under General Hood.

—I was in the Army of Tennessee, which brigade?

Isaiah hardly knew the individual brigades within the army he had served in let alone the opposing one. He was caught in a lie and the fellow before him had an itchy trigger finger.

Isaiah pointed toward the horizon.

—Yankee devils, he shouted.

The man and the boys gave perplexed expressions, but they turned and looked over their shoulders. Isaiah kicked the rifle aside and ran into the woods. A shot bellowed out behind him. Leaves crunched behind him as the trio pursued him. His ankle burned something fierce. He still wasnt used to normal movement. He zigzagged through the trees and found himself in a modest acreage with a burned-out cabin. He ran past the cabin and back into the woods.

—You better hope we dont catch you, a voice called from behind him.

Isaiah agreed.

He soon reached a rocky outcrop. There was no way other than up. He climbed. After he was about three-quarters of the way, he heard steel rubbing against steel. The grizzled man stood below him, calmly ramming down a ball into the barrel of his rifle while the two sons began climbing after him.

Isaiah reached the top and looked down and saw that the man was pointing the rifle at him. He stepped back from the ledge of the outcrop. Running to the other side, he saw a river below. There was nothing to hide behind, and something told Isaiah that the fellow wouldnt miss.

Isaiah looked at the man with the rifle and then looked again at the river below. A searing breeze cut along the supine ridge and passed over his sore, squalid body.

He jumped.

The shot followed.

The water felt like a thousand needles as he crashed into it. His lungs filled and he coughed as he struggled to keep his head above the surface. The whitewater pulled him downstream, down beneath the crashing waves, down toward death's door within the desolate cold waters of some destination where the remnants of his being would be ever forgotten. The cold water rocked him gently, asking him to close his eyes and forget. To forget about everything. Forget about his pains, his humiliations, and his dear Emma. No. He fought. He swung his arms with everything he had as he struggled to grab a branch or a rock or anything that would keep him from being pulled to God knows where.

He jammed his fingers into a bank of sand. With his other hand he pulled himself out of the river and stumbled forward until he collapsed against a large tree. He wasnt sure how far the river had taken him. He took off his boots and poured out the water.

He spent the rest of the day lying against a maple tree in the sun. His clothes hung from the low branches. His knapsack and canteen were gone and his body ached from hitting the water and crashing against protruding rocks in the river. He tried to get up to put his clothes on but slid back down the trunk of his tree. His mind wanted him to move, his body to rest.

Isaiah set out the following morning. His clothes were still damp and his boots made a squishing sound with every step. He knew he needed to get back on the main road, wherever it was. Yet the underbrush grew thick and slowed his progress. He had trouble seeing the sun from beneath the canopy of the forest, which made finding his bearings difficult.

Each step was harder than the last. He hadnt eaten and it was catching up to him. He could will away his discomfort, but he couldnt will away the weakness of his body. Still, he trudged forward through the woods. He feared if he sat down he might never stand up again.

Isaiah pushed some branches aside and saw furrowed mud. Never had he been so elated to see an ugly roadway in all his life. He stumbled onto the road and walked.

Night fell. The road was empty of traffic and passersby. He thought about sleeping. There were only trees around him, and aside from the road not a farmhouse or any other hint of civilization. The only company he had was a pack of red wolves that trailed him. They made no effort to hide their presence, yet they seemed skittish and would dart off into the woodland every time he stomped his foot and yelled. They were patient creatures.

His vision became blurry. One step in front of the other, he told himself. At least that was what he thought he was saying. The mumbled words coming from his lips didnt make sense. He weaved and stumbled from one side of the road to the other. He saw and heard a locomotive. It was just beyond the hill on the other side of the road. He stumbled up the hill and then down the hill. The train passed by. Isaiah and it disappeared into a fog.

He continued walking down the road. Footsteps approached from behind him. He turned and saw nothing but the darkness of night and the glowing copper eyes of his hungry, four-legged companions.

It was dawn. Isaiah clutched his side. The cramp shot an unusually fierce dose of pain up his spine. He stopped and bent over while squeezing his eyes tight. He tried to walk. His body refused. He sat in the middle of the road and rolled over onto his back. His heart thumped as he gazed upward at the black canvas above dotted with stars.

He awoke to a slap on the cheek.

—Are you alright? asked a voice.

Two blurry figures came into view. They stood over him and he figured the grizzled man and his bloodthirsty sons had found him. Instead, to his side was a covered wagon filled with two young boys and a little girl. They all gazed down at him with wide eyes. A man and woman stood over him.

Cold steel was pressed against his mouth. Water entered his throat as his head was propped up by the woman. They asked him what had happened. He tried to speak but his eyes rolled back in his head.

He awoke to the rattle of wagon wheels over uneven terrain. He had enough strength to sit up and he found himself in the back of a covered wagon. Three children and a woman sat behind him.

—Oh, thank heavens, said the woman.

She gave him some water and he drank it. Then she handed him an orange. When the juice hit his stomach, he could feel fresh energy pulsing through his veins. The woman must have been surprised at how fast he ate it, but she quickly handed him another. She asked what had happened. He explained he had been traveling south to Savannah and had fallen into a stream. When asked about his profession, he said he was a simple laborer.

The family was headed back to their farm not far from Savannah and said that he was welcome to ride along until then. They had planned on dropping him off at the nearest church or hospital.

The following day, he bid the family farewell. The children waved from the back of the wagon as it disappeared down the road. Isaiah had made it to Savannah. The last letter he had gotten from her said she was working as a washerwoman downtown.

When he arrived at the address Emma had given him, he got a cold reception and was told she had been fired.

The sunlight was fading. Isaiah stood in a long line at a soup kitchen. He got his bowl and sat under the shade of a sycamore and drank. He tried to sleep in the park but was told to move along by the law. He wandered out to the perimeter of the city and slept in the crumbling earthworks that surrounded it. In a way, it felt like home.

When he awoke, he continued to wander the city. He walked every street and asked every church if they had known of a woman named Emma Beaumont. He went to general stores and the city market. They all said no. A paper boy shoved a paper into his stomach.

—Would you like the news, mister?

—No thank you.

Isaiah gently pushed the newspaper back into the boy's hand. He went into the corner shop behind the boy and asked if they knew someone by the name of Emma Beaumont. They said no.

He hung his head and walked out of the store. He collapsed onto the curb and placed his head in his hands. He didnt know what to do. A feeling of dread and remorse came over him. He wasnt sure what his purpose was if he could not find Emma.

Isaiah felt a tapping on his shoulder.

—I know where she is, said the boy.

—You do?

—She's my friend. She said she's going to someplace up north.

—Up north?

—She's leaving tomorrow.

Isaiah jumped to his feet.

—Where is she?

—She said she was going to the park, the big one.

Isaiah thanked the boy and ran.

Chapter 39

ELMIRA

1866, Georgia

Elmira had arranged a special meeting with General Willard once night fell. For now, she sat next to her son's headstone and carved an inscription into the oak tree that shaded his grave. She had just finished carving the last letter when a man on horseback rode up and called out to her.

—Elmira, thank heavens. I came as soon as I heard you had been locked up.

She looked up. At first she couldnt make out the figure in the glare of the afternoon sun. He dismounted and stepped forward. It was Pierce. She rushed forward and embraced him and then proceeded to plant kisses on his cheeks. The few remaining servants watched, and even though her husband was still inside, she didnt care. They held each other for a long time. He looked at what she had carved in the tree and struggled to pronounce the words.

—What does it say? he asked.

—*Bella detesta matribus*. It's Latin for *war, the horror of mothers*.

A long silence from Pierce followed as he nodded in agreement with the phrase. Then he revealed a single white rose. He looked as if he was about to give it to her, but instead placed it atop her son's grave.

—You can speak Latin? he asked.

—And Greek, and French, and Italian, though my Russian needs work.

—You're the most remarkable woman I've ever met. I have something very important to ask you.

Pierce took both her hands into his own. She looked up at him with eagerness. To her surprise, the usual confidence in his eyes wasnt there.

—Anything, Pierce.

—Come with me. Leave this callous man who despises you so. While I only have a modest home, I'll give you any room you like as a studio, and you can hang your watercolors wherever you please. I promise to take care of you and to give you everything I'm able to provide. There's nothing here for you anymore. Please come with me.

Pierce's voice cracked several times as he spoke. Tears streamed down her face and she reached up and touched the side of his face.

—It would be a dream to live with you in your home. The size is no matter. Even if you only had a one-room cottage it would be most suitable. To be your everything and you mine, I've dreamt of it nearly every day, Pierce. I really have. How I've wished that I had been married to you and that you had been the father of my son.

—Then let us leave this place. Tonight.

Elmira gently pulled away. It took every ounce of strength she had to hold back her dreams, her selfish desire for happiness. She was a woman who kept her word and her promises, no matter what the cost, and she had made a promise to her son and to herself.

—I'm so very sorry, Pierce, but…I'm married to vengeance now.

Pierce shook his head as he pleaded with her not to do whatever she was planning to do. He told her of the cruelties he had witnessed during the war. He said at least they would have one another. Elmira listened to his every word and nodded in acknowledgment.

—I will consider what you've told me, but I cannot leave tonight. It has to be goodbye for now.

She walked up to him and held both his hands and then kissed him on the lips as the stunned servants averted their gaze.

—There are only two men in my life that I now love. One of them was my son. The other is you. Goodbye, Pierce.

Now it was Pierce who was wiping away tears. He mounted his horse and tipped his hat toward her. It was only after he disappeared down the avenue of oaks that she allowed herself to collapse on the grass below and sob.

The white moon rose steady against the violet star-blown sky. Beaumont Hall was unusually dark and quiet, for she had ordered all the servants to pack their things and leave. Elmira sat on her porch and poured herself a glass of blood-red wine. Lacrima Christi, a rare vintage she had been saving for a special moment. Indeed, it was the finest vintage in her cellar, aged thirteen years.

She folded the telegram she had received and placed it on the table before her, a response to her invitation. She had sent Ambrose the following letter several days prior:

> *Mr. Ambrose de Bellomonte,*
> *I have proof of your dealings with Sherman. I shall release it to the press unless our two families can come to an arrangement whereby we end this terrible feud that has dragged on for generations. Currently, the documents are held in trust with a confidant who shall release them if myself or my family are harmed.*
> *Most sincerely,*
> *Mrs. Elmira Beaumont*

Of course, she didnt mention that the documents showed that Ambrose was wholly responsible for her son's death. She kept that information to herself. The mosquitoes werent biting, for the air was too cold. She hesitated before taking a sip. She realized that her destiny was sealed in a box that she was compelled to open, to observe, and unleash the will of God. Elmira held her wine glass to her nose and inhaled deeply.

A lone man on horseback appeared under the avenue of oaks. Elmira took a very small sip of her wine. She savored the bitter tannins before swallowing. The horseman climbed down from his steed.

—Ambrose. It's so good of you to accept my invitation.

The lines on Ambrose's face were deeper than before.

—So, you wish to let bygones be bygones.

—Havent both our families suffered enough because of some silly feud?

Elmira invited him to sit in a white wicker chair on her porch. Miles' empty wheelchair was parked off to the side. Ambrose's eyes studied his surroundings before he cautiously accepted. He asked about the nature of the documents Elmira had.

She placed the papers on the little table between their wicker chairs. Ambrose snapped them up and sifted through them. His face grew ashen as he read. He gritted his teeth and then looked up at her with those cold blue marbles he had for eyes.

—Is this the only copy?

—There is only one more. Which can be yours, if we can come to an agreement.

Elmira poured wine into a crystal glass and pushed it toward him. He studied the glass for several moments, as if weighing his options, then slowly reached out and held the glass up.

—I suppose the big war is over now. Maybe we ought to end the small one.

—I would like that very much.

—Then it is agreed.

—Agreed, my dear Ambrose.

They raised their glasses and toasted to reconciliation. Then they both took a sip and placed their glasses down. Elmira told him she would have the papers delivered to Ambrose first thing in the morning. He seemed pleased with that.

—You are persistent, Mrs. Beaumont. I've fought Yankee generals who would have given up before you did. I'll give you that.

Ambrose was a fast drinker. Elmira figured war did that to a fellow. He was already on his third glass while she hadnt drank hardly any of hers. She only took very small sips. They talked about the importance of family mostly. She found that Ambrose wasnt much different than herself. He was utterly dedicated to furthering his family's status and reputation through any means necessary. Perhaps he had mellowed with age, or perhaps he was tired of bloodshed, but Elmira couldnt imagine having had such a conversation with him before the war.

—It's good wine, he said.

—The best.

Rarely during their conversation did Ambrose make eye contact with her. When he finished another glass, he rubbed his weathered cheeks and cast his eyes upward toward the purple sky.

—The death of your son, well, please know I did everything I could.

Elmira placed her hand atop Ambrose's. His cold gaze met with hers. She gave a gentle smile.

—I know. God knows.

—So, everything is behind us now?

—Ancient history.

—Good evening then, Madam Elmira.

Ambrose finished the rest of his wine in a single swig. Elmira tilted her head and lifted her glass.

—Good evening and good night, Mr. de Bellomonte.

Ambrose stood. He lifted his hat and gave a slight bow. He took a few steps toward his horse. Then his legs began to wobble. He patted his stomach and shook his head as he attempted to brush off the malady. Another step and he collapsed onto the ground. He choked and gagged and gasped for air. Elmira took another very small sip from her wine glass. She calmly walked over to Ambrose as he writhed in agony.

—You poisoned my glass?

Elmira took yet another very small sip from her wine glass.

—Not the glass. The whole bottle.

Ambrose's eyes registered fear and awe. His mouth foamed as he clutched his throat. The scratch of a match interrupted his wheezing. Elmira lit a cigarette and took a light puff as the man gurgled and clawed at his own neck.

—You…you said the feud was over.

—It's over now.

—Why?

—You cant honestly expect me to forget about my son's murder?

She knelt down and blew a puff of smoke into his face. Ambrose's fingers contorted into claws and his back arched as he writhed about on the ground.

—My dear Ambrose, the pain must be extraordinary. May I remind you that there is no force on earth more powerful than motherhood.

Elmira gently took his chin and gazed into the fading light of his eyes.

—You men and your pathetic cock measuring. Status seeking is for the weak. People like you and my husband. Vengeance, magnificent vengeance, is for the artist. I want you to know that you havent seen the last of me. You'll never have peace. I promise I'll follow you to hell.

Only after Elmira had finished her cigarette did Ambrose take his last choked breath. His bodily functions gave way, and the proud general and wealthiest plantation owner in the South lay dead in a puddle of his own filth. Elmira took another sip from her wine glass. She knelt down and stroked Ambrose's cheek.

—You were my greatest enemy, and now I've turned you into my magnum opus.

A few seconds later, General Willard and three men rode onto Beaumont Plantation exactly as scheduled. The old general walked up to Ambrose's body and gazed upon it for a few moments.

—Remind me to never drink one of your cocktails, he said.

—He was already dead the second he killed my son. A heart attack. I'm quite sure the coroner will agree. After all, I know a man working for the city who's very good with paperwork.

—So how does justice taste?

Elmira took another sip of wine, then knelt down and looked at him once more.

—My son is still gone and all I have is this corpse.

—What do you want us to do with the traitor's body?

—Strip off his clothes and dump his naked body in an alley next to the cheapest, filthiest brothel you can find. Release the papers of his treachery to the press in the morning.

—It will be done.

Two of General Willard's men tossed Ambrose's body into the back of the waiting wagon.

Elmira's legs began to grow weak. Her stomach burned like fire. General Willard guided her to her wicker chair on the porch.

—I do believe you have had too much to drink, madam.

Elmira flicked a match and lit another cigarette. The glow of orange embers filled the night sky as she sucked on the end of her ivory cigarette holder. A teardrop trickled down her cheek as she stared blankly into the dark horizon. The ravens cawed. General Willard gave his usual bow and led Ambrose's horse away. The horseman and their wagon disappeared under the graceful oak branches.

Elmira opened her purse and took out the charred photo of her son. She kissed it.

A figure stood in the moonlight. It was a man in gray. He was walking toward her. He wore a gray Confederate uniform and carried a rucksack over his shoulder. As the man grew nearer, she saw bullet holes in his chest. Elmira finished the last of her wine. She felt the hot poison pulse through her veins. Her vision clouded.

—Noah.

She gazed longingly at his photo for several seconds, then held it against her heart. She stood and opened the front doors of Beaumont Hall. The inside smelled of oil and kerosene. She lifted a lantern off an end table in the foyer. She held it up to her face and studied its flickering flame, then her eyes shifted downward toward the great pool of liquid at her feet.

A voice echoed from inside the great house. Miles pleaded with her to stop. He dragged his useless legs behind him as he crawled toward her on his elbows. She regarded him as he inched his way closer. He reached out to her as she dropped the lantern. It shattered, and soon the entirety of the home was ablaze. The old timbers creaked and moaned as they succumbed to the flames. She gazed outside toward the Confederate soldier walking toward her. Her crimson dress and long hair fluttered gracefully in the ensuing firestorm. She stood tall and unafraid in the doorway as the flames consumed her—alight like a goddess.

Chapter 40

EMMA

1866 Georgia

Emma sat up from the blanket she was sleeping on and rubbed her arm. They had to get up early and pack, for their steamer was to depart in the afternoon. She didnt think it was wise to go to the north in the wintertime, but Grace wanted to see the snow. Emma had warned her friend how cold it got up north and suggested that they wait to depart until the spring. Grace responded to her warning by purchasing two new coats and a blanket.

It was still dark outside when Grace and Emma finished packing their things. Emma was able to fit everything she owned in a single small suitcase while Grace required two large ones. They were able to sell their modest furnishings, and now their apartment was nothing more than a barren wood floor with a single cast-iron stove sitting atop it.

A paperboy waved the morning news in the air. Emma caught the bold letters. Though she couldnt read well, she understood a few words—including one she recognized instantly. It was her surname.

She gave the paperboy a coin and asked Grace to read the paper's headline to her. It said: *FEUD ENDS: THE FALL OF THE BEAUMONTS AND DE BELLOMONTES*. Grace told Emma that Beaumont Hall had burned to the ground and both Miles and Elmira were presumed dead. Ambrose de Bellomonte had been declared a traitor. He'd traded his command and his secrets to protect his plantation and was found dead in an alley behind a brothel. Grace said it was a place of such ill repute that even the other prostitutes considered it disreputable. It was assumed he had a heart attack.

The paper said that Ambrose's property would be divided up amongst his daughters—they all intended to sell. The patriarch's body wasnt even cold, and his children were already fighting about whose share was what. Before Grace could finish reading aloud, Emma bought another paper. She handed it to Grace to read. Another headline with her surname on it: *THE BEAUMONT LINE IS EXTINCT*.

Emma held her baby in her arms and gazed down at him. She turned to Grace.

—We need to go to Beaumont Plantation.

—What? Why?

—I need to check on Mary.

It mattered little whether the woman had any affection for Emma or her grandson or not. Emma only knew that she was someone who needed more love, not less.

They set off toward Beaumont Plantation. The avenue of oaks for it was crowded with the fire brigade and throngs of onlookers. Already she could smell the pungent odor of smoke emanating from the charred timbers of the home. Emma tried to push her way through the crowd but she was too small and the people too many. She hiked up her dress and trudged around the mass, through the surrounding pastures. The grass was covered in thick flakes of ash and the sky above the mansion was gray with smoke. The shacks still stood, although most of them were dilapidated. She made her way toward Mary's cabin. As she approached it, Emma could feel the heat emanating from the ruins. It seemed as if such a terrible blaze must have risen from hell itself.

Mary sat in front of her cabin in a rocking chair. She didnt acknowledge Emma's presence, merely sat there, rocking back and forth, as she gazed upon the ruins of Beaumont Hall. The great mansion in front of her cabin was now nothing more than a thick stone shell stained black from smoke. Emma could see crimson roses in full bloom in Elmira's garden through the empty spaces where the mansion windows had once been.

She thought it rather odd that they would bloom at such a time. She went to the other side of the mansion and took some cuttings from the roses and wrapped them in a damp cloth. She figured she would plant them at her new home.

Inside the stone shell was a smoldering pile of burnt beams and other blackened debris. The earth around the mansion was scorched, and what parts werent black had a deep yellow hue that smelled of sulfur. There was only an empty wheelchair on the remnants of the porch that had somehow escaped the blaze. She dared not stay there any longer. Even as a ruin, the edifice gave off a strange aura.

Emma returned to Mary and knelt down and looked into the woman's eyes.

—Ms. Mary, are you alright?

Mary grunted in affirmation.

—Come with us. There's nothing here anymore.

Mary looked down at the ground and then back up again at the remains of the mansion. She got up without saying anything and went into her cabin. When she emerged she had her few possessions tied up in a crimson handkerchief.

—I'll come with you, she said.

Emma didnt understand and figured she never would. It seemed whatever spell the place had had on her had been broken. She took Mary's knotted hand and helped the woman board the wagon. Mary sat inside, hunched over in her permanent stoop. Even after Emma climbed in the back of the wagon, the place still seemed to call her toward it. It was a feeling she couldnt explain. She asked the driver to leave as quickly as possible.

The driver snapped the reins and the wagon lurched forward. They'd have to buy an extra ticket on the steamer, but that mattered little. As the wagon headed down the hill, Beaumont Plantation fell out of view.

Later Emma stood at the ticket booth. The cashier looked up.

—What's your name, missus?

—Beaumont. Emma Beaumont.

—Did you say Beaumont?

—Yes, sir.

The cashier studied her face and then slowly handed her the tickets.

The steamer was due to leave in just a few hours. They waited on a bench next to the port for the white and red ship to admit passengers. Mary seemed content so far as Emma could tell.

After a bit, Emma walked out and made her way to Bull Street and passed through Madison Square into Monterey Square. As she stood in the center of the square, she closed her eyes and inhaled the fresh aroma from the early morning rain. Then she continued down Bull Street.

She had never had the time to explore the city. Her life had consisted of waking up to work and sleeping and then starting the process over again. Though she hadnt been to many other places, Emma could scarcely imagine a city more lovely than Savannah. The architecture, the squares, and the layout of the streets seemed almost divine to her.

Emma continued down the street and entered Forsyth Park. The rain brought out the many shades of gray and brown and black and even dark mauve of the cobblestones. The park was a lush green field adorned with majestic trees. As she walked along the main walkway, the moss-strewn branches wrapped her in a warm embrace, inviting her to stay.

She heard the patter of water before she saw it. The white fountain had three levels. Water trickled down from the top before collecting into the second level, which sprayed great plumes of mist and vapor into the air. Then it continued down and collected into a large circular pool. Inside sat fish-tailed satyrs and swans that poured thin streams of glistening water from their mouths. The boy was right, it was worth seeing.

Emma had known the blood-sown plantation fields and the grace of Savannah and couldnt understand how the two could co-exist at all. She only knew she lived in a peculiar world, for beauty and misery were all around her. The gray clouds were relenting to the rising sun and the salt air grew warmer. She wanted to sit on the bench and enjoy the pleasant scenery, but the steamer was scheduled to leave within the hour. She took one last look at the fountain.

As she turned around to leave, a lone figure stood up from one of the benches. She squinted. He was some distance away from her and she couldnt make out his face until a set of two very famil-iar blue eyes came into view.

Emma blinked, which flushed the growing tears down her cheeks. She shook her head side to side. Her quivering lips muttered the same phrase over and over again.

—Please Lord, dont tease me like this, dont tease me like this.

Her cheeks were wet by the time the man stood before her. She covered her mouth to hold back a storm, but the dam burst and her emotions came flooding out. She didnt think herself worthy to have her prayers answered, to have such happiness given to her. Isaiah stood before her. His cheeks were as wet as hers. They didnt say anything. They didnt need to.

Emma pulled her baby wrap around to her front. She held out their child and Isaiah carefully took the wiggling infant into his arms. He held the infant and gazed into the child's striking blue eyes. She knew things wouldnt be easy. They'd have to not only carve out a life for themselves but also clear a path for their son.

It was only the beginning.